D1483236

THE DEAD CAN'T KILL

THE DEAD CAN'T KILL

Anne Hampson

Severn House Large Print
London & New York

This first large print edition published in Great Britain 2007 by
SEVERN HOUSE LARGE PRINT BOOKS LTD of
9-15 High Street, Sutton, Surrey, SM1 1DF.
First world regular print edition published 2005 by
Severn House Publishers, London and New York.
This first large print edition published in the USA 2007 by
SEVERN HOUSE PUBLISHERS INC., of
595 Madison Avenue, New York, NY 10022.

British Library Cataloguing in Publication Data

Hampson, Anne
  The dead can't kill. - Large print ed.
  1. Inheritance and succession - Fiction 2. Women private
  investigators - Fiction 3. Detective and mystery stories
  4. Large type books
  I. Title
  823.9'14[F]

ISBN-13: 9780727875990

Printed and bound in Great Britain by
MPG Books Ltd, Bodmin, Cornwall.

One

The crunch of tyres on loose gravel brought a frown to Sally Renshawe's eyes as she carried the tray into the cosy little breakfast room. From the hall came the click of the letter box.

'Bills,' she sighed and her aunt glanced up from the newspaper she was reading. 'The electricity, and the car service, I expect.'

'But you're not hard up, child?'

Sally laughed at her aunt's concerned expression.

'Of course not. But Mother hated the buffs and it's sort of – rubbed off.' She set down the tray and her aunt immediately began arranging the cutlery and crockery on the bright green-and-yellow-checked tablecloth. Sally went back into the kitchen from where drifted the appetizing smell of bacon grilling and coffee brewing. She was humming to herself, inordinately happy because her aunt had recently stated her intention of leaving America – her adopted country – and settling here in Dorset, where she hoped to find a property close to the enchanting village of

5

Melcombe Porcorum where Sally lived, in the charming thatched cottage left her by her parents on their untimely death in a road accident three years previously.

'What made you assume there are only buffs, as you call them?' Louisa Hooke's strong masculine voice reached her niece as she was putting the eggs and bacon on the plates. 'One certainly isn't a bill.'

'How do you know?' Appearing with the two plates, Sally saw the long white envelope in her aunt's hand.

'Philpots, Layton and Clarke,' murmured Louisa with interest. 'Solicitors of Dorchester.'

'Solicitors!' Sally's heart gave a jerk. 'Not for me! I haven't done anything.'

'Don't look so scared. Of course you haven't done anything. Open it.' She held it out and Sally took it as if it were hot, then handed it back.

'You open it, Auntie. I hate solicitors' letters.'

Laughing, Louisa picked up a knife and slit the envelope.

'You hate solicitors' letters? Why, are you in regular receipt of them?'

'You know what I mean. They portend doom – or something like that – well, unpleaasant at least.'

'Unpleasant,' repeated Louisa mechanically as she perused the contents of the single

6

page. 'Well, from the sound of this you've come into a legacy. Read it.'

The letter changed hands and after a moment of blank bewilderment Sally said firmly, 'There's some mistake. This letter isn't for me.'

'The name's plain enough, and this address. You've come into money, my love.'

'Impossible!' Sally's brows puckered. 'I don't know of anyone at all who would leave me money.' She made an impatient gesture and reminded her aunt that the breakfast was getting cold. 'I'll send it back and tell them they've made a mistake – got me mixed up with someone else—' She stopped. 'It doesn't mention anything about a legacy. You've jumped to conclusions.'

'When you're informed that you will hear something to your advantage it invariably means you have come into money – or something of value.' She paused a moment, her knife and fork idle in her hands. 'Perhaps one or other of your parents did this benefactor a good turn in the past—'

'And he – or she – knew they are both dead, and passed the gift on to me?' Sally's tone was sceptical.

'It's feasible.' Louisa paused a moment. 'The sensible thing is to phone this Eric Philpots and make the appointment to see him, as it instructs in the letter. That's far more practical than speculation.' Reaching out, she took up the letter again. 'High Street, number eleven. That should be near the museum.'

With a sigh of resignation Sally picked up the coffee pot.

'All right, then. But you'll come with me?' She topped up her aunt's coffee cup. She had no wish to complicate her life at this time, when her aunt was staying with her on a prolonged visit while she searched for a house to buy. Once she had found it she would return to Boston, pack her belongings and leave her house in the hands of a real-estate company. 'Say you will,' persisted Sally, 'because I shan't go alone.'

'The man won't eat you,' laughed her aunt, then added, 'Of course I'll go with you. I'm curious, intrigued, just a little.'

At the expression in Louisa's eyes Sally said with some amusement, 'Sensing a mystery, are you? Well, Auntie, I have a feeling that you are about to be involved in one.'

'No, I don't think so.'

'But you hope so.' Sally sent her a sideways glance. 'Remember, we know all about your reputation over there – the way, on many occasions, you assisted police investigations by spotting clues they missed. How many murders have you helped to solve?'

'Crime is my hobby,' admitted Louisa, and then, briskly, 'But why this silly talk? What has your legacy to do with crime?'

8

'Nothing that we know of, but –' with a sudden frown – 'there is something not quite right about this business. As I said, there isn't anyone in the whole world from whom I could possibly receive a legacy.' As there was no response, Sally's thoughts deflected to things she had heard her mother say about the sister ten years her senior who had gone off to America 'just for the adventure of it' and had soon found herself a fairly rich husband. But Louisa had an interest other than that of the lovely home with which she had been provided: she was keenly interested in crime, and had become so clever at solving some of its mysteries that the local police had often sought her advice and help. It seemed that she possessed an uncanny insight into the criminal mind, but in her own words, her successes were 'more a matter of luck than anything else', which Sally could not believe. Her aunt was merely being modest. As a private investigator her services had been in great demand.

Louisa was again reading the letter from Eric Philpots and Sally knew by her expression that although she had lightly passed off the possibility of a mystery, she nevertheless sensed there was one. Sally had to smile and she thought her aunt looked the part, with her sturdy athletic build and firm, resolute features. She was tough, invulnerable. She loved gardening and walking but her first and most important interest was crime. Sally remembered her husband; he was a kind, gentle man, and although to some it looked like a mismatch the couple were devoted and very happy. But as Shamus had contracted a disease that would have given him years of pain had he lived, Louisa admitted she was glad he died suddenly, of a heart attack. He had been dead just two months when Louisa wrote to say she was coming back 'to live and die in her native England'.

'You're going to be late for work.'

Louisa spoke into her niece's thoughts and she replied with a smile, 'I'm off right now. Good luck with the house-hunting.'

Louisa gave a grunt of disgust.

'The trash these estate agents show you never ceases to amaze me. Are they really optimistic enough to believe some fool will come along and buy a hovel that is falling to pieces?'

'Have they all been so bad?'

'None – not one – has come anywhere near to the exaggeratedly glowing descriptions one reads on the particulars. And as for the photographs—' She stopped in disgust and shook her head. 'I can only keep on trying. I guess the right one is waiting for me somewhere.'

'Let us hope it isn't far from here.' Sally frowned as her eyes travelled to the table. 'I ought not to leave my guest to do the washing up,' she began, when her aunt interrupted her.

'You made the breakfast so I shall do the clearing up. Now, off you go – and be careful.'

'You, too, with that hired car which, you say, has its steering wheel on the wrong side.'

'It has! But then you drive on the wrong side of the road, don't you?'

'Auntie, you sound like a real American – and you are certainly not one. Another week and you'll never remember that you ever did drive on the right.' She paused, becoming serious. 'I do hope you have more luck today, Auntie. It would be wonderful if I arrived home and you could say you had found it.'

'Keep fingers crossed.' Louisa grinned as she added, 'At least I'm getting to know the countryside for miles around here!'

On the well-manicured lawn of Downland House, John Hilliard relaxed contentedly on a flowered lounger. Two of his grandchildren were playing boisterously with the dog, a King Charles spaniel puppy. It was a pleasing sight, and the satisfied smile it brought to his lips widened when his wife emerged from the black and white 'home of charm and character' (as it was described by the estate agent who had sold it to him eighteen years previously).

Monica waved to him as she strolled

gracefully to where the children were tumbling about under the impressive cedar of Lebanon, its foliage appearing almost silver in the bright sunshine of an August afternoon.

'It's good to have one's family around.' John spoke to himself; he always felt smug about his achievements. A self-made man, as the saying goes. Yes, he had been fortunate for most of his life, and especially after he had dispensed with James Devlin, his partner, all those years ago.

The children's laughter switched his thoughts and he stared at them with pride. David and Avril, his daughter's two, and there were two more, both boys, his son's children. They were at an expensive boarding school, as the carpet business was now in the hands of the capable Stephen, who had taken over from his father five years ago so that John and Monica could travel, as they had done many times already. They loved it.

When John had started the carpet business thirty-three years ago he had soon realized he had taken on more than he could handle; he got into money difficulties. James Devlin had come along in answer to his advertisement for a partner and had put everything he possessed into the business. John knew the man was going through a most traumatic period and realized at once that he was joining the firm because he hoped the new interest would help him pick up the pieces of his broken life. It was an opportunity too good to miss. John deliberately exploited the situation and within four months had declared the partnership was not going to work. James, sunk too low in spirit to fight for his rights, accepted the pittance offered and conveniently disappeared from John Hilliard's life.

Again John spoke to himself, though his eyes were on the slender figure of his wife.

'It was a crucial time for me, and after all, sentiment has no place in business. One has to be ruthless or go under, as I was rapidly doing till the business was rescued by his money. He was a fool, anyway, going to pieces over a broken engagement. I have no qualms. I'm where I am because I know how to use other people. That is an achievement.' He thought of the saying 'A fool and his money are soon parted'. He smiled and glanced around, at the small stately home he had been able to purchase despite its inflated price, at the splendid gardens surrounding it, at the children ... All beautiful, and his wife, too. No, he had no troubled conscience over getting rid of the encumbrance of a partner. He would never have been where he was now, running a Rolls, travelling on Concorde and the famous *Queen*, being able to buy his wife jewels and furs, and anything else her heart might desire.

His reverie was cut by Avril's racing towards him across the lawn.

'Postman's coming up the road on his bicycle,' she exploded. 'I want him to bring a card from Mummy and Daddy. Why did they go on holiday without us? Nana said Mummy needs a rest, but I need a rest, too!' She paused for breath. 'I'll go and get the letters—!' Off she sped before either of her grandparents could say a word.

Monica sat down on the vacant lounger and turned to smile at her husband.

'Having the children around keeps us young,' she commented, though she did add that she would not be happy if Susan, the treasure of a nanny, were not here as well. Her attention was diverted by the reappearance of Avril, who rushed up to flourish an envelope close to her grandfather's face.

'No cards!' she pouted. 'Only a letter, for you, Grandpa.'

He took it from her, watching her with a smile as she ran off, towards the swing. Monica came and looked over his shoulder, frowning in puzzlement as she read the names in the left-hand corner of the envelope.

John took out the letter and for a few minutes there was silence.

When he looked up there was an expression of bewilderment on his face.

'From a solicitor.' He tapped the paper.

14

'I've to phone, when I shall hear something to my advantage. Sounds like a legacy.'

'A legacy? But who—?'

'I'll go and phone,' he decided, rising from his chair. 'It's no use debating; we'll soon learn more once I have spoken to this Eric Philpots.'

Ten minutes later he was back, his brow creased in a frown.

'I've to go to Dorchester – the appointment's for tomorrow afternoon, when I shall be given instructions.' He paused as if reluctant to go on, then said in a strangely hollow voice, 'James Devlin has left me some money. He died last Friday and his will is to be read at his home.'

'James Devlin? We don't know anyone...' She tailed off, the colour receding from her face. 'The man who was your partner?'

Her husband nodded his head.

'He must have prospered after all.'

'It might not be much.'

'Apparently there are six beneficiaries. This Philpots fellow says complying with the conditions will be worthwhile for all of us.'

'Conditions?' A cold finger seemed to be running along her spine. 'What kind of conditions?'

'I'll tell you tomorrow when I return.'

Monica thought: Why should James Devlin leave money to a man who had cheated him of almost all he possessed?

15

Emma Smallman was on holiday in Tenerife when the letter arrived. Millie, her young Irish maid-of-all-work, knowing it must be important, phoned the hotel at which her mistress was staying.

'Open it,' ordered Mrs Smallman after a moment's indecision. 'And read it to me.'

'But it's from solicitors, as I said,' began Millie, who was swiftly and rudely interrupted.

'I said read it!'

'Yes, madam.' Millie slit the envelope and read the letter over the phone. The pause which followed became so prolonged that Millie asked if her mistress were still there.

'Yes. Put the letter in the top drawer of my dressing table. There is no urgency from what I can see and as I shall be home in two days' time there is no need for me to cut short my holiday. Now, have you cleaned out the garden shed as I told you?'

'Yes, madam.'

'And scrubbed the small statues in the rockery?'

Statues? Ugly little gnomes with silly crinkled faces!

'Yes, madam.'

'I want you to clean the carpet in the small sitting room. You can buy a shampoo in Bridport. But be careful! I don't want to see any streaks or patchiness. Don't wet the carpet too much. It's elbow grease that will get it clean, not gallons of water. Understand?'

'Yes, madam.' Anyone else would employ the experts, whose charges were said to be quite reasonable.

'Make sure you water the plants in the tubs every day.'

'I will, madam.'

'That is all.' The line went dead.

Though a simple girl from a remote village in Ireland, Millie was not the duffer her mistress assumed her to be. Well aware that she was being exploited, Millie was saving every penny for that day – not too far away now – when she would delight in saying goodbye to the woman whom she had always despised.

'... *something to your advantage...*' Millie stood by the telephone table and re-read the letter, slowly this time. And she would not have been human had she not said in disgust, and not without a tinge of envy, 'Lucky you, you old skinflint! Much gets more, my gran used to say. Something to your advantage. And you are very rich already. Whoever has left you money doesn't know you very well!'

Bernard Wilding was talking to his doctor, who was also his friend of long standing.

'So my heart's still sound.' He sometimes wondered why he bothered with these six-monthly check-ups, since the verdict was

17

always the same: he was in perfect health – blood pressure, heart, the lot. All as sound as when he was twenty.

'You'll live to be a hundred.' Leonard Fulham, noticing the sudden grimace, added in some amusement, 'You don't want to live that long? Yet you don't want to die. That's why you come here for these check-ups. You want to be very sure you'll be taking tablets just as soon as they become necessary.'

'Correct.'

'None of us wants to die...' He tailed off, frowning. 'I'm wrong. There are some of us for whom life no longer holds any attractions.' He fell into a thoughtful silence and presently his friend asked, 'Is something wrong, Len? I mean, you're all right, and Lucy and the kids?'

Leonard spread his hands then and explained that he'd dealt with an attempted suicide the previous day.

'A sad case. The chap had lost both wife and baby in a terrible accident. She was wheeling the pram on the pavement when a crane overhead dropped some of its load.'

'And they were killed?'

'Not outright; that was the worst thing. The husband kept screaming to his neighbour about the pain they had suffered. It finally became too much for him to live with.'

'He is dead?'

'No, we saved him, although God knows

whether or not he will ever be able to thank us. Certainly at present he is cursing us.'

'For your meddling interference,' murmured his friend reminiscently. He glanced at Leonard. 'Brings it all back, doesn't it?'

'James Devlin? Yes, it certainly does. I've sometimes wondered about him – whether he ever forgave us.'

'He swore he never would.' Bernard paused reflectively. 'Strangely enough, I have sometimes brought it all to mind – you know, some incident can spark off a memory?'

Leonard nodded his head, recalling the man's violent reaction.

'He cursed us both to hell; said if it hadn't been for our interference he'd have been dead by now.'

'And out of his misery. I wonder if he tried it again, and perhaps succeeded.'

'Sometimes it happens that they try it again,' returned Leonard, 'but normally that initial courage doesn't come so easily a second time.'

'So you don't think James Devlin would be likely to have tried again?'

'That's something I can't answer. He seemed so determined to die and he was positively murderous when we saved him. You remember his violence?'

'I'm not likely to forget. I fully expected to be attacked.'

'I've never seen such fury.'

Bernard made no response. He was living again through that rage, those few moments when he was cursed and told he would pay dear for his meddling. It was put down to the ravings of a man temporarily insane, and in fact, nothing more was heard from him.

'I wonder if he ever made anything of his life – presupposing of course, that he didn't make another attempt, and succeeded.'

'He's probably a happily married man by now, and a grandfather.'

'And thankful that we both acted so swiftly.'

'It was your quick action that saved him.'

'But your medical expertise.' Another switchback of memory took Bernard to that house where he saw through the window a man slumped in a chair. At the time Bernard was going through a difficult period, reduced to accepting a job which entailed house-to-house calls. Having rung this particular bell several times, and wondering why it was not answered, he went back to the window. He saw that the man had never moved and assuming he had taken ill, he hurried to the nearest phone box and spoke to a doctor. That call was the start of a long-standing friendship.

It was soon after that that Bernard's fortunes changed, and from the small corner shop of which he had obtained the tenancy there had grown a chain of quality grocers spread over the counties of Surrey and Sussex. And now, with the transfer of the business to his son and a nephew, Bernard and his wife were taking things easy, living quietly and happily in simple retirement.

A week after his medical examination by his friend, Bernard received a letter from a Dorchester solicitor, and on phoning Leonard he learned that he, too, had received one. They had each been left a legacy by the man whose life they had saved. They arranged to meet in Dorchester after each had had their interview with Eric Philpots.

'So he was grateful after all,' Bernard said over the coffee they were drinking in Judge Jeffreys' cafe. 'This is his thank you.'

But, strangely, his friend was silent, and thoughtful. At last he murmured, almost to himself, 'I wonder ... Yes, I wonder.'

'But it's obvious,' insisted Bernard in some surprise at his friend's strange manner. 'He's had a happy life and wants to show us his gratitude.'

Leonard looked straight at him.

'How do we know he was happy? He swore, viciously swore, to get his own back for what he called the hell we had condemned him to. Over and over again he said he would now be out of his misery if only we had minded our own business and left him alone.'

'He was hysterical.'

'I wouldn't say that,' argued Leonard. 'He

21

was in deadly earnest and I'd swear that if he'd thought he'd get away with it he'd have murdered us. So all he could do was curse us.'

'It's a long time ago, Len. He changed; he came to know the value of his life. I expect he fell in love and married, and when he died it was in the bosom of a loving family.'

Leonard had to smile.

'Conjecture, Bernard, pure conjecture. It could have been the opposite; he could have died alone and unloved, could have lived in mental pain and misery all these years.'

'Nonsense. Why, if that were the case, would he leave us money?'

'And why,' returned Leonard with soft emphasis, 'has he made this stipulation: that all the six legatees must gather at his home for four days? Surely that strikes you as strange, and also unnecessary if all were straightforward. The normal way is for the legatees to meet in the solicitor's office and hear the will read, not to be involved in what can only be described as a mysterious and mightily puzzling situation.'

Bernard shrugged and said they could only wait and see.

'We'll drive there together, of course,' he added. 'Your car or mine?'

Despite the driving rain, with which his wipers could scarcely cope, there was an expression of extreme satisfaction on Joseph Powell's florid face as he drove along the short road leading from the motorway to his home.

He was returning from a visit to a firm of Dorchester solicitors.

His wife, a nondescript, grey-haired woman with sagging skin and eyes of an indeterminate colour, was at the door even before he had inserted his key.

'What happened?' she asked breathlessly. 'Have we – you – come into money?'

His smile was smug; he took off his gloves, tossed them on to the hall table and, brushing past her, he swaggered into the living room. He looked around at the shabbiness, the patch of damp to one side of the window, the cracks in several tiles which formed the outdated fire surround. He turned and said with a sort of triumphant flourish, 'Are you asking me if, at last, we can think of doing this place up? Repairing the roof? Installing that bathroom we've so often looked at—?'

'Joe!' She actually stamped her foot. 'Stop messing about. The thing in the letter – about you hearing something to your advantage? What did the solicitor say? Is it a legacy? It is, isn't it? You're looking so pleased with yourself.'

'Sit down, Amy, and I'll tell you all about it.'

'Yes – yes! But first of all, are we coming

into money?'

'We are, and from what I've deduced, it's going to be more than we'll ever need to make this house decent, up to the standard of the one we had to leave.' His face creased into a broad smile that reached his small, closely set eyes.

'The one we...' Danefield House. Lost owing to Joe's recklessness where investments were concerned. A gambler, was Joe, and he had ruined them.

'What did the solicitor say? He obviously gave you some idea of the amount?'

'No, but I have reason to believe it will be substantial.' He went on to say that all six beneficiaries must spend four days at Hazeldene Manor. He drew a piece of paper from his pocket. 'This is the full address. There are five other legatees, two of whom are women. We're to stay for what appears to be a social weekend together, then on the Monday the will's to be read and we can all come home.' He saw the puzzled expression on her face and went on before she could speak, 'That was all from Mr Philpots. He was, to say the least, uncommunicative.'

'But surely you questioned him? I mean, it's so unusual – mysterious, staying at this manor for four days. Why?' She stared at him, baffled and uneasy, her flushed face emphasizing the orange-peel texture of her skin, and the thin, faint veins that lay beneath the surface like threads of dull red cotton. Her eyes fell to the paper she still held. 'This manor's not too far from Dorchester. You've quite a long drive from here.'

'I did it to Dorchester in two hours today – each way, of course.'

'I don't like it, not at all. You say this Mr Philpots didn't tell you anything else?'

'That's right. He said all would be revealed at the reading of the will on Monday. However, he was called away and handed me over to a young clerk to show me out. But the man was talkative and I guessed I could get something more out of him than I did from his boss, so I asked him some questions.'

'What did you ask him? He wouldn't know all the details, not if he was only a clerk.'

'Well, I thought I'd have a try.'

'And?'

'He couldn't answer most, but he'd accompanied Mr Philpots to the manor yesterday when he went to give instructions to the married couple he'd hired to look after us. He said Mr Devlin must have been a recluse because not only was the house neglected but the only servant he had had was an old gardener...' He tailed off, amused as he waited for what he knew was coming.

'Devlin? James Devlin?' Her face paled. She had a dazed look as she managed after a long pause, 'The man you – robbed? It isn't possible that he'd leave you money!'

'I did not rob him!' thundered her husband, glowering at her. 'I merely took what was my own!'

Half his own. Even though she knew his temper was rising she just had to say, 'Those two paintings you took from the house were part of its contents, and those contents, along with the house and the land, were left to you and James jointly.'

'He never knew. And what the eye doesn't see...' He shrugged.

'I believe he did know. He wasn't stupid, as you assumed at the time.' She threw him an accusing glance. 'You did rob him, Joe, and you know it.'

An ugly expression came into his eyes and she heard him grit his teeth. Fury hung in the air but he did not speak.

So long ago, Amy reflected. James Devlin had been the victim of Joe's greed and yet he had left him money. Why? There was something radically wrong with the whole situation. The paintings had been in the attic, thick with dust. Joe recognized their value at once. But the large amount of money he received from Sotheby's didn't do him much good because he took reckless chances on the stock market. She said at last, 'You've no idea how much he has left you?' All her eagerness had evaporated the moment she learned who had left the money.

'I didn't get the amount, but as I said, I

deduced it will be substantial, because of what the young man said about the manor. It's an estate of over seventy acres, and a firm of builders is interested in buying it. The lad had heard Mr Philpots telling one of the other partners that it was worth over two million.'

'James obviously spent his inheritance more wisely than you,' she said. 'Two million pounds. Incredible.'

'Plus a houseful of antiques. The lad said he'd never seen so much silver. He'd been poking about while his boss was outside and it seems every cupboard is full of it – it's all right, woman! I'll not take anything from there! I'm no common thief, for Godsake!' His face was crimson with anger. 'In any case, it was as well I took those paintings, in view of what happened later.'

Amy said, as if his fury had escaped her, 'Doesn't it strike you as very odd that a man who had been served such a dirty trick should leave money to the perpetrator of that infamy?'

'Infamy!' he spluttered, rising to stand menacingly over her. 'How many times do I have to tell you that I only took what I was entitled to! I don't want it mentioned ever again! Get that?' He turned and left her sitting there, to become lost in memories of the past.

So long ago ... two distant cousins – so

distant that they'd never even met until they were left, jointly, the estate of Frank Wareham, an 'uncle' so distant that he too was unknown to them. The house and contents were very valuable but there was little cash. It was left to the two as to which should live in the mansion; the other would receive half the valuation price. James had set his heart on it but Amy also wanted it. But because she felt blameworthy on account of her husband's theft of the paintings, she told Joe she could never live in it. Her conscience was assuaged by her sacrifice. But Joe had lost both her respect and her love and there were times now when she felt she hated him. At times she even wished him dead.

Her thoughts were interrupted by his reappearance. He had calmed down and his voice was almost placating as he said, 'Look, Amy, we mustn't quarrel over this. It's a matter for rejoicing. We'll have a great time spending some of the money. The rest, I promise, will go into the bank to supplement our present very modest income. I'm sorry I lost my temper, but please don't keep on accusing me of robbing James.'

She opened her mouth, then closed it again. Best to keep certain thoughts and convictions to herself. But nevertheless she just had to say, 'Leaving the matter of the paintings aside, you must admit you bled him over the half of the house. We had the correct valuation but you'd only settle for much more. That wasn't fair, Joe, and it's one reason why I am so troubled about this legacy. It doesn't make sense that he'd leave you money.'

'That's where you're wrong. This legacy is conscience money. You are so busy accusing me that you're forgetting the fact that it was James, in the end, who made a fortune out of that house.'

'But at the time neither of you knew that in years to come the motorway would run through the estate, that heavy compensation would make a wealthy man of James. No, there wasn't any excuse for your action *at the time.*'

He gave a sigh of exasperation but managed to contain his temper.

'Not only was he paid a fortune for the house and immediate lands, but the rest of the land, which would normally have been valueless since no one would want to build on it, was, by some miracle, spotted by that frozen-food firm who bought it for growing peas, or something, thereby giving James another tidy lump of cash. This legacy is conscience money, given to me as part of what he received from the government.' He paused but she remained silent. 'Another thing, if only you had liked the house it would have been *our* good fortune to sell out to the government. But you said you disliked the house, though I never did understand why.'

'James wanted it,' she said shortly.

'But he had no *right* to it. And as he was single and I married we could have forced him to let us have it.' The envy in his tone, the tightness of the mouth – these were like a rasp on her nerves. She thought: how wonderful to have some peace, to be away from him, if only for a while. James had been altogether different, a thorough gentleman. She would have welcomed him as a friend, but he had made it plain that he wanted nothing more to do with them, and it was this attitude which convinced Amy that he knew all about the theft of the paintings.

She said at last, 'When do you have to go to this manor?'

'Next Thursday and we stay till Monday.' He shook his head. 'I wish you'd bring yourself to rejoice over this news. Whatever you say, James left me this money because he considered it to be part of my original share. You can't argue the fact that he gained at my expense.'

She drew a breath, exasperated by his logic – or, rather, lack of it.

'His later gains had no bearing on what happened *at the time*. And he was *forced* to leave his home – it was no voluntary move, so if the motorway hadn't been going through he'd never have received the money which you say ought to have been half yours.' She thought about the paintings and the large sum they had brought. She also thought that most of what he would shortly receive as a beneficiary would go the same way – in gambling on the stock exchange. They'd soon be poor again; she had no doubt of that.

Sally drove her Beetle out of the village and on to the dual carriageway. The sun was brilliant in a clear summer sky and the calm sea could be discerned in the distance.

'Before we drive to the manor,' her aunt was saying, 'I want to go into the village.'

'Hazeldene, you mean?'

'Yes. Stop at the post office, if there is one. I want to make a few enquiries.'

Sally cast her a sideways glance. 'The amateur sleuth's already at work?'

Louisa replied lightly, 'Just curiosity, my love. This Eric Philpots is an old fogey – with the mistaken belief that he can keep us in total ignorance about your benefactor until the very last moment.'

'Not total—' Sally swerved to miss a Rhode Island Red that had somehow escaped from a field into the road. 'He did give us his name, when we went for the interview and to receive our instructions.'

'That you and five others had to have a long weekend at the manor. And what else did he tell us?' added Louisa in a grim tone.

'Not much. But at least we know his name.'

'And a fat lot of good that is! Who was this James Devlin, and what was he to you?'

Sally shrugged and drove in silence till her aunt spoke again.

'You've never even heard of him. You know nothing whatever about him – was he old, young, a gentleman or just an upstart? Is the bequest large or small—?'

'Mr Philpots did assure us it was worth our while to comply with the terms of the will.'

'After you'd said you didn't want to come and stay at the manor.'

'I didn't want complications in my life, Auntie. I'm so much enjoying having your company, seeing you pottering about in my garden, and the walks we have together. You'll be gone once you've found a house so it's only natural I'd not want any annoyances interrupting this happy time.'

'You are very flattering, Sally. But as for "gone" as you say – well, we have hopes – high hopes – of my getting Mrs Millsom's delightful cottage by the river. If I do get it then I shan't be more than two minutes' walk away from you.'

Sally again drove in silence, thinking of the fantastic bit of luck in hearing that old Mrs Millsom had decided to go into sheltered housing just outside Dorchester.

It was only two evenings ago and her aunt had suggested they go to the Golden Pheasant for a drink. It was a homely little pub run by Bill Scott, who was always the first, naturally, to hear the latest gossip or learn the latest news. Knowing Sally's aunt was looking for a small house he mentioned it and without delay Louisa went off to knock on the old lady's door.

Oh, yes, certainly Louisa could buy it. Save advertising it and having dozens of nosy people coming round. Yes, she would be delighted if Louisa had it, because of the garden, which had been planted and tended for over forty years by Mr Millsom before he died just over a year ago.

But there was a snag which deflated the jubilation: David Millsom, the son and only child, put in his oar with the intelligence that homes in the village of Melcombe Porcorum were so greatly sought after that they brought far above what would normally be termed the current market price. Did Mrs Hooke know this?

She suspected it, and was prepared to pay over the odds, she told him obligingly. But his price made even her stagger. She would have to think a lot more about it, she said. Nevertheless, all was not lost yet because Mrs Millsom, who thought a great deal of Sally who collected her groceries for her from Bridport and would always take her into Dorchester on a Saturday if she had other shopping to do, dug in her heels at the very suggestion of her home being put into the hands of an estate agent who would advertise it widely. She told her son in no uncertain terms that it was her house and she was definitely not having strangers trampling all over it, just so she could obtain more money which she would never spend, but would leave to him one day.

Greed, she told Louisa in his presence, was destroying the world, nothing else, just greed. Well, if her son was going to be greedy, it was not with her property!

The matter was left in abeyance until Louisa and Sally returned from Hazeldene Manor.

Sally spoke at last.

'Another thing we learned from Mr Philpots, Auntie, was that James Devlin was a recluse and an eccentric.'

'Obviously an eccentric, wanting you all to meet and gather at his home for four days. Why? That's what's continuing to baffle me. I can't find any reasonable answer.'

'And to a detective, that is frustrating.' Sally's voice was amused.

'Yes, I'm riled all right. And that's why I want to make some enquiries in the village.'

'I must admit,' began Sally, 'that I myself am puzzled by the strange fact that Mr Philpots has never even seen James Devlin. Do you think he was lying to us for some reason?'

'He'd not lie; there'd be no cause for him to

do so. I agree with you that it's most odd, very odd indeed.' She paused in thought. 'When I asked Mr Philpots about James – what he looked like – and he admitted he'd never set eyes on him, I own I was inclined to treat his statement with some scepticism, but then I saw it was illogical for him to lie about a thing like that.'

'Mr Devlin made the will out himself...' Sally was speaking in a low voice, almost to herself. 'And had it signed, obviously.'

'We shall begin by trying to discover, then speak with, the two who witnessed his signature. They must be people living close, seeing that he was a recluse and never went outside the manor grounds. Ah, here's a sign: Hazeldene – the next turn right.'

The village postmistress proved to be a cheerful, middle-aged spinster with ruddy cheeks that owed nothing to artificiality, and frizzy hair that undoubtedly did. The colour had gone drastically wrong, but Miss Baker's philosophy was that the reddish-purple would not last forever, so why worry? A few months hence it would have grown out and she could begin all over again. She eyed with some curiosity the two strangers who entered her shop, produced a smile and asked what she could do for them.

'We want some stamps,' began Louisa opening her purse. 'And do you have picture postcards?'

'Of Hazeldene?' She shook her head. 'It's a pretty enough village but we don't get tourists, so no postcards.'

'Just the stamps, then. Six first class.'

They were produced and paid for, and while Sally was wondering how her aunt was intending to seek information about the late James Devlin, another woman entered and the two greeted each other like old friends.

Miss Baker said cheerfully, 'I expect you've only come in for a chat?'

'Yes. I don't want to buy anything today.' She shot a glance at the strangers and added with a note of curiosity in her voice, 'You can carry on serving these ladies.' Mrs Gates, from Rose Lodge, then subjected Sally to a prolonged stare. Pretty thing, but skinny. All these young ones are too thin. Mrs Gates turned her attention to the older woman. A bit on the mannish side – well, no, not exactly. Severe, yes, that was it, with that Harris-tweed suit and the shirt beneath the jacket having a high uncompromising collar. Gloves, well fitting – those you had to push every finger into. Sensible walking shoes and matching brown leather handbag. The girl could be her daughter, mused Mrs Gates, thoroughly enjoying herself. Bit of a diversion, this, strangers coming into Hazeldene post office. She said with a smile which showed two gaps in her top teeth, 'Here visiting friends, are you?'

'We're to be staying at the manor for a few days,' replied Louisa, noticing the postmistress's jolt of surprise. 'A long weekend, as a matter of fact.'

The two exchanged glances across the counter. It was Mrs Gates who spoke at last.

'But no one lives there – except the old gardener.'

'And we were given to understand he was leaving any day,' put in Miss Baker. The question in eyes and tone brought a half smile to Sally's lips and she turned her head to hide it. 'Old Mr Devlin died, you know,' went on Miss Baker.

'Perhaps it's another manor,' suggested Mrs Gates, fishing for more information that she could carry to her cronies. 'Ours is called Hazeldene Manor.'

'That's the place.' Louisa tucked the stamps into a pocket of her handbag. 'We know of the death of Mr Devlin. I expect –' she paused to throw a glance between them – 'that you all feel sad at losing the local squire, the lord of the manor?'

At this Miss Baker – whom Mrs Gates had called Dorothy – gave an expressive grunt, while a grimace was her friend's reaction.

'We can hardly miss someone we've never even seen. Mr Devlin was a recluse.'

'No one ever saw him in all the twelve years he's lived there,' said Mrs Gates pettishly. 'He was the mystery man of Hazeldene.'

'Now what do you make of that, Sally? In twelve years no one has ever seen your uncle.'

'Uncle!' Both women uttered the word together. 'You're his niece? It was thought that he had no relatives, not even a distant one.' Dorothy stared at Sally and added perceptively, 'So that's why you're here – to claim the money and house.' It was a statement which brought the colour to Sally's cheeks. Uncle, indeed! But it was certainly one way of explaining their presence here, at the manor.

'Yes,' replied Louisa calmly. 'My niece has come to hear the will read.'

'I had a notion the young lady might be your daughter.' Mrs Gates looked Sally over again, and decided she was too pretty to be the woman's daughter. 'So you're the old man's heir? Did you get along with him? I mean, it was said he never spoke to anyone except his dog and the gardener.'

Louisa decided to veer the subject in order to avoid Sally's having to flounder for an answer to Mrs Gates' question.

'If Mr Devlin never went out—' She shook her head. 'He must have gone out sometimes. What about haircuts and shopping for clothes?'

'The gardener did it all – not that anyone saw much of him, either, because the groceries were ordered by phone and delivered twice a week. The gardener used to keep hens and a cow, and he grew all their own vegetables and fruit.'

'Did they not have help in the house?'

'No. Most rooms were shut up...' Miss Baker looked at Sally and added perceptively, 'You've never met Mr Devlin, have you? I guess you are one of those long-lost heiresses, aren't you?'

'Well – er...'

'We are not able to say more,' broke in Louisa, smiling. 'It's all very confidential, you understand.' She produced an encouraging look. 'You were saying that groceries were delivered to the manor. The delivery man, therefore, would have met and spoken with Mr Devlin?'

Both women shook their heads. It struck Louisa that although there were certain things the villagers knew about the manor's two strange occupants, there was far more that was causing them some considerable frustration.

'The gardener always paid the delivery man – a youngish lad who started with Meg the Corner Shop when he was sixteen.'

'Ah ... so there is no one at all who has actually seen Mr Devlin?'

'That's what I have already said.' Mrs Gates spoke as though she had a personal grievance against the elusive lord of the manor. 'He never supported anything to do with the village except the Home of Rest for

Horses, which is up the road – you passed it if you came by the church?'

'No, we came from the other direction.' A pause and then, 'So Mr Devlin cared about animals, it would seem?'

'Always had dogs,' supplied Miss Baker. 'You could see them and hear them sometimes but they never came past the gates.' She stopped rather abruptly as a tall, immaculately dressed gentleman came into the shop. Both Sally and her aunt swung round on hearing him ask, 'Can you direct me to Hazeldene Manor? I seem to have taken a wrong turning somewhere.' His voice was low and cultured; he smiled charmingly at the woman behind the counter.

'Another of our party,' observed Louisa sotto voce. 'Looks as if he's a millionaire already.'

'You're going to the manor as well?' There was no mistaking Mrs Gates' mystification. The whole village would be buzzing before the next hour was out, decided Louisa with some amusement.

'I'm on my way to the manor, yes,' replied the man with a glance at Sally and her aunt. 'Am I on the right road?'

'Are you staying for a weekend too?' enquired Mrs Gates with unashamed curiosity. His manner changed; he became forbiddingly austere.

'That,' he replied arrogantly, 'is my

business. I merely asked this lady for directions.'

Silence. The air could be cut. Louisa decided to intervene.

'You will find it if you take the next turn right and then a left. From my map I estimate it to be about half a mile along that lane, on the right-hand side.'

'Thank you very much.' His tone was less severe as he added perceptively, 'I believe we shall be meeting again later?'

'Your assumption's correct,' responded Louisa somewhat curtly. She did not care much for the man; his arrogance had been out of place, totally unnecessary. A successful man with an inflated ego was her verdict, and she hoped the others would prove to be a little more attractive.

A slight bow and he was gone. The four women listened automatically to the quiet rhythm of the car as it purred away into the distance.

'A Rolls, I shouldn't wonder,' sniffed Mrs Gates, 'judging by the edge on him!'

Sally drove the car along the tree-lined drive – a bumpy ride, she noticed but before she could comment her aunt was saying:

'There's an air of neglect about the house, which one would expect in the home of a recluse, but just look at the gardens! They're delightful. It's easy to see they've been tended with care for a number of years.'

'Yes, they're very beautiful. James Devlin's gardener must enjoy his work.'

'Gardening might be work to some, but to me it has always been a real pleasure. I can relax and also do some deep thinking when I'm among the trees and flowers. I rather think I'm going to have pleasant chats with this old retainer.' She glanced around after alighting from the car. 'Cuttings,' she murmured with relish. 'I intend to take many cutting from here.'

'For River Bank Cottage? Oh, Auntie, I do hope you get it!'

'Fate shall decide, my love. Meanwhile, let us enjoy ourselves in this beautiful place.'

Sally grimaced. The gardens might be special, but the house ... when did it last have a coat of paint on the door and window frames? she wondered. She lifted the lion's head knocker and let it fall.

'No eerie echo or ghostly moan,' commented her aunt with a laugh. 'Disappointed?'

'Relieved,' returned her niece briefly.

The door was opened by a tall thin man with gaunt features and a sallow skin stretched tightly over the high, prominent cheekbones. His mouth was thin and pale above a receding chin, his eyes almost black. Sally shuddered and thought he was like something out of a horror film.

'Good afternoon,' was his brusque unsmiling greeting as he pulled open the door wider and took a step backwards. 'You are Mrs Hooke and Miss Renshawe. Please come in.'

A woman emerged from the shadows as they entered the wainscotted hall, where antique weapons adorned the walls and the general aspect was made more effectively gloomy by the dusty suits of armour standing guard, one on each side of the massive oak door which they were soon to learn led into the main drawing room.

'My wife.' The man stood aside as he made the introduction. 'Mrs Thorpe.'

'How do you do?' Louisa's tone was cool; Sally remained silent. 'Mr Philpots said you would receive us and – er – make us comfortable.' Her tone carried doubt; she felt these two were concerned only with the financial aspect of the situation and cared nothing about the comfort of the guests. Where on earth had old Philpots found them? She asked if he were here yet and learned that he was expected within the hour. 'And any of the others?' she added.

'Mr Hilliard is here and two other gentlemen, Mr Wilding and Dr Fulham.'

'Mrs Smallman hasn't arrived yet, then?'

'No. She and her maid are coming by train as Mrs Smallman cannot drive her car, due to an accident. Perhaps you already know?'

'About the accident? Yes, we do know.'

'The introductions will be made at teatime by Mr Philpots,' inserted Mrs Thorpe in a cold dispassionate voice, her colourless mouth as unsmiling as the ice-grey eyes set beneath heavy black brows. Sally thought: there is something sinister about these two. 'The tea will be served in the lounge at four o'clock,' supplied Mrs Thorpe. 'The gardener informs us it is called the Blue Drawing Room,' she added with the hint of a sneer. She began to move towards the elegant balustraded staircase that rose centrally from the hall to a galleried landing off which were the bedrooms. 'Please follow me.'

'Our luggage is in the car.' Louisa glanced at the man, who said at once:

'I shall be bringing it up, madam.' He added that cars must be taken round to the back. 'There is plenty of room for yours alongside the two already there.'

'Splendid.' Louisa turned to Sally. 'Give Mr Thorpe the key so he can see to your car.' And she added with a sort of acid sweetness, 'You will do that, won't you – after you've dealt with our luggage?'

He glowered at her but his voice was low and respectful as he replied, 'Very good, madam.' He accepted the key and went out to the car.

'These are your rooms.' Mrs Thorpe pushed open one door and indicated the adjoining one. 'You share the first bathroom along

44

the landing.'

Louisa glanced around, noticing the two single beds.

'You have sufficient accommodation to give us separate rooms?'

'There is another wing,' replied the woman shortly. Her manner was frigid, her face expressionless. Her jet-black hair was scraped back from her forehead with forbidding severity and formed into a bun. Her heavily veined hands were long and thin, the fingernails cut very short. She wore a black dress, black shoes and stockings.

'She reminds me of a vampire,' shuddered Sally a few minutes later when she and her aunt were in Louisa's room. 'And her husband's not much better.'

'It's only for a few days,' Louisa reminded her cheerfully.

'We'll share at night, won't we?' Sally glanced about her. 'I told you it would be creepy.'

Louisa laughed and declared it was not creepy at all.

'However, we'll share a room for sleeping if that is what you prefer. You choose. Both rooms are alike from what can be seen.'

'We'll sleep in yours, then.' Sally's hands were icy cold; she rubbed them together. 'It does have an atmosphere, no matter what you say, Auntie.'

'I'll agree about that, but it's not creepy. All

houses of this age have an atmosphere.'

'Because of all the people who have died here.'

'And been born. This house is at least three hundred years old. These walls could tell interesting tales if they could speak.' She went to draw back the heavy velvet curtains to their fullest extent. 'That's better. The sun can now warm up the room a bit.'

'I wonder which room Mr Devlin died in?' A sudden note of awe edged Sally's voice. 'It was bound to be one of these six.'

'There's another wing, so that woman told us.'

'But this is the main wing. I have an idea the other will be secondary – they often do have a less superior part where the servants usually slept.'

'Well, we shall ask. And if it happens to be one of these two then we'll use the other. Now, go off and unpack and we'll take a stroll in those lovely gardens. We've an hour before tea,' she added with a glance at her watch.

'All right. I'll be as quick as I can.'

Louisa was by the window. She said as Sally reached the door, 'Here come Mrs Smallman and our Millie.'

'I'm glad you put it like that, our Millie.' Sally joined her by the window. 'I'm sure she'll soon be with us – or, rather, you. I'm dying to meet her; she sounds very nice.'

Sally was in time to see Mrs Smallman getting out of the taxi. 'It was a bit of incredible luck, your running into Millie like that yesterday afternoon.'

Her aunt smiled reflectively. A remarkable coincidence, the meeting with the young maid of one of the other legatees.

'I didn't run into her. We met in Judge Jeffreys' cafe, as I told you.' Turning from the window she sat on the edge of one of the single beds. 'I was reviving myself with a cup of tea after the exhausting and abortive run around the countryside viewing all those "homes of charm and character" which those rogue estate agents had glorified for my benefit—'

'If only you'd think positive about Mrs Millsom's place you wouldn't have been running around,' broke in Sally chidingly. At which her aunt declared it was not sensible to count one's chickens. Then she went on, 'Into the cafe came this young woman, very shabbily dressed, and with an air of one who intrudes. And I'm sure she would have turned and run if the waitress hadn't come along to put her at her ease. The place was packed so I invited her to share my table—' Louisa broke off, frowning. 'I've told you all this, so why am I repeating it?'

'Because it's so interesting. Just imagine her laying an envelope on the table addressed to our solicitors. No wonder you pounced.'

Sally produced a broad grin as she added, 'To the amateur sleuth that was a windfall if ever there was one.'

'Certainly a piece of unexpected luck,' agreed her aunt, but mildly. Whatever excitement might affect her inwardly, Louisa Hooke always maintained an exterior of cool composure, along with – more often than not – an unreadable expression. 'I did not pounce. I merely enquired if she had a letter to deliver as I saw it had "by hand" written in the corner where the stamp would have been.'

'And within minutes you had managed to turn the situation to useful account.' Sally was now by the mirror, using a comb she had taken from her handbag. Fair and gleaming, her hair was styled into a kind of pageboy bob, although some of the ends flicked out with a hint of unruliness that was most attractive. 'The girl was shy, you said, but she seems to have opened up to you easily enough.'

'We took to one another instantly. I felt sorry for her, knew she was unused to the luxury of afternoon tea in a cafe...' Louisa allowed her voice to trail away to silence, thinking of the girl's rich and attractive Irish brogue. Millie had explained the letter. Her mistress had fallen and broken her wrist so she had to have her maid with her at the manor, Mr Philpots had said it would be all right, but Mrs Smallwood had been anxious in case she had to pay anything for her maid's keep. Of course not, Mr Philpots had told her over the phone. But later Mrs Smallwood decided she did not trust the man's word; she wanted it in writing, and as there was no time for letters in the post she sent Millie with the note by hand, asking for written assurance that there would be no charge for Millie.

What kind of a woman was she, wondered Louisa, who would not trust the word of the solicitor?

'She can't dress herself,' Millie had said, 'and so she has to have me with her.'

'Why haven't you delivered the letter?' was Louisa's question.

Millie reddened and said with a hint of guilt, 'I've never been to Dorchester before and I wanted to look at the shops, seeing that I was here. My mistress told me to get the two o'clock train back but I thought I'd say I missed it, blaming the solicitors for keeping me waiting. So here I am, having a lovely time. I'll deliver the letter and hope they'll not be too long with the reply as I must catch the quarter to four.' She had accepted a huge cream puff offered her by Louisa, who never ate such things but had ordered a plate of cakes purely with the intention of giving the girl a treat. 'This is lovely. I do thank you, Mrs Hooke.'

Having a lovely time ... Louisa possessed a

49

much softer heart than her austere exterior would in any way have revealed, and suddenly she wanted to help the girl. Millie had spoken of her intention of returning to Ireland, but what chance had she there, in her remote village living with an aged aunt? Louisa would need help in the house once she was in a home of her own...

Before they parted company it had been arranged that Millie should change her job immediately Louisa had acquired her own place. And Millie also learned, much to her delight, that Louisa would also be at the manor, that her niece, Sally, was a benefactor.

'You'll like Sally,' she was assured. 'She's much the same age as you, so I have every confidence that you'll get along famously together.'

Sally's quiet voice brought Louisa from her reverie and she glanced up.

'I'm ready for that walk,' she said. 'I can unpack when we get back.' Sally looked up at a painting of a lady and her two children, all dressed in seventeenth-century costume. 'Why did they make their children replicas of adults? A ruff looks stupid on a child – and how uncomfortable it must have been.'

'All the same, that painting would be most attractive if it were cleaned up.'

'You'll have to come to the sale when the contents of the house are auctioned. You're

so keen on old things that it's bound to interest you, and you might get a bargain; one
never knows.'

'I noticed some magnificent Georgian
silver as we came through the hall. I'd not
mind a piece of that.' Louisa picked up her
handbag and slung it over her shoulder. She
stood looking at the painting for a moment
longer. 'When I was talking to Mr Philpots
the other day and he mentioned the forth-
coming auction, he said the gardener had
first pick of everything. He has been allowed
to take what he needs to fix up his own
house. I wonder where the poor old fellow
will live?'

Sally had scarcely heard; she was feeling
between the sheets, and suggested the beds
were damp.

'Dare we ask for hot-water bottles?'

'Dare?' with a lift of her aunt's brows.
'Watch me.'

They encountered Mrs Thorpe in the hall.
She had the telephone receiver in her hand
but she hastily replaced it on seeing them.
Louisa thought: there's a guilty and furtive
manner about this woman. She requested the
bottles, was subjected to a cold unfriendly
stare and added with acid politeness, 'If you
cannot find any, then I am sure you will go
out and buy some.'

The woman gritted her teeth. 'I'll see what
I can do.' Her eyes flitted to the phone. It was

plain that she was wanting to get back, to continue her conversation with whoever it was on the other end of the line.

'She's deep, that one,' Louisa was saying as they stepped from the gloom of the hall into the bright sunshine. 'And her husband.'

'An unhappy pair.' The voice came from behind a perfectly trimmed yew hedge and at the same time a black-and-white mongrel dog bounded towards them. Sally bent immediately to stroke it, then straightened up as the man, bearded and dressed in a light brown overall coat, added in a voice edged with apology, just as if he were to blame, 'And unfortunately they're to be here with you all for the whole of the four days, I'm afraid.'

'Not to worry,' from Louisa cheerfully. 'There's an abundance of beauty out here to compensate those of us who care to take advantage of it.' She gave him a smile and went on, 'You are the gardener we were told about. We owe all this –' she made a sweeping and comprehensive gesture – 'to you. I'd like to have a long chat when you have time. I'm most interested in gardening and would like to take some cuttings.'

'That's very flattering, madam. You are Mrs Hooke and this is your niece, one of the benefactors under Mr Devlin's will.' He subjected Sally to a stare so long that it became embarrassing. But she used the time to examine him, also, noting the vivid blue eyes, frank and widely spaced, the luxurious beard that effectively hid any expression; but the mouth was full and as she looked it widened in a smile. 'Forgive me,' he said to her. 'I've had so little to do with young people – do forgive me if I stared.'

He would have ambled away but he had taken only a few steps when Louisa halted him with, 'You have the advantage of us. We weren't given your name.'

'Albert Forsythe. I'd like it if you called me Albert.' The dog had gone off after a dove which had been pecking on the lawn and he called to it, 'Tessa, come,' and it obeyed at once. 'She never catches anything,' he said to Sally. 'I'd stop her at once if ever she did.' He did go this time and they saw him bend a couple of times to pat the dog as they went along the tree-lined path to disappear eventually round a wide curve.

'Pleasant sort of bloke,' observed Louisa. 'But what a life he's had, living like a recluse.'

'He must be odd, too,' returned Sally without pause.

'I agree. But some people want to be away from the world. And this is a most restful and beautiful place in which to spend one's time.' She paused, thinking how effectively the thick grey beard hid his face. But the eyes were set wide apart, the bronzed forehead high and lined below a healthy head of hair that showed no sign of thinning. She had liked him instantly and so had Sally. Not so the Thorpes. They were deep, unfathomable, and in her opinion not to be trusted an inch. Why had the woman been so furtive? What was the reason for the hasty cutting off of the conversation? Louisa would have given much to know the gist of that conversation.

'Wasn't Tessa sweet?' Sally's comment interrupted the train of Louisa's thoughts and she turned her head. 'So patient, sitting there. And then so obedient when she did run off. You must get a dog, Auntie.'

'I shall, once I'm settled. I hope Millie likes dogs.'

'She will. She's that kind of person.'

'I'm sure you are right. Well, love, let us go for our walk.'

They had not gone far when Eric Philpots appeared, strolling ahead in a slow and appreciative way. He turned and stopped; they came up to him and greetings were exchanged.

'It's a lovely afternoon for a walk,' he commented, making polite conversation before adding, 'You're happy with your rooms?'

'They could be delightful,' returned Louise, 'if they'd received a bit more attention. A spot of furniture polish wouldn't have come amiss.'

Sally had to smile. Mostly her aunt adopted

a subtle, polite manner but on occasions she could be unashamedly outspoken. Mr Philpots was in no way put out, though. He merely smiled and shrugged resignedly.

'My room is the same. A cloth to remove the dust, and a vacuum cleaner run over the carpets seems to be all we can expect.'

Louisa asked curiously, 'Where did you pick up a couple like the Thorpes, Mr Philpots?'

'The letter with the will instructed me to engage a couple to act as butler and housekeeper-cum-cook. The agency sent three couples but these had such excellent references that I had to favour them despite their outward appearances.'

'So you admit they are peculiar?'

'Peculiar?' His manner changed; he assumed a rather haughty mien.

'You've admitted their outward appearances did not impress you.'

'Yes,' intervened Sally before the solicitor could speak. 'You obviously found them weird, too. Doom and gloom. Didn't that bother you at the time?'

He stiffened and said coldly, 'Outward appearances are not what influences me. As I said, they had references far superior to either of the others. They've worked for titled people.' He cleared his throat. 'And now, if you'll excuse me...?' He swung around and walked briskly back to the house.

Sally made a face. Her aunt murmured thoughtfully, 'References are easily come by.'

'Forged, you mean? *You* would certainly go by appearances, I know. But then you're a physiognomist, brilliant at reading a person's character from their face.'

Louisa nodded in agreement. It was a gift, and had proved invaluable on many occasions in the past, when she had helped the police to apprehend the guilty person. With the Thorpes, she was puzzled. It was not merely that their whole demeanour was repellent; there was something else, something shifty beneath the assumed cold dignity which all butlers acquire during their training. Louisa resolved to keep a close watch on them – as far as her position at the manor would allow.

Two

'Shall we sit on that seat for a while?' Sally indicated a little shady arbour where a rustic seat had been placed. She and her aunt had strolled round the gardens before wandering into the wild region, the thickly wooded area which was part of the extensive outer grounds of the manor, beyond which stretched fields rented out to local farmers whose cows were grazing on the lush green pasture.

'Yes, why not?' agreed Louisa after a glance at her watch. 'The Thorpe woman mentioned tea would be served at four so we have half an hour or so – ah, here comes the man we met in the post office.'

He came towards the seat, tall, distinguished, perfectly clad in a dark grey suit, his shirt gleaming white against a deeply tanned skin.

'Good afternoon, ladies. We meet again.'

'Mr Hilliard, I believe. I'm Mrs Hooke and this is Sally Renshawe, my niece, and one of the beneficiaries. Won't you join us?' She moved closer to Sally, making room for him. 'Aren't these roses over the trellis lovely? The perfume's intoxicating.'

'This is certainly a beautiful place.' He sat down, hitching up a trouser leg. 'Pity about the house, though. I'd like to buy it when it comes up for auction. Do it up a bit and a fortune could be made on a resale.'

So he wasn't averse to speculation, thought Louisa. She had taken a dislike to him on that first meeting in the post office and she was unlikely to change her opinion. His features came under examination. His mouth was too thin, his eyes were a little too small for his face and set too close together. Not an honest face, and yet a handsome one. She was aware of Sally's close scrutiny and smiled at her. John Hilliard broke the silence by commenting on the strangeness of the circumstances which had brought the six beneficiaries together. An opening. Louisa intended to use it.

'You are of the opinion that there is a mystery, Mr Hilliard?'

'Of course. There has to be a mystery.' He glanced sideways at her. Severely cut suit of quality tweed; a severity too, about the blouse with its high, buttoned-up collar. No makeup other than a hint of lip rouge. He decided there could be a formidable austerity within her personality. He sensed an inquisitiveness in her eyes, and a glimmer of optimism betraying her hopes that he knew something which she did not. She was in for a disappointment. 'I was told practically nothing by that man Philpots, and I expect it was the same with you?'

'We've decided that patience is the practical attitude,' returned Sally with a sigh of resignation. 'So we're concentrating on enjoying the weekend.'

'I suppose that is one view. But why the secrecy? Do you know that Philpots has never set eyes on James Devlin?'

'Yes, he said so, and I must admit I was sceptical at first, then realized there was nothing for him to gain by lying. It seems James made out the will himself. Two people must have signed it. The gardener couldn't

have been involved because he's a beneficiary. And as James never left the grounds
here, who did sign it?'

'It's no use asking me. I'm completely in
the dark; this whole show's stupid. We are
here at the whim of a recluse, James Devlin,
who always was an odd one.'

'You knew him?' Louisa shot him a glance.
'He was a friend of yours?'

'We were once business partners.'

'You were?'

'It was over thirty years ago. We lost touch
after the partnership was dissolved.'

'The partnership didn't work?' The question came so swiftly that Sally was left in no
doubt that her aunt was fishing for information – something, anything that might
provide her with a lead from which she could
make some progress in her intention of dis-
covering more about the situation here at the
lonely manor, where six beneficiaries were to
meet and mix for four days and nights.

'Partnerships rarely do work,' John Hilliard
was saying, 'it isn't at all wise even to consider such a thing.'

Louisa paused in thought. Why hadn't the
partnership worked? Whose fault was it?
More important, which man lost the most?
John Hilliard had obviously prospered ... but
then so had James Devlin.

'Was there some major disagreement?' she
enquired presently.

'Not major, no. It just wasn't working out, that's all. We didn't see eye to eye on several important matters. Our decisions didn't coincide.' He had been leaning forward, his head turned so he could look at her, but suddenly he glanced away as if unable to meet the eyes which had become fixed with fine-drawn intentness on his face.

'So there was a major disagreement,' persisted Louisa.

'I've said no. It was merely a clash of personalities!' His tone was sharp-edged but, decided Sally, it would take more than that to daunt her aunt. 'We parted amicably.'

Louisa made no immediate response; she was soon lost in thought, endeavouring to analyse what had been said. Vaguely she heard the man questioning Sally, heard her niece say that she had never known of James Devlin's existence until the interview in Dorchester when she learned she had been left some money by the man. John Hilliard repeated what he had said earlier, that this coming here was stupid, but it was when he said he hoped there was nothing sinister about it all, and she noticed the sombre frown the words had brought to her niece's face, that Louisa decided it was time she intervened.

'There wasn't a quarrel, then?'

'Certainly not,' he snapped. And he added as if the thought had only just occurred to him, 'I'd hardly be here if we'd quarrelled, would I? You only leave money to those you like.'

To those you like … To Louisa's mind, neither Mrs Smallman nor John Hilliard were what could be described as likeable … yet James Devlin had left them money in his will. Had he really liked them?

'How long did the partnership last?'

'Four months,' answered John Hilliard tightly. What was the object this woman had in view? Was she bored and seeking for some diversion by probing into other people's affairs? Politeness was becoming difficult to sustain but he managed it as he added, 'It was long enough for me – us – to realize it wasn't going to work.'

'Four months?' And he, Hilliard, was the one who decided it was not going to work. How much had James put into the project? More important, how much did he get back? 'Four months doesn't seem very long to me. Did you become friends during that time?'

'We became friends, yes, but mainly it was a business relationship.' His temper was rising. If it were not for the fact that they were to be together for the next four days he would have snubbed her once and for all, ensuring there would be no more questions.

'You became friends and yet you didn't keep in touch?' Louisa was well aware of his rising temper; the narrowed eyes and tight mouth, the clenched fist resting on his knee ... 'You lost touch thirty years ago. It seems most strange that he included you in his will. Surely, Mr Hilliard, the fact that he did so poses you a question?'

He drew a breath and for a moment Sally thought he would avoid an answer, change the subject or something. But after a moment she heard him say, 'I'm puzzled, yes. But what about young Miss Renshawe here? She didn't even know him.'

'So another question posed.' She turned her head to look straight at him. 'I believe you are at a complete loss as to why you've been made a beneficiary, Mr Hilliard. I know that Sally and I are, very much so.'

He paused as if carefully choosing his words.

'James Devlin was an eccentric – Mr Philpots will have given you this information as a reason for our being here, and it is my belief that he became morose, alone but for the gardener who, although he has an apartment in the house, appears rarely to be in it – I've just had a word with him and gathered he has always wanted to be outside. He's made one of the garden sheds comfortable and he said he goes in there when it rains. As I was saying, James Devlin, living quite alone, would become a little off-balance...' He tapped his forehead demonstratively. 'He had no relatives – he told me that. And my wife explained his action in a way I have come to accept. He had this estate and he wanted to leave it to someone, as otherwise the government would take it.'

Sally was frowning at this and she shook her head.

'You are saying he just – well – rummaged round in his memory and left his money to people he knew in the past? But then how do I come in, Mr Hilliard? He didn't know *me* at all, remember.'

'He could have known one or both of your parents.'

'That is a possibility,' acceded Louisa, and then she fell silent for a space after casting a glance in Sally's direction. She was musing on things her sister had said about her husband. Frederick Renshawe had turned out to be – well, not exactly a 'bad lot', but certainly his personality, when one got to know it properly, left much to be desired. In other words, Sally's father had not been a likeable man. Louisa asked herself the question which was logical, in the circumstances: if Frederick were alive, would it have been he who would have been included in James Devlin's will? If so, she mused, it would mean that the other beneficiaries would be unlikeable people too. 'The whole thing doesn't make an atom of sense,' she said, speaking her thoughts aloud. Impatience gripped her; she hated groping in in the dark.

'We shall know it all on Monday,' put in Sally in an attempt to bring a lighter note to the conversation. 'Meanwhile, we ought to enjoy ourselves in these beautiful surroundings.'

Louisa smiled affectionately at her and spoke a few words of agreement. But she was mystified, and the fact of John Hilliard's mentioning the word 'sinister' seemed to have fixed itself in her mind.

John Hilliard was remarking on the house and its neglect, then saying how different the grounds were.

'What is your house like?' asked Sally with a smile.

'On par with this, valuewise. Immaculately kept, though, and we have a clever and efficient full-time gardener.'

Louisa looked at him with a hint of contempt. She had sized him up instantly when they met in the post office, and she hadn't needed to see the Rolls with its plate, HIL 1, parked at the rear of the manor to tell her that here was a man whom fate had treated with rather more than average generosity.

'You have a family?'

Sally spoke with genuine interest and he gave her a smile. He told her of his wife, children and grandchildren and all the time the note of pride was apparent.

'You have obviously made a great success of your life,' observed Louisa and he said yes, he was satisfied that he had not missed any chance that came his way. In business his success had been all that could be desired.

'I've been able to buy lovely homes for both my children,' he added almost pompously, 'and my wife has some exquisite and valuable jewellery – diamonds, rubies, emeralds – and of course masses of gold.'

'Your wife is a very fortunate lady.' The sarcasm in Louisa's voice was not lost on him. He glanced at his watch, rising as he did so.

'I must be off,' he said curtly. 'I promised to phone my wife, so if you'll excuse me?'

Sally said when he had gone, 'Well, what did you deduce from all those answers to your pertinent questions?' She was laughing with her eyes and Louisa thought how pretty she was.

'Not a lot,' came the swift admission. 'However, it has set me thinking. I'd like to know more about that partnership. Obviously Mr Hilliard was the winner, so how did James Devlin become rich, too? I did ask Eric Philpots if he had been in business and he said no.'

'Maybe he was left a fortune,' suggested Sally.

'But he had no relatives.'

'No ... no, he hadn't. So where did he get all this?' She spread a hand.

'That partnership,' mused Louisa, bypassing Sally's question. 'John Hilliard got the business, while James was thrown out.'

'Bought out. Mr Hilliard said so.'

'For how much? I'll bet you anything that our Mr Hilliard made a substantial gain at your benefactor's expense.'

They were on their way back to the house when they encountered Eric Philpots again. He informed them that Mrs Smallman had arrived with her maid, at which Louisa told him that they already knew.

'You will meet her at teatime, which is in about twenty minutes,' he added, his previous arrogance apparently dissolved.

Louisa asked carefully, 'Do you know anything about the lady – Mrs Smallman? The reason I ask is because of the puzzling aspects of this business. Sally here has never heard of James Devlin – or she hadn't until a week ago. Mr Hilliard had had no contact for over thirty years...' She tailed off on an unasked question.

He shook his head; he too was baffled.

'I know practically nothing. She's a woman who keeps her distance, but I was given the information that she and her husband had been friends of James Devlin – over twenty years ago.'

'Twenty?' Louisa's brow creased. 'I understand that Mrs Smallman is a widow.'

'Yes. She lost her husband eight years ago, but they had lost touch with Mr Devlin twelve years previously.'

'Curiouser and curiouser,' murmured Louisa to herself. Aloud she said, 'If Mr Smallman had been alive, do you suppose the legacy would have been his, rather than his wife's?'

'I can't answer that, Mrs Hooke – but it's a thought,' he added musingly. He saw the gardener with a watering can in his hand and gave him a salute. 'A most conscientious man is Albert Forsythe. He's no need to do much at all now that the house is being sold. But he keeps on – takes great pride in his work.'

'We've noticed.' Louisa glanced at him and added, 'He's due to take a well-earned rest, you were saying. Where will he live?'

'He mentioned a cottage he wants. But the price is high and he's having doubts.'

'Surely he's been left sufficient to get himself settled,' cut in Sally with a touch of indignation. 'All those years with Mr Devlin—'

'It's not that. I'm sure he will have more than enough to buy it. But he was telling me he is so ignorant of values that it might be overpriced. Obviously he doesn't want to lose money. He is hoping for some cash left over to invest as a supplement to his pension.'

'Poor old man.' Sally looked at Albert and smiled. 'He's been cut off for so long he's probably lost his confidence—' She turned to her aunt. 'You've had enough experience lately of house prices, so you could take a look at this cottage and proffer him some advice?'

'I'm sure he would welcome help like that,' said the solicitor.

'Very well,' smiled Louisa. 'I'll see what arrangements we can make for him to take me to see it.'

Mrs Smallman was sitting in the lounge – the Blue Drawing Room – as Louisa and Sally passed through the hall. Louisa stopped, her brown eyes flickering.

'Let us introduce ourselves.' She moved towards the door with Sally close behind. 'We might be able to succeed where Mr Philpots failed.'

'You're going to question her?'

'I am going to ingratiate myself with her,' was Louisa's half-amused reply. 'Come on – and wear your sweetest smile.'

The woman was the only occupant of the room and her sudden change of expression revealed that she was not averse to company.

'Please do,' was her reply to Louisa's asking if they could sit down. 'You must be Mrs Hooke, and her niece, Miss Renshawe. Mr Philpots said you were already here. Well, what do you make of it all? Having us come here, to stay for four days. I only hope it proves to be worth the trouble.'

'I'm sure it will be,' smiled Louisa, settling in the deep armchair opposite to Mrs Smallman and with a small piecrust table between them. Sally took possession of the other vacant chair and leant back, ready merely to listen with interest to whatever tactics her aunt intended to employ. 'You've had an accident, we heard. Is it still painful?' Louisa showed interest by glancing at the plaster.

'Very painful. It's my wrist – broken. My maid's fault entirely. She'd scrubbed the steps – they're tiles – and didn't dry them properly.' Her teeth snapped together. 'I slipped and fell. I might have been killed. The result is that I've had to bring her with me because I can't do much for myself at all. It's going to be a holiday for her. Just think, having to allow her so much free time when there is so much wants doing at home. She's upstairs unpacking now.'

'It's only for four days. You'll be resting it. I do hope you'll feel better soon and be able to enjoy this little break. This is a lovely place, don't you agree?'

'It's all right.' The woman paused a moment and then asked, 'Which one of you is the beneficiary? Mr Philpots seems reluctant to tell me anything.' She had a chill incisive voice that grated on Sally's ears.

'Miss Renshawe is the beneficiary,' submitted Louisa. 'I came along with her for company.'

'It's a funny business. I tried to get something out of that weak-livered solicitor but all he could say was wait till Monday!'

'We've decided not to tease ourselves with questions we can never hope to answer, and you should do the same, Mrs Smallman. Enjoy it here. The weather seems to be set fair. Do you walk much?' added Louisa with specious affability. 'I should imagine the lanes around here provide some pleasant, leisurely strolls.'

'I'm having trouble with my feet!'

'Oh, I'm sorry to hear that.' Louisa ignored the irascible manner of the other woman. 'Then it will be equally pleasant to sit in the garden and perhaps read?'

'I forgot my books! That maid could have remembered but she didn't.'

'I have some I can lend you,' promised Louisa obligingly. 'I'll bring them down and pass them to you at dinner.'

'Thank you.' Curt and grudging, the two brief words, and silence prevailed while Louisa recharged her batteries of politeness. She smiled presently and asked if Mrs Smallman had come far. Sally suppressed a smile; her aunt knew exactly how far Mrs Smallman had come.

'From Exeter. And you?'

'From a delightful little Dorset village called Melcombe Porcorum.'

'Never heard of it. But Dorset villages often

do have stupid names, I've noticed.'

Sally drew a breath. The woman was deliberately offensive. What a life poor Millie must have had. Five years...

Louisa, managing a smile meant to be one of encouragement, said quietly, 'Were you a friend of Mr Devlin?'

'My husband went to school with him and they became good friends. We used to visit him regularly at the other house.'

So her tongue was becoming loosened. Sally smiled to herself. Her aunt's tactics might after all pay off.

'Not here, then? He lived elsewhere?'

'Yes. Though the house was similar to this. Better kept, though, as he had a manservant living in.'

'He did?' Louisa's eyes opened wide. 'But for many years he's been a recluse, having only this gardener fellow working for him.'

'He wasn't always a recluse. He was getting married at one time. But the girl jilted him and he never bothered again. I didn't know him then because it must have been well over thirty years ago. Jack Smallman and I were married twenty-four years ago.'

Louisa cast a tentative glance in her niece's direction. Had Sally grasped that certain things were linking up?

'You say "over thirty years ago".' Louisa was calculating and paused before adding, 'Can you be a bit more specific?'

The woman sent her a sharp look through eyes that had suddenly narrowed.

'Just what is the object of all these questions?' she demanded aggressively. 'I don't think I like them.'

Louisa gave a careless shrug of her wide shoulders.

'I was merely making conversation. I hadn't realized I *was* asking too many questions. I suppose,' she went on thoughtfully after a pause, 'I was hoping, as you must be hoping, to clear up some of the mystery surrounding this matter of our being here. You see, Mrs Smallman, Sally has never set eyes on James Devlin and we were looking for similarities. But apparently you and your husband knew James well, so you are not surprised by the legacy?'

'I wouldn't say I'm not surprised,' returned the woman with unexpected amiability. 'We lost touch, remember.' She seemed for a moment to be making up her mind, while Louisa watched the changing expression with growing optimism. At last the woman said quietly after glancing around, 'There was a tiff on account of— Well, the cause of it is not important. It was a lot of fuss about nothing and I told James as much. We were right in the middle of one of our visits and he told us to leave. I gave him a piece of my mind and he told us never to come again; he never ever wanted to set eyes on us. Peculiar, he was. I told him to get his priorities right, said he couldn't see straight—' Suddenly she winced. 'My wrist. Drat that girl! I curse her every time the pain begins to shoot!'

'I'm so sorry about the pain. Perhaps you should see a doctor.'

The woman shook her head.

'Time alone is required, so my own doctor said. He warned me of the occurrence of shooting pains. I shall just have to bear them.'

'You have painkillers with you?'

'Of course I have.'

'Perhaps Sally could go to your room and fetch them for you?'

'If I wanted them my maid could be told to fetch them, but I was warned not to take too many.'

'You were talking about the tiff,' began Louisa tentatively. 'In view of it, doesn't it strike you as most strange that James Devlin left you money?'

'I'm puzzled, yes, but I reached the conclusion that he'd forgiven Jack and was making amends for being so rotten with him – with us both. The legacy is his way of saying he was sorry.'

'You mentioned the word "forgiven". What was there to forgive? Had your husband wronged James Devlin?'

Suddenly the woman's eyes blazed and pure fury filled the air.

'Who the devil are you to ask all these personal questions? Mind your own business! You're just a nosy parker who wants gagging!' And with that unexpected outburst she rose to her feet and left them, making her way somewhat awkwardly to the door. Her parting shot was, 'You meddlesome bitch!'

'Phew!' exclaimed Sally, bursting into a laugh. 'So much for your ingratiating tactics. You now know her opinion of you. Will it curb that inquisitive tongue?'

'What do you think?' Louisa joined in the laughter. 'But this business becomes increasingly mystifying,' she added on a more sober note. 'Do you realize that the two we have spoken to have both treated James Devlin badly? It doesn't make sense. I want to talk to the other three.'

'You suspect that they, too, have treated him badly?' Sally's brow was puckered in a frown. Why, if these people had treated James Devlin badly, were they here, with the promise of a legacy? She added, 'If that is what you think, Auntie, then where do I come in? I haven't done any harm to the man.'

Louisa became guarded. She had no proof that Sally's father had done some harm to James Devlin, but even if she had she would not disturb her niece by mentioning it.

'Obviously you don't fit into the pattern. And for that reason I now see that my train of thought has taken the wrong direction.'

'Auntie...' There was a chiding note in the slow and quiet voice. 'You're merely trying to put me at my ease, but I can guess what your conclusions are – even though you have not yet spoken with the other three. You're thinking that these people from James' past have been brought here to be punished in some way. But are you expecting James Devlin's ghost to appear one night and murder us all in our beds?' She was laughing, oblivious of the fact that her manner had brought a great sigh of relief to her aunt's lips.

Louisa laughed and said, 'It seems I shall make a detective of you yet. However, as I haven't had the opportunity of weighing up the others, I'll admit I'm trying to create a mystery just so I can occupy my mind in solving it.'

'Well, no one denies there is a mystery, so you haven't created one. We decided to relax and enjoy the break, so I for one intend doing just that.'

Afternoon tea was served in the Blue Drawing Room promptly at four o'clock. Eric Philpots was standing with his back to the massive oak fireplace, waiting to make his introductory speech. Louisa and Sally had been taken by Mrs Thorpe to a round table by the window. Mrs Smallman was alone at a table which had been set for two. John

Hilliard was sitting opposite to Joseph Powell on a table for four. When the two friends, Bernard Wilding and Dr Leonard Fulham, had joined them the solicitor began his speech by welcoming them to Hazeldene Manor and expressing the hope that they would all have a pleasant sojourn in this delightful home and leave on Monday afternoon feeling it had all been worthwhile. John Hilliard came in on a pause to ask why they had been brought here when it was normal for the will to be read in the solicitor's office.

'Your benefactor wished that all the legatees should get to know one another. Call it a whim if you like; we all know by now that he was an eccentric and as I have said to several of you, eccentrics are unpredictable. This is puzzling to some of you and perhaps a little frustrating to some as well.' His glance flicked to Louisa because she had been more persistent than any of the others in her questions, both on the phone and during the several uninvited visits she had made to his office. 'I believe someone has put forward the idea that James Devlin had some ulterior motive for all this but I'm sure he was not that kind of a man.'

'How *can* you be sure,' Louisa wanted to know, 'when you have never met James Devlin?'

Before he could answer Joseph Powell asked how he could know anything at all when he had not even had anything to do with the making of the will.

'Most of you have already asked these questions,' returned the solicitor imperturbably, 'and my answer now is as it has always been: wait until Monday.'

'Have you seen the will?' Again it was Joseph Powell who spoke. Louisa looked hard at him, deciding he was a cocky little man with an inflated ego. He was as unlikeable as Mrs Smallman.

'I have not seen the will.'

'He made it out himself, I think you said?' Dr Fulham spoke quietly, in contrast to the harsh and over-emphasized accents of Joseph Powell. 'But if he never left this place, who signed it? The gardener couldn't have, being a beneficiary.'

'Monday,' almost snapped Eric Philpots.

The Thorpes appeared, each carrying a tray. Albert Forsythe was standing by the sideboard, looking smart in a navy blue jacket and trousers a shade lighter. His shirt was white, but if he possessed a tie he had elected not to wear it.

'Where is Millie, I wonder?' Sally frowned and glanced all around. 'I hope she isn't ill, or anything.'

She had scarcely finished when the solicitor asked curtly, 'Where is your maid, Mrs Smallman?'

'I've told her to get a sandwich in the

kitchen.' The voice was arrogant and harsh, with some of the words stressed unnecessarily. Everyone turned to look at her but she remained coldly indifferent to the stares.

'She must eat with everyone else. My instructions are that no one shall be separated during meals.'

'Instructions? Where, my man, did you receive any instructions?'

'Your maid, madam, must join us.'

'What a stupid condition!' Her face was purple, her eyes glaring. 'My servant does not sit at the same table as I!'

'Then she shall be found another.'

'As you please, Mr Philpots!'

Millie was brought in by Albert. Louisa said quietly, 'We have room and we would like the young lady to join us.'

A smile lit Millie's eyes. The gardener seemed to hover longer than was necessary and so he heard Millie say, 'Thank you very much. You're kind, Mrs Hooke,' but no one else heard because Millie's tone was not much above a whisper.

'Meet my niece, Sally Renshawe.'

'Pleased to meet you,' murmured the Irish girl shyly. And she whispered, 'Your aunt told me a lot about you. You're fortunate,' she added wistfully. 'It must be a wonderful feeling, coming into money.'

Albert was bringing over the cutlery and crockery from Mrs Smallman's table; he smiled benignly at Millie as he bent to put the things on the table.

'It is wonderful,' admitted Sally but she did add that she hoped it would not be too much. This was heard because someone laughed and said, 'Not too much? It can be as much as it likes for me!' Another loud guffaw; Louisa eyed Joseph Powell with disgust. What about you, Mrs Smallman?'

'Oh, a hundred thousand would be acceptable; twice that would be even better.'

'What would you do with it?'

'Live in a luxury hotel – then I'd be rid of a maid who doesn't like work.'

A murmur arose; Millie's eyes filled up and her cheeks turned crimson. Louisa challenged Eric Philpots with a narrowed stare and he rose to the occasion.

'Mrs Smallman, I must remind you that this is meant to be a happy, social occasion for all of us. Your remarks can clearly be seen to be objectionable to other guests and I would ask you to refrain from any further public criticism of your maid.'

She stood up. 'I didn't come here to be insulted! How I deal with a servant of mine is no one's business but my own—'

'I'm afraid it becomes the business of everyone here if you cause unpleasantness, Mrs Smallman, and your offensive behaviour is most certainly creating an atmosphere which will not be tolerated. You are at liberty to leave this room if you wish.'

'If I do, my maid comes with me!'

Sally spoke in a whisper to her aunt, who nodded.

'I've room for Millie, until you are ready to employ her.' Sally turned to the unhappy girl. 'Tell her you're no longer in her employ; come back with us and stay with me—'

'No, it is kind of you, but I would rather do it properly, give Mrs Smallman a month's notice. It is only right.'

'But you owe her nothing, Millie, not after this exhibition.'

Louisa intervened, saying she fully under-stood Millie's desire to do what she herself considered right and proper. Nevertheless, Louisa spoke to Mrs Smallman across the room, her voice decisive and stern.

'Millie happens to be a friend of ours – I've known her for some time, and as her friend, I also would ask you, Mrs Smallman, to refrain from any further criticism in my hearing. Should you forget my injunction I shall ask Millie to leave your employ at once and take up residence with my niece and me.' There was a general buzz, and immediate interest in the rather manly woman who had spoken with such strength of purpose and, it would seem, taken the wind completely out of the other woman's sails. She glowered but sat down. Her stay was short, though, for after eating only one sandwich and sipping her tea for a minute she rose with what dignity she could muster and swept from the room.

'Well,' said the doctor, 'the air seems fresher for her departure.'

'Imagine James including a woman like that in his will.' Bernard Wilding's voice, though quiet, was of the carrying kind; it reached Louisa's table and she became interested in the man. He seemed pleasant enough, as was his friend, the doctor. Neatly dressed in a lounge suit of good-quality tweed, with spotless shirt and a general air of wholesome cleanliness, he was in her opinion more fitting to be a legatee than either John Hilliard or Joseph Powell – and of course, the woman who had just left.

'It seems they're a rum mixture.' Albert was serving tea from a Georgian silver pot and spoke as he poured the piping hot beverage into Louisa's cup.

'Don't you know any of them?'

He shook his head.

'Not one; they were all before my time.'

All so long ago, she mused, not for the first time. And from bits of conversation she had heard during tea, James Devlin had not kept in touch with the three to whom she had not yet had a chance to chat. That meant that not one of the legatees had seen James for at least twenty years. He had loved animals; he had disliked people, and yet it was to people he had left his money – most of it, probably. Mr Philpots had intimated that some had gone to animal charities. But why not everything?

'Auntie, what do you make of it all? I wasn't going to worry about the situation here, but it's becoming more and more puzzling all the time.'

'And what's troubling you most is that James Devlin left money to a horror like Mrs Smallman.'

'Yes, it is. He's never seen her for twenty years and yet he includes her in his will. It's the stupidest thing I've ever heard. She must always have been objectionable. I don't believe she was ever nice to him, that she ever did anything to deserve what he is doing for her. She spoke of his forgiving her husband for something or other, but that doesn't make sense to me, either. It was all far too long ago.'

They were in Sally's room and Louisa was sitting on the bed. Sally was by the open wardrobe, choosing a dress for dinner. Would it be formal? They ought to ask, she decided, taking up a flowered ankle-length dress.

Her aunt was saying, 'We've agreed that Mrs Smallman doesn't deserve a legacy, but what about the Powell man?'

Sally swung around.

'Yes, him as well.' And she added darkly, 'I can easily see him doing James a dirty trick.'

'What is termed these days as a nasty piece of work.'

Sally looked at her. What exactly was going on behind that unfathomable expression? Her aunt would tell her in her own good time, and not before, she decided resignedly and asked if the dinner would be a formal affair.

'Not too formal. I should wear that pretty midnight-blue cocktail dress. I expect the men will wear jackets and ties.'

'OK, the blue it is. What are you wearing, Auntie?'

'The silk suit. A sensible form of attire – no unnecessary fuss.'

Sally only laughed and suggested they go for a stroll before dinner.

'Are you fit, Auntie?'

'As fit as I shall ever be. You know me; I'm ready for a walk any time.' She added as they left the house, 'I must have a word with Albert about my seeing his cottage. I also want to ask him about some cuttings. He might just offer to pot them up for me.'

They found him replenishing the bird feeders, two of which he had already hung on the branch of a tree.

'Ah, the two ladies out walking again,' he smiled. 'Er – I was talking to Mr Philpots and he said you wouldn't mind giving me some advice about the cottage I'm thinking of buying?'

'I shall be delighted to have a look and tell you what I think,' she replied at once. 'I suggest we go in Sally's car?'

'That'll be nice.' His eyes had brightened. 'I usually go on the train – taking a taxi to the railway station.'

'You've seen the cottage more than once, then?'

He nodded his head. 'Three times, and I like it very much. It's just the right size, and it has a garden. It's just the price. It seems high for what it is.'

'Country cottages are at a premium. So many people want to get away from the noise and bustle of the towns. That's the reason why the cottages command such high prices; people buy them as a second home, to escape to at the weekends.'

It was arranged that they would go on the Saturday afternoon. It was only twenty-five miles away at the most, he said. Louisa then introduced the matter of the cuttings and he immediately offered to pot them up for her. Perhaps they could walk around now and she could say which she wanted?

'Some roses, certainly,' she said for a start. 'These are quite special. Have you some secret, magical power?' She laughed. Then became instantly serious. 'You must be sad at leaving all this.'

'Sad, yes. I've admitted it. But also I want to own my own place, to be my own boss after so many years in service.'

'It's understandable,' interposed Sally, but added that it seemed a shame that he would not still be enjoying the fruits of all his years of labour. At which he informed her that the gardens would be destroyed anyway, when the building firm who were buying the estate started work with their bulldozers.

'So you see, Miss Renshawe, change is inevitable. It happens all the time.'

'Houses are to be built here?'

'Two hundred, just for starters. Trouble is there are too many people in the world.' He hooked up the third feeder on to a tree. 'I must go. I have to see to the graves. I shall probably see you at dinner. Mr Philpots asked me if I would help at all the meal times. That pair have told him they can't manage.'

'Graves?' repeated Louisa ignoring the rest. 'What graves?'

'The dogs' graves.' He pointed. 'Just over there, where the clump of trees is.'

'You mean, you have dogs buried there?'

'Mr Devlin was a dog lover, remember. He always had dogs, often three at a time. Tessa was his. He'd take in any lost dog that happened to stray on to our land. So he had this cemetery made – we did it between us.' He suddenly seemed a long way off, far from them.

'Can we see this cemetery?' Sally was eager

85

and he turned his head to subject her to a look of interest so fixed that she was reminded of another occasion when he had stared at her like this.

'You're such a charming young lady,' he said apologetically, 'so enthusiastic and impulsive. Knowing you is a most happy experience for me.'

'Oh, Auntie,' Sally was saying a moment later as they followed him towards the rise, 'he's so lonely. I wish he'd buy a cottage closer to us, so we could look after him.' Her voice was edged with concern; the gardener cocked his head, and slowed his steps, as if he would catch her words. 'What will happen to him when he's no longer able to look after himself?'

Louisa said nothing. There were so many lonely people in the world; one could not concern oneself with them all. But she knew her Sally, with her soft heart, and she laid a gentle hand on her shoulder.

The cemetery was on the slope of the rise and it faced east. Tall cedars and yews and other evergreens surrounded it on three sides with the eastern side open to the first light of dawn. Louisa counted five graves and a swift glance at the one closest told her that a mother and daughter were buried here. But it *was* only a swift glance because the centre-piece, the thing of beauty that caught the attention, was the white marble, delicately carved and supported by perfectly fashioned miniature Corinthian columns in polished granite.

Sally gasped, and could only stare in speechless admiration and wonderment. She heard her aunt ask, 'Why this? Why was Bess so special?' She was still reading the inscription.

The gardener came and stood beside her. 'Bess saved Mr Devlin's life. It was before my time but he told me about it. He was out on a long tramp and fell and broke his leg. It was a desolate region with, he said, no possible hope of anyone coming along because for one thing he was miles from a road. Bess stayed with him for a while but then she up and sped off. Help came before nightfall, with the dog leading the rescue party.'

'What a lovely story,' breathed Sally. 'No wonder he had a very special grave for her.' She moved closer. 'But ... how sad for her to die so young.' She lifted her eyes to meet those of the old man. 'What happened?'

'Four years old.' Louisa shook her head. 'How old was she when she saved James Devlin's life?'

'Four. She died two weeks afterwards.'

'Good God...' Louisa glanced at her niece. Sally's eyes were filled with tears; she was too choked up to speak. 'James must have been devastated.'

'He told me, actually admitted, that he

wept for days. He said he loved that dog more than he'd have loved a brother, and I used to think he never did get over it. He always had her photograph – just a snapshot, of course – on his bedside table. I took it away and I'll show it to you before you leave, if you want to see it, that is? I felt he would want me to put it away.'

'Yes,' eagerly from Sally. 'We'd love to see it.'

Louisa said slowly, 'The inscription – Bess died twenty years ago. James Devlin came here twelve years ago.' She knew the explanation but waited with interest to hear it voiced.

'We moved the grave, piece by piece. The casket is of oak and brass so it was easy to lift. In fact, the whole thing was easy enough to move.'

'You moved the grave?' Sally gazed at the inscription for a long moment and then, 'What will happen to it now? I mean, if these builders—' She shook her head vigorously. 'You can't let them demolish it, It wouldn't be right. Auntie...?'

'You're asking me to have it – to move this grave into my garden—'

'It will be quite big enough, if you get Mrs Millsom's cottage.'

The old man said gently, 'Mrs Hooke wouldn't want it. After all, it doesn't mean anything to anyone but the man who is now dead.'

'But for it to be demolished, thrown into a rubbish skip, or something. It just can't be allowed to happen. I'll have it!'

He laughed.

'You want to remove a dog's grave from here to your garden? You would have to have a large plot or otherwise you'd be looking at it all the time and you wouldn't want that, I'm sure.'

'There's much logic in what Albert says, Sally.'

'Your garden would be large enough, though. You have an area to one side which is hidden by trees. Maybe you haven't seen it, but I have; it would be a lovely peaceful place for Bess's grave.'

Louisa reminded her niece that it was by no means certain that River Bank Cottage would be hers.

'The young lady is persistent. She has a soft heart.'

'It's just that I can't bear to think of this lovely thing, the grave of such a faithful friend, being thrown away, maybe ending up in one of those crushers—' Sally shuddered and her aunt put in swiftly: 'If it's all right with Albert, and if I get the cottage, I'll agree to have Bess's grave.' Whatever next? she asked herself. What other complications would this tender-hearted niece of hers bring into her life?

The old man said in a strangely affected tone, 'I'm sure that James, if he could know of this, would be very happy at your action, Mrs Hooke.'

'Mr Devlin, wherever he might be, has Sally to thank much more than he has me.'

The gardener was on his knees, pulling up a few tiny weeds that had sprung up between two of the marble slabs. They left him there, tending the grave, the dog sitting very close, its head touching his knee. Louisa had stopped and turned, her grey eyes narrowed and puzzled. Tessa had been James Devlin's faithful friend ... but had very quickly transferred her affection to Albert. Had he and the dog always been this close?

Three

Louisa was in her room changing for dinner, but every now and then she would glance down to consult the notebook that lay open on the dressing table.

'One,' she murmured to herself. 'Mrs S and Mr H definitely not the kind of people whom James would ordinarily include in his will, as each had done him some injury. Two: it was twenty years since she told J that he had his values all wrong. Quarrel. She and husband ordered away. Three: Twenty years since the dog died.' Louisa's eyes widened with sudden perception. She glanced at the clock, swiftly finished her toilet and made a hurried exit from the house. She was probably too late. The gardener was most likely already in the house, helping with the dinner.

'Ah!' She found him winding up his hose-pipe. He spoke before she did, with a flattering remark on her appearance. 'This dress? I've had it for years.' And then, without further preamble, 'Can I ask you how Bess died?'

He gave a slight start, plainly surprised by her question. His hesitation caused her to ask if she had upset him by her query.

'No, of course not,' he replied. 'After all, she wasn't my dog. You just took me by surprise since it wasn't a question I would have expected.' A pause followed before he looked straight into her eyes and said, 'Bess was shot.'

'Shot?' Louisa stared at him. 'How was that? It was an accident?'

'Yes, it was an accident, but...' He tailed off, to become thoughtful for a space. 'It was before my time, you understand? But from what James told me – and he only ever spoke once about the matter – Bess didn't die immediately and was in great pain. He said he knew he should have asked the man with the gun to take another shot and kill her, but instead he had hopes of saving her and rushed off to the vet with her in his car. By doing this he subjected her to another hour's suffering and it left him with a feeling of self-blame and, to my mind, Mrs Hooke, he never did get over it.' He glanced at his watch and she knew he wanted to go. She pondered on what he had been about to say after the 'but...' Whatever it was had been left unsaid. He hadn't mentioned the name of the man who shot the dog, so obviously he had not guessed – as she had – that the man who shot Bess was the husband of the woman who was here with her maid.

Louisa said slowly, 'The death of Bess seems to be the cause of James' withdrawal from human society, to become a recluse. Rather drastic, wasn't it?'

The old man nodded in agreement.

'Not many would have reacted like that. But I believe it was the final straw.'

'Final straw?' How much did this man know, wondered Louisa. How much could she learn from him?

He was shrugging his shoulders; plainly he was impatient to be off, since there was not much time before dinner and he would have to change. Nevertheless, he paused to say, 'He mentioned several other instances of his being what he described as a sufferer from the infamy of the human mind.'

'I had not imagined James Devlin as being of the confiding kind, but obviously he confided in you.'

'Very occasionally. There were a few times when he would seem almost eager for conversation, as if he had temporarily returned to normal. It was then he would ask me to have a drink with him and we'd sit for an hour and chat. At other times he would let slip things which proved to me he'd suffered some very hard knocks in his earlier days.'

'Everyone suffers knocks, but most people stand up to them.'

'True, very true. Others take it hard, and suffer. It depends on their temperament. I guess he wasn't tough. I wouldn't know because, you see, before I went to him fourteen years ago I was sixteen years with a widowed lady who also kept herself to herself for the most part. So I, too, have led what you'd call a sheltered life.'

'You are saying that as you yourself haven't suffered any knocks you cannot say what your reaction would have been?'

He nodded; he was uneasy because of the time. But as he made to turn away Louisa remarked that he himself appeared to be deeply moved when talking about Bess.

'I am,' he agreed. 'I feel it especially when I'm tending her grave. You see, James had a strange way of affecting one's emotions. It was a particular way he had of relating something. Maybe it was something left over from the time when he was in amateur dramatics – when he was very young.' With a word of apology he left her staring after him ... and remembering that her sister – Sally's mother – had once been in an amateur dramatic society.

Louisa made her way slowly and thoughtfully back to the house. Once in her room, she took up the notebook and a pencil. But she made no attempt to add anything to what was written there. Instead, she began turning over in her mind all she had learned up till now.

It was Mrs Smallman's husband who had shot Bess – by accident. So apparently he had been allowed to go out with a gun into the grounds of the estate. Probably he was shooting pigeons. But he had hit another target. There had been a quarrel and Mrs Smallman had told James Devlin to get his values right. 'Why all the fuss? It's only a dog!' Louisa could almost hear her saying it, in that harsh and arrogant voice. The amateur dramatics ... James had been jilted at one time – when? Could it possibly have been Sally's mother...? Louisa began reckoning the time factor and – yes, it could have fitted perfectly, could have been about thirty years ago. Sally's mother was 'getting on a bit' when her daughter was born.

'So what have we up till now?' she asked herself aloud and with pencil poised. 'Three of the beneficiaries should not be beneficiaries at all.'

Sally and Millie were already at the table when Louisa arrived in the dining room. Both greeted her with smiles and she thought how pleasant her life was going to be from now on. She was glad she had decided, on becoming a widow, to return to her own country. Her niece was already like her own daughter, and with this charming little Irish girl living in her home Louisa felt that the days of her semi-retirement would be just about as happy as they could be.

'Sorry I'm late.' She sat down and soup was put before them within seconds. After casual conversation had taken up the time to eat it and the plates cleared away, Louisa asked casually, looking at her niece, 'When was it that your mother was a member of the amateur dramatic society in Surrey?'

Sally stared at her aunt in some puzzlement.

'Why do you want to know?'

'Oh, I was just remembering it and could not quite recall the exact time. You weren't born, of course, but I wondered if she had ever mentioned it?'

'She did, on a couple of occasions. It was when she was quite young, living at home with your parents – in Surrey, as you say.'

'Oh, well, never mind.' Louisa felt it wise not to continue with the subject but Sally was speaking again, saying her mother had shown her a photograph of herself, on a beach.

'The man with her wasn't Father, so I suppose it was another of the actors.'

'You have this photograph?'

'Yes – somewhere among all the papers Mother left. I've not even been able to go through them all yet,' she went on to confess. 'It'll be an unhappy task which I continue to shirk, I'm afraid.'

Her aunt nodded understandingly and offered to go through the papers herself. Sally was only too willing. Louisa fell silent, allowing the two girls to chat. She wanted very much to see that photograph.

Was she on the right track? Was the man in the photo James Devlin, the man jilted by Sally's mother? It would certainly explain why Sally was in the will.

Her reverie was cut by Sally's suddenly saying, 'You're miles away, Auntie.' A hint of suspicion entered her eyes. 'I would very much like to know what is occupying your mind. I'm sure I fail to see why you should suddenly want to know about Mummy's brief association with acting.'

It was half a question but Louisa merely laughed and said, 'Take no notice, dear. I'm not quite sure myself what I'm about.' She was exasperated by her inability to fit the pieces of this jigsaw puzzle into place. Of course, it might be a lot easier when she had talked with the others included in the will.

The two girls began chatting again and it was plain that both were excited about Millie's coming to work for Louisa.

'If you get Mrs Millsom's cottage, Auntie, then everything will be just perfect.' She paused. 'Why don't you give her a ring? She's probably managed to get her son round to her way of thinking by now.'

'I might just do that.' Louisa's eyes slid to Millie. If the cottage did happen to be hers, then she could persuade Millie to give in her notice to the detestable Mrs Smallman.

It was a pleasant meal despite the dour faces of the couple who waited on them. An unfathomable pair, mused Louisa. Something deep and devious beneath the stolid exterior of both of them. Louisa was sure they had some plan in mind, a plan which would be carried out before Monday. She must try her best to watch them closely.

Albert's smile was a welcome change when he came to their table to serve the coffee. Very different he looked now, with his white shirt, black bow tie and dark grey trousers. His hands had been scrubbed clean, so that his fingernails looked far different from when they had been poking about in the soil.

Liqueurs were served by Thorpe while his wife put a dish of petits-fours on each table. Mr Philpots drank his coffee and left the room.

'This is doing us grand.' The loud voice of Joseph Powell grated on Louisa's nerves but she sent him a swift and inviting smile. Sally suppressed a grin; she turned to Millie and they began chatting together again. A friendship was already being cemented.

'Most pleasant,' returned Louisa turning in her chair, the more easily to see the man's face. Florid and lacking entirely the refinement seen on the faces of the other men, it reminded Louisa of a bloated and unwholesome ape kept as a pet by a neighbour of hers in Boston. 'You're obviously enjoying yourself.'

'Up till now.' He picked up his glass. 'Here's to Monday and the visit of Lady Luck!' He quaffed the cognac, oblivious of the contemptuous glances of almost everyone present. Only Mrs Smallman from her table by the window returned any comment.

'Can't come quickly enough for me. This place is depressing, this idiotic stay here unnecessary. I resent being manipulated like a puppet, just to satisfy the whim of a man who isn't even here to have his laugh – if a laugh at our expense was intended.' She sniffed and added, 'I only hope it's substantial after all this.'

'It will be,' replied Joseph Powell confidently.

'You seem very sure, Mr Powell.' Again Louisa produced one of her charmingly specious smiles. 'Perhaps you know something we others don't?' Her eyes flickered round the room. All the others were keenly interested. 'Mr Philpots didn't say much at our interview and I expect it was the same with you.'

'If you say so.' Probing old busybody! She'll get nothing out of me!

Mrs Smallman spoke again. 'Maybe you and I can have a chat, Mr Powell? I believe there's a quaint little pub about a mile and a half along the road. Can I buy you a drink? You could drive us there in your car.'

'Not tonight, thank you,' he returned shortly. Another of them, he thought. Fishing for information. Well, he was keeping what he knew to himself. 'I've nothing in particular I want to say to anyone.'

A silence followed, as indeed it would after an interchange like that. It was Louisa who broke it at length, to say in a deceptively casual tone of voice, 'I expect all of us have some scraps of information we wish to keep to ourselves, Mr Powell. However, all will be revealed on Monday. Meanwhile I for one intend deriving full enjoyment from having this break in such delightful surroundings.'

'Delightful!' exclaimed Mrs Smallman.

'The house is like a morgue!'

A murmur of protest brought an instant tightness to the woman's small mouth. Louisa told Sally to drink up and they'd have a stroll in the grounds before dark. She asked Millie if she were coming too.

'I'd like to very much, but...' The girl looked at her employer. 'Will it be all right, madam?'

'No, it will not be all right! I need you. I'm helpless – can't even undress myself. What do you think I pay you for?'

Millie went bright red.

Louisa checked her temper with the utmost difficulty. She said tersely, 'It would seem you're intending to go to bed now. If that is so, Millie should be free to join us in, say, half an hour's time. She can join us—'

'I don't know what time I'm going to bed. Millie won't be free at all tonight – or any other night for that matter.' She glowered at Louisa. 'I would remind you that Millie is *my* maid. She is not a guest here in the sense that you and I are. Had I not met with this accident – of which she was the cause – she wouldn't be here at all. Come, girl, I need you upstairs!'

Louisa's teeth snapped together.

'If Millie wasn't so far away from home, and lacking most of the self-confidence possessed by others of her age these days, you'd not be able to adopt this attitude.' She stopped, almost adding that it would not be for much longer now. But with Millie present Louisa decided it were best for the girl if she curbed her tongue.

She and Sally went out into the garden. The evening was balmy as the setting sun's rays contributed to the atmosphere of warmth and peace. An idyllic place, mused Louisa. If one had to be a recluse, then what more pleasant a place in which to indulge one's whim?

They came to the little arbour where they had rested earlier and made to sit down, but at that moment the doctor and his friend appeared from around a bend in the path. Both smiled and Bernard Wilding commented on the fragrance of the air, while his friend added his supplement by saying it was all due to the wonderful work done by the gardener. Louisa smiled in agreement then invited them to sit down.

'I think there'll be enough room for us all,' she added taking her own place next to Sally. 'We haven't had much opportunity of getting to know one another yet.'

'No.' Bernard made a grimace. 'The attitude of that dreadful woman was rather off-putting.' He sat down next to Louisa. 'I think we all wanted to get out into the fresh air.'

'A deplorable display,' agreed Louisa.

'Her long-suffering maid was almost in tears.' The doctor's rugged, good-natured

101

face became stern as he added, 'People like her are totally immune to the hurts they inflict on others.'

'Yes, they are.' Louisa was thinking of the hurts inflicted on James Devlin. She turned her head to examine his features even though she had already done so. A firm chin and strong bone structure, brows wide apart, high forehead. Eyes open and frank. She gave a small sigh. Her earlier detailed examination of both men's features had left her with the conviction that neither would deliberately wrong another human being. She said curiously:

'Did you know James Devlin, Doctor? I mean, was he ever a friend of yours?'

'Not a friend, no.' The brief reply sounded curt, though it was not meant to be. But in any case, it would take much more than that to silence Louisa's tongue.

'But you have some idea why he should leave you money?' Her eyes slid from the doctor's profile to that of Bernard. He turned immediately when she added, 'And you, too, Mr Wilding?'

'Yes, we do know why. It's in gratitude. Yes, we know exactly why.'

'You do?' Louisa could see her theory falling apart. 'It is a reward for something?'

'For saving his life.'

'You – which one of you—?'

'Both,' supplied the doctor, but went on to

admit it was nothing heroic. 'We saved him from taking his own life.'

Sally felt slightly sorry for her aunt because judging by her expression her calculations had suffered a severe setback.

It was Bernard Wilding who related what had happened, while both Louisa and Sally listened with avid interest.

'When was this?' Louisa wanted to know when presently Bernard stopped speaking.

'A long time ago. Over thirty years. He later prospered and naturally would be grateful for our saving him from self-destruction.'

Louisa said thoughtfully, 'But he apparently didn't have a happy life. He's been a recluse for over twenty years.'

'So long as that? Mr Philpots gave us scant information about him.'

'You said that at the time of his attempted suicide he was passing through a traumatic period. Did he tell you anything about it?'

A small silence followed; she wondered if she would find herself being snubbed, as she had been with Mrs Smallman. But no – these two were of a different breed.

'He'd been jilted only a month after the death of his mother, to whom he was devoted. She herself committed suicide. A sad story: her husband had gone off with a girl of eighteen. James said his mother collapsed and was in hospital being treated for nerves. She was discharged a week later and a few days after that she took her own life.'

'How terrible!' exclaimed Sally, her eyes filling up. 'How very terrible for him.'

'That wasn't all, apparently,' supplemented the doctor. 'He had tried to rebuild on the ashes and was persuaded to sell his house in order to go into a partnership with someone who had begun a carpet business. James told me he felt this might occupy his whole time – he worked all hours, it seemed. But after only a short while the partner told him to go, and he robbed him, that was a certain fact. James hadn't put up any sort of a fight; he felt the easiest way out was to leave the world behind. He said people were all rotten and only animals were fit to live.'

'He was in a bad way,' murmured Louisa almost to herself. Her thoughts were shooting forward and she enquired interestedly if they knew how, in the end, James Devlin became rich.

'It must have come as a surprise to you to be left a legacy by a man who had had nothing?'

'Naturally. But by a strange coincidence information came to me through my locum when I happened to mention I was coming here and that I'd been left a legacy by James Devlin. Why I mentioned his name I don't know, but my locum, Grantley, said he'd taken part in a project when at school. It was on changing land use and he remembered

104

that a James Devlin's house and much of his land was required for a projected new motor-way and was subject to a compulsory purchase. There was a great deal of publicity, owing to the fight James put up – along with others similiarly affected. They lost, of course, but he did receive a vast sum as compensation. The rest of the land, which would otherwise have been worthless, was bought by a frozen-food firm for the growing of pulses, thereby giving James another substantial sum of money.'

'Hmm...' murmured Louisa when the explanation came to an end. 'That has cleared up one question that has been on my mind.'

'Only one?' from Bernard Wilding in some amusement. 'If you'll forgive my saying it, Mrs Hooke, your mind is far more curious than most.'

She laughed, but it was Sally who said, 'Auntie likes mysteries. She always feels she must clear them up.'

'I'm sure we'd all like to learn more about this business,' agreed the doctor. 'You see, we've been totally out of touch with James since the incident of which we've spoken, and so it did come as a complete surprise when we learned from the solicitor that he'd remembered us in his will.'

Louisa said, ignoring all that, 'The other thing that isn't cleared up is where, in the first place, did James get this estate which later proved to be a gold mine.'

'Oh, that. It also came out during the publicity – which lasted for months, by the way – that James had inherited the estate from an uncle whom he did not know he had, along with a cousin who took his share before the profitable house sale and went off. It had been in the family, apparently, for over two hundred years.'

'He inherited it...' Louisa wondered about the other cousin. He had lost out, apparently.

'It was a happy ending for Mr Devlin,' interposed Sally. 'But yet he never was happy, was he?'

'He certainly didn't make the most of his good fortune,' agreed Bernard.

'He never did get over his dislike of his fellow men.'

'So he shut himself away,' murmured Sally on a little note of sadness. 'He only had Albert, no one else at all.'

Louisa became lost in thought. Vaguely she heard Sally and the two men talking, heard Sally's answer to a question from the doctor.

'I can't think why. It's a complete mystery why he should have left me anything. I had never even heard of him until I met Mr Philpots.' One of the two men responded; Louisa was still preoccupied. She came to presently to ask the doctor if he really believed James Devlin was glad to be saved.

'But of course.' He slanted her a look of

surprise. 'Why else would he be leaving us money?'

That, said Louisa to herself, was to her mind a question still unanswered.

'Tell me, what was his reaction at the time?'

A small pause ensued before Bernard replied: 'To tell the truth, he wasn't at all pleased.'

'Ah! I thought so.'

'You...?' The doctor gave an impatient shake of his head and asked what this was all about.

'That particular curiosity of my mind spoken of by Mr Wilding a moment ago. You see, I am of the firm opinion that James Devlin wished, all through his life, that you two had left him alone to do what *he* wanted to do.'

The two men exchanged glances.

'As a matter of fact, that was his attitude. He cursed us for our interference. But I cannot agree with you, Mrs Hooke, that his attitude remained the same throughout the next thirty years or more.'

She shrugged, unwilling to reveal her thoughts, her conclusions.

Sally helped by observing that dusk was falling rather quickly and a faintly damp chill was affecting the air. Neither she nor her aunt had brought out wraps and so with goodnights to the two friends Louisa and her niece went indoors.

The following morning Louisa was up early, intending to take a brisk walk before breakfast. At ten minutes to seven she had left Sally fast asleep, collected her clothes and gone to the bathroom for a shower. Half an hour later she was dressed and treading softly along the landing so as not to disturb anyone who was not already up and moving. All was silent until suddenly she was aware of a voice from the room occupied by Joseph Powell. Although deliberately quiet, the voice carried a distinct quality of anger. Louisa stopped, and thought how convenient mobile phones were, as otherwise he could not have phoned from his room. Her musings cut short as she heard James Devlin's name mentioned. She moved to the door, unashamedly listening, and soon knew who was on the other end of the line.

'... What kind of a wife are you to accuse me like this, to think I'd be stealing some of his silver or something!' A pause, and then, 'Look here, Amy, isn't it time you stopped accusing me of robbing James? I took only what was legally mine— What do you mean, not legally? I inherited half of everything—' Silence followed and Louisa would have given anything to know what his wife was saying. He spoke at last, in an explosive voice.

'Those paintings were in the attic, thick

with dust, and if I hadn't spotted their value they'd probably have been thrown out with the rubbish. Certainly James had no idea of their value, so what the eye doesn't see the heart doesn't grieve about.'

There followed another silence while Louisa waited in impatience and frustration. But suddenly she was calm; as she could not hope to know what Amy was saying she must concentrate and gather all that was possible from the part of the conversation she *could* hear.

'You keep on saying he *did* know I'd taken the paintings and sold them at Sotheby's ... All right, it was a large sum, but in view of what happened afterwards it was as well that I did help myself to those paintings. He made a fortune when the motorway was to take up his land—' Another long silence and Louisa began to wonder if the conversation had stopped. But just as she was turning away Joseph Powell's voice reached her again.

'Blast you, Amy! I did not rob him over the share-out of the house. Why do you keep saying I lied over the valuation? In any case, you should talk; if you hadn't disliked the house *we* would have had it, and made the fortune instead of him. No, I have never had a guilty conscience, but evidently he had and so made amends by leaving me this legacy. He believed it was due to me. Look,' he went on in a more subdued voice, 'why can't you look forward instead of going forever into the past? We'll be in clover; we can do the house up and have some over for an investment. I'll not gamble any more, I promise you.'

Yet again there was silence, and when Joseph spoke again the topic had changed.

'It's a little neglected but the house is being demolished anyway, as an estate is to be built here. I'm unable to get hold of any figures but even with six beneficiaries I guess we shall all be happy with what we inherit.' A pause and then, 'Well, I haven't been here long but this afternoon I'm going to explore the countryside. I'm told there is a spectacular walk along the cliffs so I intend to take that after lunch ... What time is lunch? One o'clock and I'll be out for two. It's a few miles' drive to this cliff but I shall have plenty of time to do the walk and be back for tea, which is served at four by these two oddbods I mentioned earlier. There is a doctor and his pal and a busybody who's always asking questions, rather in the manner of a private investigator. She's here with her niece, who's also a beneficiary. There's another woman with her maid and a stuck-up bloke who owns a Rolls.' A long pause and then, 'You seem very interested in the countryside around here but I can't tell you much. Look at a map and visualize it for yourself.' He said goodbye and Louisa hurried away, to sort out the information she had so fortunately come by.

'So the mystery deepens.' Sally looked at her aunt across the breakfast table. Millie had not appeared and it seemed that her employer had decided to have her breakfast in bed, in which case it would fall to Millie to attend to it, since it was most unlikely that the Thorpes would provide that kind of service.

'In a way it does seem that the mystery deepens, but one thing stands out clearly: all the other five legatees have wronged James Devlin – in the case of the doctor and his friend not intentionally, the fact being that by doing their duty they upset James'intention of ending his life in order to find peace.'

Sally had become thoughtful. She reminded her aunt that she was the odd one out.

She was not the odd one out; Louisa was sure it was her mother who had jilted James. She'd stake her life on it. 'And the man she jilted him for,' she said to herself, 'turned out to be of little good to her. They got by, after a fashion, as so many married couples do, but my sister was never really happy with him.'

Aloud she said lightly, 'I expect I'm reading things into this situation that don't exist. It wouldn't be the first time, you know. I'm not infallible, always, when I'm helping the police to solve a crime.'

Sally's glance was sceptical, and a little accusing.

'Aunt Louisa, you are not convincing: you've a brilliant brain for probing the depths of a mystery, and coupled with this talent you have the rare gift of physiognomy, and this ability to read a person's character from facial features and bone structure has proved to be of immeasurable value both to you and the police.' She sighed. 'I believe you are being very secretive, but I expect you'll satisfy my curiosity in your own good time.'

Four

'Mr Powell is missing tea.' Mrs Thorpe stooped to place a small tray on the table; it contained jam and cream.

'He told you he was?' from Sally.

'No, but it's obvious, isn't it? He's not here.' The woman walked away. Sally shrugged a dismissal of the matter and remarked on Millie not being present.

'It's quite likely that woman has her sitting up there, probably to spite me as much as to torture the poor child.'

'You said you'd phone Mrs Millsom,' Sally reminded her.

'I'll do it immediately after tea. I wonder what happened to Joseph Powell?'

The abrupt change of subject brought a slight frown to Sally's forehead.

'Do you care?' she queried briefly.

'Not particularly ... but he went out immediately after lunch with the intention of taking a walk along the cliffs.'

'You think he got lost?'

Louisa shook her head.

'One couldn't get lost there. From the map it looks like open country – behind the cliff, that is.'

'You've looked on the map?' Sally's expression was curious.

'I did so because, as I told you earlier, I heard him say he was to take a walk along the cliff. And as you and I enjoy walking I thought we might take the same route one day.'

They had scarcely finished tea when, after Mrs Thorpe had whispered something in the solicitor's ear, he rose swiftly from his chair and hurried from the room. His voice was heard, and that of another man.

The solicitor's face was pale when he re-entered the room. He was followed by a constable in uniform. Mr Philpots just stood there, undecided and shaking a little. Louisa said sharply, 'What's wrong? What has happened?'

Mr Philpots passed a tongue over dry lips.

'Mr – Powell – he's— There's been an accident. He fell off the cliff...'

'Fell?' from the doctor tersely. 'Is he badly injured?' He rose as he spoke.

'He's dead, sir,' inserted the constable. 'A couple collecting fossils at the bottom of the cliffs found him. A nasty mess he was in. The ambulance came and he's been taken away. I found a paper in his pocket with this address on it but nothing else.' He glanced around the room. 'Is his wife here?' he asked as his eyes came to rest on Louisa.

'No,' replied the solicitor, 'his wife was not with him. I'll get in touch with her right away.' A few minutes later he returned saying there was no reply. 'I'll keep ringing,' he said.

Amy Powell arrived at eight o'clock, having hired a car and driver. She was pale, her lips trembling, but otherwise she was remarkably composed. However, she asked Louisa if she would accompany her to the mortuary.

'It's just that I feel so alone,' she confessed apologetically. 'You wouldn't mind, would you?'

'Of course not,' Louisa replied sympathetically. 'My niece will take us in her car – er – won't you, Sally?'

'Certainly.' Sally was not too happy about it but she felt so sorry for the widow. The shock must have been dreadful for her.

It was half past nine when they returned. Mr Philpots suggested that Mrs Powell should stay the night. The Thorpes unbent sufficiently to serve them supper at ten o'clock, after which Joseph Powell's widow went to the room given to her, while the rest of them sat in the drawing room discussing the tragedy.

'I suppose the legacy will automatically pass to her?' John Hilliard looked questioningly at the solicitor who nodded his head.

'As next of kin Mrs Powell will receive whatever was left to her husband.'

'Poor thing,' whispered Sally to her aunt. 'Apparently she's all alone in the world now.'

Louisa's mouth curved in a half smile. She said bluntly, 'Don't you think she's better off without a man like that?' She was naturally recalling the deplorable way her husband had spoken to her on the phone.

'He wasn't a nice man, certainly,' agreed Sally. 'But I expect she cared for him and will miss him.'

Louisa said nothing. John Hilliard was speaking again.

'Will she stay on, Mr Philpots, to hear the will read on Monday?'

'I cannot answer that. She has the funeral arrangements to see to so I rather think she will be anxious to have the body taken nearer her home.'

Sally shuddered. The body ... A man alive and well only hours ago was now referred to as the body.

The following morning, when Mrs Powell entered the dining room, she glanced around, her whole manner one of lack of confidence, of awkwardness. And it was almost as if Louisa was ready because she beckoned invitingly and asked would she care to sit with them. Millie was again absent, but Sally knew for sure that even had she been able to join them for breakfast, Louisa would have asked for another chair.

'You're very kind.' The woman sat down, and when Louisa addressed her as Mrs Powell she said with a quiver in her voice, 'My name's Amy. I'd – I'd feel better if...?'

'Of course we shall call you Amy.' The necessary words of condolence had been expressed last evening but Louisa now added a few more words of sympathy. And then fell silent as Amy told the housekeeper what she wanted.

'Just toast and coffee, please.' She glanced around covertly; it was clear that she was still ill at ease. Sally thought: it won't take Auntie long to draw her out. She studied the pallid features, aware that her aunt would be doing the same, but in more detail, and with an end product in view. It had always been a matter of puzzlement to Sally how her aunt could so accurately read a person's character from his or her facial bones and contours. What was she reading from the full lips, at present seeming almost bloodless, the hollows in the cheeks, the rather thick eyebrows above dark brown eyes that were never still? The chin was slightly receding but although her aunt had once told her this meant weakness of character, Sally sensed a certain strength about the woman, a secret strength which she had no wish to reveal and so she was adopting this pose of being ill at ease. Sally smiled at her own conclusions and she wondered just what her aunt's were. Did she see a good woman, a mean one, a conscientious one? From what her aunt had heard early yesterday morning it would seem that Amy Powell did have conscience trouble over those stolen paintings.

Louisa was asking what Amy's intentions were. Was she staying on till Monday?

'I spoke to Mr Philpots on the landing – he came from the room two doors up from mine – and he said I could stay if I wanted.' She shook her head, not in a negative gesture but because she was utterly at a loss; the expression of helplessness was very plain to see.

'You are alone, we understand,' said Louisa in a kind and gentle tone, 'so if you need help or advice do come to us. Both Sally and I will be only too glad to do anything we can.'

'I can't think of any help you could give me, but if there is I shall certainly come to you. It is so kind of you, Mrs Hooke.' She heaved a deep sigh. 'Perhaps I should go home and then come on Monday to hear the will read— Oh, I wish my Joe had never come here!'

Louisa watched as she brought out a handkerchief to dab at her eyes. The woman's lips quivered; she seemed to be in great distress. Louisa's eyes narrowed.

'You were not happy at his coming here?'

'I felt there was something – w-well – mysterious about the whole thing.'

Louisa became alert to the possibility of drawing the woman out while she was in this unhappy state. She said gently, 'There must have been a very good reason for your misgivings?'

Amy Powell hesitated a moment then said in quivering tones, 'My husband – he – he—' She lifted her eyes. 'I don't like to say things about Joe now he is – is dead...'

'Mrs Powell – Amy – anything you say here will go no further, and as it is sometimes helpful, when one is troubled, to confide, then we are willing to listen.'

'You are very kind. I feel so alone and do want someone to talk to. Mrs Hooke, my Joe was the last person James Devlin should have included in his will!' The words came out in a small explosion, as if the woman had much bottled up inside her. 'He – you see, he treated James very badly.' She glanced around;

118

the two friends smiled at her and John Hilliard lifted a hand in salutation. 'It is so peaceful here ... on the surface.' A sob shook her body. 'Yes, I do want to confide in someone. I warned Joe that there was something not quite right because James would never leave money to a man who had – had robbed him.'

'And of course you are saying that had your husband taken notice of you and perhaps not come here, then the accident would not have happened?'

She nodded her head at once and Louisa wondered why the gesture had come so quickly.

'You say your husband robbed James Devlin. Would you like to talk about it?'

'Yes – yes, I would.' Her eyes went to Sally, and Louisa smiled at her niece and asked if she would mind leaving them when breakfast was finished.

'Of course. I'll stroll along and have a look at the village church. Albert says it is five hundred years old.'

Half an hour later the two women were seated in the arbour and there was a sombre frown between Amy's eyes; her voice when she spoke was unsteady and strained.

'You did say it would go no further,' she began. 'You wouldn't repeat any of it?'

'I have said you can depend on my silence.'

'Well, it goes back a long way,' began Amy,

'when, quite out of the blue, James Devlin and my husband discovered they were related. This came about owing to their jointly inheriting an estate from another distant relative, a sort of uncle several times removed.'

'That kind of thing does sometimes happen,' said Louisa as the other woman paused.

'There was a beautiful old house and it was full of treasures. All this – everything – was to be divided equally between the two cousins, but – but—' She stopped, plainly affected emotionally. 'I don't want to sound disloyal to my – my dead husband, but, Mrs Hooke, Joe robbed James. He took two very valuable paintings from the attic and sent them to Sotheby's. He – he kept the money.' Again she paused, blinking rapidly as if holding back tears. 'I was dreadfully upset but of course couldn't tell James. However, I let James have the house – he wanted it, you see, but I'd have loved to live there.'

'Your husband was compensated, though, receiving half the value of the house?'

'Yes, he did get money from James. But I'm sorry to say that Joe robbed him a second time – by charging him almost twice the price he should have done. I mean, the house had been valued by an estate agent, but Joe altered the figures on the letter and so James paid twice as much as he should have done.'

Louisa was silent for a while, digesting

this. She was seeing that cocky little man with the narrow shoulders and noticeably podgy hands. A florid complexion, and eyes set too close together. He had the typical inflated ego found in those with smallness of stature. His wife had not had a happy time, and Louisa was sure that Amy Powell would not be long in mourning.

'I now understand,' she said at last, 'why you told me that your husband was the last person one would expect to be favoured by James Devlin. He had wronged him most seriously.'

'Yes. And I myself felt so guilty about it. It was so unfair of Joe because there was plenty for both of them.' She paused a moment. When she spoke it was to say she would rather have believed James would have wanted revenge rather than rewarding her husband for his callous behaviour.

'Revenge?' Louisa was interested. 'How would you imagine revenge could be carried out?'

'I don't really know. But it was just an idea.'

'James Devlin would have to come back from the grave to have revenge,' Louisa returned with a hint of amusement. Then as she saw that Amy was distressed she reminded her that she'd had a severe shock and the idea of revenge was perhaps a result of it.

'In the light of things you have told me

about your husband, it took courage to confide but I am sure it has taken a load off your mind. I agree that it is puzzling why your husband should have been left money by a man he so greatly wronged.' Louisa's thoughts naturally shot to the others – the two friends who had deprived him of the peace he had craved; Mrs Smallman, whose husband had killed the dog whom James had loved more than he would have loved a brother; and Sally, who was here instead of her mother, the girl who had jilted James in his youth. Yes, Louisa now had no doubts; it was her own sister who had jilted James Devlin. 'However, Amy,' she continued at length, 'I am sure your husband's death was an accident. You must accept that and forget all about revenge.'

'Of course. It isn't logical to think of revenge, is it?' Louisa merely smiled and the woman went on, 'Thank you for listening, and for reassuring me. My doubts are put at rest, once and for all.' She paused then added confidingly, 'The money will be such a godsend, Mrs Hooke. Our house is in a mess – you see, Joe was a gambler on the stock exchange and we lost everything he inherited. Taking the pictures did him no good either. I learned only yesterday that he'd mortgaged the property. Now, though, I can clear off all the debts and also spend a bit on the house. I only want to be comfortable, that's all.' Her voice quivered to a stop; she was overcome by emotion.

Louisa said briskly, 'I expect you will stay till Monday?'

'I feel I'd prefer to go home and come back. Mr Philpots said it would be all right.'

'When are you going?'

'This afternoon if possible. I – I don't think I want to drive Joe's car, as suggested by Mr Philpots. I'll hire a car and driver.'

'I'll see to that for you. And, Amy, if there is anything at all that I can do for you, let me know. Have you a friend near to where you live?'

'Yes, I do have one. She'll be a great help.' She glanced at her watch. 'I'll leave immediately after lunch. I'd like to have a look around. It seems to be a lovely place. Oh, I suppose I'll have to pack Joe's things.' Her lip quivered and she brought out a handkerchief to her eyes.

Quite a clever actress, thought Louisa. Amy Powell might have had a modicum of affection for the husband she had lost, but certainly no love at all.

Albert was ready and waiting when, immediately after lunch, Sally brought the car round into the drive. Louisa had been having a talk with Mr Philpots, who assured her that it would be all right for Albert to go off for the afternoon.

'He isn't needed until dinner time,' he went on affably. 'As a matter of fact, I had no authority to force him to help in the house but he was most cooperative when I explained that the Thorpes had said they couldn't manage both the dishing up of the food and the waiting on.'

'An odd pair,' returned Louisa repeating what she had said before. 'You could have done better than that, Mr Philpots.'

'As I have already pointed out to you, Mrs Hooke, their references were well above those of the other couples I interviewed.' His tone was stiff, and all cordiality dissolved with Louisa's forthright declaration.

'References – bah! Anyone can produce references,' and with that she turned on her heel and strode, straight-backed and impressive, to the door, where she met Sally who was just opening the rear door of the car for the gardener to get in.

'This is most kind,' he murmured. 'You are two very charming ladies – which is more than can be said for the other female staying here. I heard her speaking to her maid and it was disgraceful. Why does the girl put up with it, I wonder?'

'Necessity.' Louisa fastened her seat belt and leant back comfortably against the soft leather upholstery. 'But quite soon now Millie will be free of her. She's coming to live with me as soon as I'm settled.'

'That should be very nice for her.' He leant back, obviously intending to derive the full amount of comfort the car had to offer.

'We think it will be quite soon,' interposed Sally on an eager note. 'Auntie phoned the owner of River Bank Cottage and she said she did want Auntie to have it but her son was still wanting it auctioned. It could then bring a very high price.' Sally had driven slowly, but now she put her foot down, having left the drive and reached the open road. 'The lady who owns the cottage,' Sally resumed once she had the car in top gear, 'has a forceful nature, which makes me feel optimistic that she'll override her son and sell it to Aunt Louisa.'

'It's close to where you live, you said?'

'That's right. It's going to be wonderful. You see, Albert, I've been on my own since my parents died and now, to have not only my super aunt living close, but Millie as well. She and I are good friends already.'

'Even though you see so little of one another.'

'She did get out this morning, though. Mrs Smallman had a chair taken out to her balcony and told Millie to get—To leave her.'

'To get out...' Albert was shaking his head. 'Just the way she would talk to her maid.'

Silent and thoughtful, Louisa left conversation to the others, who were discussing the accident. Louisa was recalling how solutions to problems had come easily, but now she was unable to clear the fog from her mind. She had the strange conviction that Amy was not all she appeared to be: the grieving wife. But yet again nothing concrete emerged from the haze. Why this block? Correct mental deduction had always come so naturally to her that, it being an inherent trait, she took it for granted that nothing was beyond her ability to solve. Yet here she was, with yet another incident – if one could call an accident resulting in death an incident – to add to her confusion of mind. She frowned and tried to dismiss the matter by listening to the other two. It was merely inconsequential conversation, though, and Louisa allowed her thoughts to return to what she now considered to be a major problem. It had to be admitted that Joseph Powell's death was a most strange occurrence, and any strange occurrence was grist to the mill for her.

'I think I shall go and take a look at that cliff path ... and especially the spot where he fell from it.'

'Were you speaking, Auntie?'

'To myself, love. How far have we to go now?' she enquired of Albert.

'Only a couple of miles. It's beautiful country around here, don't you think?'

'Very beautiful. You'll be very happy – should you get the cottage, of course.'

'Tessa will be taken for lots of lovely walks,

I expect,' put in Sally.

'Yes, I shall have to walk her because she won't have the large grounds she has now to romp about in.'

'You could have brought her, you know. I'd not have minded her being in the car.'

'She's dropping hairs at the moment, Miss Renshawe, and so I'd not want you to have them all sticking into the carpet.'

'She won't like being fastened up in that garden house.'

'It won't be for long.' A pause and then, 'You're a kind young lady ... and they don't come in bunches any more. On the contrary, people like you and Mrs Hooke are becoming very hard to find.' He gave a little sigh; Louisa turned her head. His eyes were closed.

The cottage turned out to be far more attractive than either Louisa or Sally had imagined. Set right in the middle of a patch of old-fashioned country gardens, it was thatched in the Norfolk reed manner with no sign that any immediate attention to the roof would be necessary. It was perfect, declared Sally even before Albert had obtained the key from the greenhouse and opened the front door.

'The gardens are a bit overgrown,' observed Louisa but went on to say that with his skill and love of the work they would very soon be as delightful – in their miniature way – as those at the manor.

'Just look at that wide fireplace! And a bread oven! Oh, Albert, you must buy it. No matter if it is overpriced, you must have it, you must!' Sally swung around to look at him, her eyes bright and eager. 'Auntie, you must admit it's a little gem, and just right for Albert and Tessa.'

'And Tessa...' He murmured the words almost to himself. 'James would certainly have taken you to his heart, Miss Renshawe—'

'Sally,' she broke in swiftly. 'Call me Sally as I know we're going to be friends. We have no need to lose touch and we shan't.' The last word was stressed and spoken in the nature of a challenge. He laughed and seemed exceedingly happy at the suggestion that they would remain friends. 'You must visit us and we shall visit you.'

'And I shall always be on the cadge,' laughed Louisa. 'For cuttings and probably some plants as well.'

'You will be welcome to them, I'm sure.' He glanced through the latticed window to the rose bed outside. 'So you advise me to buy it, then?'

'I advise you to get a move on,' she replied promptly, 'or you could be in danger of missing it.'

'It was just the price...'

'The question is,' put in Sally, 'have you the money? Can you buy it without leaving yourself short?'

'Just about, but I really wanted to have some over to invest.'

'You could get a mortage,' began Sally then stopped, shaking her head. 'No, that would not be practical, would it?'

'Or possible,' he grimaced, 'for several reasons. Firstly, at my age, and on this type of property, I'd be refused a mortgage. But even if I could get one I'd not be able to pay it back out of my pension.'

He seemed to be pondering and Sally with her usual impulsiveness said brightly, 'I will lend you whatever I get from this legacy. I don't need it – in fact I didn't want it—'

'You didn't want it?' he interrupted, staring at her with an odd expression. 'Why?'

'Well, I don't really know. I've never had much money and yet I'm happy, so—' She spread her hands in a casual gesture. 'I've Auntie now, and I already own my own home, so I'm sure I shan't be needing whatever it is that Mr Devlin has left me. You could have it, for that matter, but I suspect you wouldn't accept it as a gift, so I'm offering to lend it to you. Mind you,' she added with a sudden frown, 'I don't know how much it will be.'

'We were given to understand it would be fairly substantial,' interposed Louisa. 'I'm sure it will be enough for what you want.'

A long and strange silence followed. The old man shuffled around the living room; he scraped some ashes from the hearth as if he would begin tidying up already. He went into the kitchen, which was in need of some renovation since it had a brown stone sink with a well-worn wooden draining board. The brass taps were green but would look good when cleaned; the floor was of large, uneven slabs between which the underlying soil had forced a way and one or two weeds were actually thriving there. But as Sally and Louisa came up behind him they were both still enchanted with the cottage. Louisa said practically, 'I should accept Sally's offer of the loan, Albert, because this kitchen needs a good deal of money spending on it. New floor, new plaster to the walls and a larger window would be nice.' She went on and still the old man said not a word. What was wrong, wondered Sally anxiously. Had she upset him by her offer? Insulted him – hurt his pride? She was about to speak when he turned and she saw his eyes were bright, and the mouth behind the beard quivered slightly. She herself was full up suddenly and Louisa, aware of something in the atmosphere, said in a businesslike way, 'Come, Albert, and show us the rest of it. We're delighted and of course you must have it, but let us see the bedrooms – and is there a bathroom at all?'

'No, but there are three bedrooms and one of those could be made into a bathroom.' He led the way up the narrow curving staircase on to a landing which was surprisingly wide.

'This is great,' said Louisa. 'You can have a sofa here and perhaps a couple of chairs. You're lucky to have a landing like this.' The bedrooms were small but adequate and the smallest was most suitable for a bathroom to be fixed up in it.

They came down and went outside. The sun was shining, the birds singing. There was a steady buzz from the bumble bees in a colourful patch of heather.

'This is a bit of heaven,' breathed Sally. 'You know, Albert, it's awfully similiar to the one Aunt Louisa is having, and not much different from mine.'

'But Sally's has been modernized,' said Louisa. 'Her mother was a lady who believed in cutting down a housewife's work.' She was suddenly attracted by a pair of blue tits flying in and out of a piece of earthenware pipe which was sticking up from the ground. 'You have a nest in that pipe,' she told him, but he already knew.

'I saw the male going in and out when I was here at first, so guessed the female was sitting on eggs.'

'We who live in the country are privileged,' said Sally, whose attention was also with the tits. 'I never cease to be grateful that I don't have to live in a big city.'

'I could never live in one,' he returned, 'or even a big town.'

He had lived in seclusion for so long, thought Louisa, that he would have to continue like that till the end of his days. She wondered, not for the first time, how old he was. With anyone who had a beard it was always difficult to tell.

'I had better put the key back now.' The gardener paused, though, as if asking was there anything else they wanted to see.

'Yes, I suppose you must,' agreed Sally, but went on to say he should heed her aunt's advice and contact the estate agent at once.

'Will he be open this afternoon?' she asked.

'Yes. They all open on Saturdays now. Shall I phone from a box along the way?'

'You could do. But if you don't see a box you can phone from the house. I don't expect Mr Philpots will have any objection.'

Albert laughed as if at some joke.

'There does happen to be a box just along this road.'

The phone box was found and Albert left the car and went over to it. He was all smiles as he came out, and he walked back to the car with a jaunty step.

'I've made a deal,' he told them, and Louisa said it called for a celebration, so they eventually pulled up at a quaint little village inn which had the obvious signs that it had once been a coaching house – the mounting-block, the stables, the yard at the side where once the ostlers would have been busy.

Louisa ordered a bottle of champagne; the old man seemed to have become shy, yet at the same time happy. This pleasant company, he thought, these two delightful people … bothering their heads about me, a mere odd-job man, a servant.

Louisa smiled at him; she had no difficulty in reading his thoughts for they were reflected in his vivid blue eyes.

Sally was to say later, when he excused himself and said he needed to wash his hands, that it was a wonderful feeling to know one had made another person happy.

'It sort of – uplifts you, doesn't it?'

'You're absolutely right, love. He's been a lonely man, equally as isolated as his employer.' She paused in thought. 'It would seem, though, that he prefers it that way. He has had many years in which to adapt and now it's a way of life – his way of life.'

'But he'll visit us, and let us visit him? Oh, surely he will!'

'You can content yourself that he will. He's thoroughly enjoyed our company this afternoon, and he will want more of the same. Just you wait and see.'

'Do you think he'll accept the loan?'

'I'm not sure,' was Louisa's response

spoken on a note of doubt. 'You know, Sally, I rather think he doesn't need a loan. I feel he can very well afford the house – in fact, if you remember he said so. But his fear is that it's overpriced and if ever he has to sell it he'll be out of pocket.'

Sally was shaking her head.

'You can't think like that. If you want something then have it. Otherwise, as you say, it could slip away and the opportunity never come again.'

'I love your youthful philosophy,' laughed her aunt. 'You're a most refreshing lass and it's no wonder Albert likes you so much.'

He returned; they drove back to the manor, having been away much longer than intended. They had almost reached the entrance to the house when an ambulance came through.

'Good heavens, what's been happening—?' Louisa stopped abruptly. It was Sally who said, a nervy element to her voice, 'A police car, and – and another...'

'My God!' Louisa was out of the car almost before it had stopped. The solicitor was hurrying towards them from the house.

'A terrible thing has happened while you've been out. Mrs Smallman has – has been – murdered. Mrs Thorpe found her – her – dead body.'

'*Murdered!*' The exclamation was uttered simultaneously by both Sally and her aunt.

Behind them, standing by the car, Albert was staring at Mr Philpots in a sort of shocked disbelief.

'But how...?' He shook his head dazedly. 'Who could possibly have done it?'

'That we don't know. She was felled by a blow on the back of the head and the doctor said she'd died instantly. They think she disturbed an intruder who was stealing some of the silver.' He spread his hands in a gesture of bewilderment. 'For a thing like this to have happened, and so soon after the other death—'

'You have a constable here,' broke in Louisa on noticing how pale her niece had gone. 'And...?' Her glance had slid from the police car to the Rover.

'Inspector Corlett,' submitted Eric Philpots in precise tones. 'Constable Hall arrived within minutes of my calling him at the local police station. It was he who phoned for the inspector. The police surgeon left half an hour ago.'

'The body has gone,' frowned Louisa. 'I'd have liked to see it.'

'You see it?' The solicitor drew himself up. 'This is police business, Mrs Hooke. They'll not allow just anyone to poke – er – to interfere in their investigations.' This was the one, he thought, who was always wanting to know more about the will and the legatees and had actually demanded to know about

135

James' private life. He wouldn't have satisfied her curiousity even if he had the knowledge himself. 'The inspector told me I must not let anyone into the Blue Drawing Room, where he is to interview everyone, or into the small Green Drawing Room, where the body was found, until he gives the word. So, like all the others, Mrs Hooke, you will be required to keep away from those two rooms. Mrs Thorpe and her husband have made the dining room comfortable with a few arm-chairs. For the present that will serve as sitting room and of course dinner will be served there this evening.' He seemed, Louisa thought, puffed up with his own importance as he uttered these instructions in his customary stiff and precise manner. She made an impatient gesture. Turning, he left her and she swung around to see where the gardener had gone. He was still standing by the car – in fact, he appeared to be leaning on it for support. She watched him fingering his beard, his expression one of blank bewilderment, incredulity. He shook his head as if he would throw out what he had just heard, throw it out as if it were completely impossible that anyone could have been murdered in the house of his late employer.

Five

'Auntie,' quivered Sally as they entered the hall, 'another death. Two of the legatees dead and – and only f-four of us left.'

Louisa took hold of her hand.

'I agree it is grim, love, but things like this do sometimes happen. Mr Powell met with an accident. I don't suppose it is the first time some unfortunate has slipped and fallen over that cliff. As for Mrs Smallman – well, this is a grave occurrence. But, my dear, there is nothing for you to become scared about. Now, just you go and find Millie and take her to that little roadside cafe we passed and buy her some tea. She's bound to be upset.'

'All right.' Sally looked up at her aunt, saw that the eyes had a certain sparkle; she was ready to throw in all her resources in an endeavour to find the murderer of the woman who had made herself so obnoxious to everyone around her.

Contrary to the solicitor's prediction, Louisa was treated rather like an old friend when, without much effort, she had successfully made her entry into the Blue Drawing Room without the solicitor's seeing her, and confronted Inspector Corlett, the burly detective who was in charge of the case.

'I feel I know you, Mrs Hooke—' He shook hands heartily and even she, tough as she was, winced at his strength. 'Remember the Carston case? I was on holiday in Boston – one of those "New England in the Fall" tours where you have a nightly stopover – and I was intrigued by the way you assisted the police. In fact, I later learned that it was actually you who solved the whole thing.'

She smiled reminiscently.

'I did my bit, yes, but I'm sure they'd have fastened the murder on Carston in the end.'

'I'm not so sure.' He shook his grey head. He was a large robust man well over six feet tall. He had a genial face which she examined critically. A full wide mouth spelling compassion; widely set brown eyes below rather bushy grey brows. A slightly bent nose was suggestive of a period of boxing in his youth, while the somewhat pugnacious, jutting chin also told its own story: he was a man who would pursue a course to its bitter end. Louisa liked him on the instant. 'No, Mrs Hooke, you are being too modest. I am sure that without your extraordinary powers of deduction that man would have escaped the law and most likely have committed another murder by now.'

'Well, Inspector, I am naturally flattered by your comments and – well—' She looked up at him. 'I expect you know what I am about to ask.'

A light laugh escaped him.

'Mrs Hooke, I am the last man to ignore your reputation. I shall be delighted to have your help.'

'Mr Philpots said Mrs Smallman was felled by a blow on the back of the head. You have found the weapon?'

'The poker, from that set in the hearth. It's gone for examination but I don't expect there'll be any fingerprints.'

Louisa fell thoughtfully silent. How much should she tell the inspector? Was it her duty to tell him of her suspicions? And if she did, he would probably ask her what she had already asked herself: who on earth would want to push Joseph Powell off the cliff? However, she did say, as the thought struck her, 'You know of course about the other death?'

'The other death?' He stared at her. 'What death?'

'I assumed Mr Philpots would have mentioned it. Another of the beneficiaries died yesterday – had an accident. He fell from the cliff when he was out walking. His widow was here until a few hours ago. She'll be returning on Monday to hear the will read.'

She sent him a glance. 'I expect you know why these people are here?'

'The solicitor gave me a scrappy outline of the situation but perhaps you will fill me in with the details before I begin questioning the others.' He turned to the constable. 'Wait outside and see that no one disturbs us – unless,' he said to Louisa, 'you want some tea, or perhaps coffee?'

'You would like something?'

'I wouldn't mind a cup of tea.'

'Then perhaps Constable Hall will inform Mrs Thorpe we'd like a pot of tea and some biscuits?'

'Certainly,' he smiled.

'But do make sure we're not otherwise disturbed.'

'Yes, sir, I'll be outside the door all the time.'

The door closed behind him and the other two sat down opposite one another with a lovely Bouille table between them. Louisa sat staring in front of her for a moment or two, ready to fill him in as requested, but wondering just how much to leave out. She soon found herself yielding to the insistence of her mind that she had every right to withhold – for the present at any rate – most of what she had discovered for herself. It was not incumbent on her to reveal the fact that all the beneficiaries had, many years ago, done James Devlin grave injuries – all except Sally, that was, who was here because her mother had jilted James.

Nor did Louisa feel it necessary to reveal her doubts about Joseph Powell's accident or the 'revenge' voiced by his wife. She wanted to take a look at that cliff before even considering telling the chief inspector that the man had been an experienced fell-walker and, therefore, would be most unlikely to take risks when walking along a cliff top. For the present it suited her that everyone else should accept the obvious: that it was an accident. Louisa was particularly concerned that her niece should not, for one moment, suspect murder. One murder was bad enough; two would assuredly send Sally scuttling back home.

A slight cough from the inspector brought her thoughts back and she began to talk, telling him of the condition laid down in the will, and giving him a rough description of those involved. But her narrative provided little more than that and when she had finished she found herself subjected to a prolonged scrutiny – and was there a glimmer of scepticism in that piercing gaze? Was he doubting the sincerity of her final, 'And that is all, Inspector'?

At last he gave a small sigh of resignation as if telling himself that, if she *were* holding anything back, there was nothing he could do about it. Nevertheless, he did venture a query as to the opinion she had formed about each one of the guests here.

'You must have formed one,' he added by way of a challenge. 'It is well known, remember, Mrs Hooke, that you have this gift of physiognomy, and so—' He sent her a chiding glance. 'And so one must naturally assume that you have used it to the full in the time you've already had here.'

This brought a light laugh and an admission that she would be telling an untruth if she were to deny it.

'Briefly, Inspector, the two who are dead were not what one would describe as likeable people, while the man on his own, John Hilliard, also comes under the same category, although I have to add that his character is slightly more acceptable than the two deceased, his main fault being that he is a braggart with a highly inflated ego.'

'And the others – these two friends Philpots mentioned? One's a doctor, he said.'

'Yes. These two are far more acceptable. They appear to be good-living, responsible men.'

The glimmer of a smile touched his lips.

'You make them sound dull and uninteresting.'

'On the contrary,' she denied at once.

'Did you take a liking to them?'

Again she laughed.

'Am I to infer that if I like them it lets them

off as regards being suspects?'

'Well,' he admitted with a grimace, 'that fact would certainly be in their favour.'

'I like them,' she offered briefly. She thought of the part they had played in prolonging James Devlin's life, truly believing his legacy to them was by way of a thank you, gratitude for their prompt action. She knew otherwise. How his life must have dragged. Had he cursed them with every birthday that had come along?

Why hadn't he tried again? But it was plain that lack of courage was the reason. And so James Devlin had lived on, cutting himself off from his fellow humans except for the gardener who had been with him for fourteen years – that was, two at the other house and twelve here. It would have been supposed that the two men would have become friends, but that had not been the case.

Louisa glanced across at her companion to find him deep in thought, staring into space. His manner advised her that any verbal intrusion from her would be most unwelcome at this time so she herself lapsed once more into thought.

Louisa's musings were cut by Hall's light knock on the door. He held an envelope in his hand.

'For you, Mrs Hooke. Your niece found it on your dressing table and asked me to give it to you. She says she and the other young lady will be back in about an hour.'

'Thank you.' Louisa slit the envelope. Vaguely she was aware that the constable had left the room. She read the contents of the note. Silence prevailed as a decision was being made. It would be more sporting of her to let the inspector read this, but...

'It's nothing of importance,' she said lightly and with a smile. And she was saved of any questions that might just have been asked, by the appearance of Mrs Thorpe with the tea tray.

Louisa sat in the little arbour and brought out the note which Sally had found in her room. But she did not read it again for the moment; her thoughts were elsewhere as she went over the interviews conducted by the inspector. John Hilliard had an alibi. He had walked into the village, called at the post office for stamps, then gone along to the cafe to which Louisa had sent her niece and Millie. He had arrived back at the manor just as the police surgeon was leaving in his Mercedes. The two friends had alibis also; each had never been out of the other's company during their visit to the town, to which they had driven soon after lunch, returning a few minutes after John Hilliard. The Thorpes were questioned, and Louisa mentally went over the interview with the wife, who was interviewed first.

The woman had come into the room, a tall gaunt figure whose sallow-skinned face was entirely without expression. She walked with an air of dignity and stood looking down upon the detective as if he were her inferior.

'You wish to speak to me?' She threw Louisa a glance. 'Does she have to be here?' she demanded harshly.

Corlett's eyes narrowed; he leant back in his chair and deliberately kept the woman waiting. Her mouth went tight and Louisa half expected her to turn and stalk from the room. However, Corlett spoke at last, ignoring the ill-mannered reference to Louisa.

'Will you give us a full description of what you saw – and did?'

'I've already told the constable,' she snapped. 'Must I repeat it? I have work to do—'

'It can wait, Mrs Thorpe. We are wanting to know exactly what happened.'

'How should I know what happened?' she began haughtily, when Louisa interrupted her with a gentle: 'You found the body, Mrs Thorpe. Perhaps you can fill in the details for us?'

The woman glowered at her but any negative retort that leapt to her lips was stemmed on her seeing the severity of the inspector's expression.

'I went in, as usual, to set the tables for afternoon tea. Mrs Smallman was lying there, by the fireplace. There wasn't any sign of blood but she was dead. The poker was obviously the weapon since it had been taken from its stand and was lying in the hearth. I went to find Mr Philpots, who phoned the police. The constable came – from the local station, and he phoned for you.' She threw a glance at the inspector and added with a careless shrug, 'That is all.'

The inspector asked, 'In your opinion, had she come upon an intruder, a thief maybe?'

'I am not here to offer my private opinion. To my mind conjecture at this stage would be profitless, and most likely misleading.'

Arrogant bitch, thought the inspector. Pity he couldn't charge *her* with the murder. With what patience he could muster he asked if anything was missing. 'Any silver, for instance? There seems to be a large and very valuable collection here.'

'I have no idea if any of the silver is missing. My husband and I were engaged to look after the housekeeping. Making an inventory of the contents of the property does not enter into the scope of our duties. In any case, an inventory should have been made long ago, but the gardener says it wasn't.'

The inspector and Louisa exchanged glances. She then looked hard at Mrs Thorpe, watching for any change of expression – of any readable expression at all. The woman stared her out for a long moment until Corlett said curtly, 'You may go, Mrs Thorpe. Send in your husband.'

She strode out.

Louisa said thoughtfully, 'I disliked that woman the moment I set eyes on her. She's deep, sly – must be with eyes like those. Her husband is the same. I'd not trust either of them to tell the truth.'

'I shouldn't think she'd lie over what she saw,' he returned. 'There would be nothing to be gained by it that I can see.' He was stroking his chin. He added after a space, 'I can't say I'd trust her either, now I think more about it.' He looked up. '*Was* she lying, Mrs Hooke?'

She hesitated, trying not to let her dislike of the woman distort her vision.

'As you say, it would appear that lies would not benefit her anything.'

'No,' was his decisive rejoinder. 'Lies could not possibly gain her anything.' A small silence prevailed until the inspector said reflectively, 'Getting back for a moment to the reason for these six beneficiaries being here. From what you have said – the conclusion you reached as to their respective characters – it would appear that at least two of the beneficiaries were undeserving of the legacies, while one other, this John Hilliard, also seems to be the last man one would favour.' He glanced speculatively at her across the table. 'Have you any theories regarding this?'

She hesitated, a circumstance which she knew he was bound to notice and on which he would draw his own conclusions. So she decided to open up, just a little, supply just sufficient information to satisfy him for the present. But first she asked a question.

'Did Mr Philpots tell you that none of the beneficiaries had been in touch with James Devlin in the last twenty years – and in some cases, much longer?'

'No,' he answered, puzzled, 'no, he didn't.'

'It's true. And therefore I have naturally asked myself why the man should leave them money—'

'With the stipulation that they all gathered here for four days before the will was read,' he broke in swiftly. 'There's a mystery here, Mrs Hooke, and,' he added with slow deliberation, 'mysteries are right up the street of the world's most famous amateur sleuth – no, do not interrupt me. You are world-famous and you know it! What I am hoping for now is your complete confidence. You have learned much, of that I am in no doubt, and I'd appreciate your sharing your know-ledge with me.' It was a request which she found difficult to ignore; it would be like slamming the door in his face. And yet, she was loath to give him her full confidence at this stage, mainly because of Sally. Louisa would hate to have to leave here with the mystery unsolved, but this would be the case should the inspector decide to consider the 'accident' as murder. Sally had not cared if she had lost the legacy in the first place, by refusing to comply with the condition that she come here and stay. So it was logical to assume that with the implication by the inspector that there had been two murders, not one, her niece would abandon the idea of the legacy and leave the manor. There was of course the promise she had made to Albert, to make him a loan of her money, but Louisa was fairly certain that he'd have refused it anyway.

She said at last, 'I have a very good and important reason for keeping certain information to myself, Inspector, so please forgive me. I promise that you will share my knowledge just as soon as it is expedient for me to confide. However, there are a few facts that I can share. One is about a suspicion I have that all the beneficiaries did at one time harm James Devlin. As to the doctor and his friend: they were both instrumental in saving his life—'

'That doesn't sound like harming him!'

'He wasn't grateful, Inspector, quite the opposite. He cursed them and said they ought to have left him alone to control his own destiny. I feel that he never did forgive them, never.'

'You have a reason, obviously.' He paused

but she did not speak. She felt she had said enough already, perhaps too much, she thought with belated regret. He was deep in thought and when he spoke it was almost to himself.

'The law of retribution...'

Louisa said swiftly, and perhaps a little speciously, 'How on earth can you say that, Inspector, when the only man who would want to punish them is dead?'

'I know,' impatiently and with a not-too-friendly glance in her direction. 'Give me credit, Mrs Hooke, for knowing that dead men cannot kill!'

Louisa came from her long reverie and paid attention to the note in her hand. She read:

Mrs Hooke,

I know you and I have not been very friendly, but I need to talk to someone before I go to the police, and there is no one here. In any case, I would rather talk to a woman. It is about something I saw from the taxi in which I was riding and concerns the so-called accident of Mr Powell falling from that cliff. The reason for the delay is that I did not want to get myself involved with the police, but what I saw has bothered me and at last I have made up my mind. I am sorry for entering your bedroom but I want you to get this immediately you come in. I shall be waiting in the arbour ... Mrs Smallman.

150

Louisa said aloud, 'The so-called accident...'

She again lapsed into thought, vaguely aware of the distant bark of a dog, probably Tessa racing over the fields with the gardener.

So Mrs Smallman saw something which she wished to talk about. She had left the note and should have been waiting right here, where Louisa herself was sitting. On the surface it would seem that she had been killed because of something she had seen, but Louisa failed to fit this into any pattern. She felt sure her murder had not been premeditated. Once again she was going over the interviews and now it was Millie who was being questioned. The two girls had returned and soon it was the Irish girl's turn to be brought in to face the inspector. Her answers to his questions were concise even though the girl showed signs of stress.

It seemed that, yesterday afternoon, Mrs Smallman had told her maid to get a taxi, which she did, from the Yellow Pages. They were driven into town where Mrs Smallman did some shopping, then instead of having a taxi take them back to the manor she had decided to go for a drive, leaving Millie with the parcels and instructions to wait, on a bench outside one of the shops, for her employer to come back.

Having just read Mrs Smallman's note,

Louisa asked, with an air of the question not being of any great importance, 'Do you know where Mrs Smallman went, Millie?'

'No. She just said she would like to be driven round the countryside for an hour.'

'That was when she was leaving you, but when she came back?'

'She didn't speak – just told me to get in and the taxi drove us back here.'

The detective was watching Louisa intently and it was plain that he was curious as to the point of these questions.

Louisa said carefully, 'How was she? I mean, did she seem – er – troubled about anything?'

'Just what are you getting at?' from the inspector with a hint of impatience. 'What has the way the victim was yesterday to do with the murder?'

Louisa shrugged her shoulders.

'Nothing, I suppose. I was merely wondering why she should decide to drive around. Not what I'd have expected her to do.'

'I think it was because it was such a nice day,' submitted Millie. 'She said it was early to go back and there was nothing to do here, so she went for a drive.'

'Seems straightforward enough.' The inspector was obviously satisfied and Louisa did then have a pang of conscience in keeping the contents of the note to herself. However, she did still keep the contents to herself and now she was sitting here, in the spot where Mrs Smallman had planned to meet her and talk ... and tell her what she had seen to make her use the phrase: 'the so-called accident'. To Louisa there was only one conclusion to which she could come: someone had pushed Joseph Powell off that cliff, and that someone had been seen by Mrs Smallman from her seat in the taxi.

Dinner was late owing to the inspector's questioning each of the Thorpes for a second time and also the three men. Louisa, Sally and Albert, having cast-iron alibis, were not questioned at all.

John Hilliard was heard to say, 'Why this second interrogation? He can't suspect me. I wasn't even in the house.'

Bernard Wilding and Leonard Fulham were far more tolerant of the inspector, although Bernard did remark to Louisa, as they sat drinking an aperitif before the meal, 'I'm beginning to wish I'd never come here. Whatever the legacy, it's not worth all this. I suppose you know that none of us can leave?'

She nodded. 'That is usual,' she replied.

'We can't leave?' from Sally with a frown. 'Do you mean, Auntie, that we have to stay even if we want to go home?'

'Do you want to go home?'

'I think I do. Two deaths, Auntie, not one.' She seemed to shudder and her aunt leant across to pat her hand.

'One was an accident,' she said, avoiding her eyes.

'It doesn't make any difference. Two of the six who came here are dead.'

Bernard frowned and appeared to have some difficulty in swallowing. He admitted that this same thing was troubling him.

'You must admit, Mrs Hooke, that it is an extraordinary circumstance that two of us are dead?'

Louisa was saved from any reply by the appearance of Mrs Thorpe to say that dinner was served.

'Auntie,' said Sally as she and Louisa strolled through the shrubbery in the gathering dusk, 'I have been doing some thinking myself – about this mysterious situation, I mean.' They had come out immediately after dinner. They had invited Millie to accompany them, but the girl was upset about the death of her employer; she had a headache and had decided to go to bed. Even though she had disliked Mrs Smallman exceedingly, the woman's death had disturbed her, and she had even had a little weep over it.

'Thinking?' Louisa repeated. 'What kind of thinking?'

Bypassing that for a moment Sally said, 'I had wanted to go home, as you know. But now I can't because of you. This situation is a major challenge to you – oh, yes, I too can do a little in the way of reading expressions and you would be greatly disappointed if we left here, and,' she added with unexpected candour, 'I myself am interested in what has happened. Two deaths out of six people who came here.'

'One of which was an accident,' began her aunt when Sally interrupted her.

'I have a strong suspicion that you have already decided against that idea. Auntie, admit that you believe there have been two murders here, not one.'

'You *have* been thinking,' returned her aunt, not without a hint of amusement. 'I fear I have some competition.'

'Oh, I'm no sleuth, but anyone with a modicum of nous can make certain deductions, and mine are that James Devlin brought us here to be punished for wrongs done to him in the past.'

'I see...' thoughtfully and after a small pause. 'But you, my love, have never harmed James.'

'No, but I have been thinking – as I said – and it could be that Father once did him a dirty trick. I have never pretended that Father was all honesty and upright truth. Mother had a hard time with him on occasions.'

'I see,' said her aunt again. She decided to let Sally assume it was her father and not her mother who had done James an injury. 'And who, might I ask, have you designated as the one willing to mete out these punishments?'

'That's the snag. I've decided to leave that to my clever aunt, who with her uncanny insight is bound to pick him out.'

Louisa had to laugh.

'Murder by proxy, eh?'

Sally shrugged in a little self-deprecating gesture.

'It would have to be, wouldn't it? James isn't the killer.'

'How very simple it would be if he was,' returned her aunt with a small sigh of frustration. 'The law of retribution...' She paused then enquired curiously, 'You, Sally, you don't appear to be afraid any more. You're suddenly so complacent.'

'I was a little bit apprehensive,' she admitted after a moment of thought. 'But, somehow, I have this strange feeling, a sort of sublime confidence that whatever else happens here I shall not be murdered.'

'Good God, child, I hope not! You say it so calmly.'

Sally stopped abruptly in the path and turned to face her aunt.

'You are also confident, Auntie, because if you had any doubts or qualms at all you'd have me away from here. I know the inspector has said none of us must leave yet but he'd allow you to go.' Her aunt made no comment and Sally continued, '*He* would be most disappointed, too, as he is relying on your help in the solving of a problem for which you will let him collect all the kudos.'

Again her aunt laughed.

'Ten out of ten for perception. Yes, he can have the credit ... if this crime *is* ever solved.'

'Oh,' returned Sally with a careless gesture, 'you will solve it, Auntie; there'll be that special moment of enlightenment – you used to tell me all about the way you worked things out, remember?'

'An avid listener you were, too.' She lapsed into thought as they again strolled on, making for the secluded little arbour they liked so much. A moment of enlightenment ... It was true that such pieces of amazing luck came to her, but this time she had seen not one glimmer of light up till now. She said aloud: 'Six people promised a legacy if they came here and spent four days. Why four days? Surely it was to allow enough time for something to happen—'

'For the whole lot to be murdered,' broke in Sally and her aunt shot her a sideways glance. No fear, not even a glimmer of apprehension for her own safety. In fact, there was a sort of detached, impersonal manner about her. From where, wondered her aunt, had she come by this serene confidence? She decided to tell Sally what was in the note, adding that she had refrained from telling her sooner in case she, Sally, became scared.

'However,' went on Louisa with a smile, 'as it appears you are not in the least scared, there is no reason why you shouldn't be told what the note contained.'

Sally was a few moments digesting this.

'So you've known that Joseph Powell was murdered ever since I gave you the note? Did you tell the inspector?'

'Not yet. I want to do some investigating first. Tomorrow morning I want you to drive me along that road. I want to see the cliff.'

Sally became thoughtful again. When she spoke it was to herself.

'Mrs Smallman was murdered soon after she wrote that note...' She was frowning, grappling with this new implication. She looked up. 'She was murdered because of what she saw – but that only adds another complication. My theory that we were all brought here to be punished falls apart – that is, *if* she was murdered because of what she saw. And that must be the case, mustn't it? Otherwise we would be stretching coincidence too far.'

'Strangely, I don't accept that she was murdered because of what she saw up there on the cliff. If there is any coincidence, it's that, after writing the note, she just happened to be killed—'

'Just happened!' exclaimed Sally. 'You don't "just happen" to be murdered.'

'I don't believe the murder was premeditated, Sally. Someone grabbed that poker on the spur of the moment and struck her with it.'

'So you don't think her attacker meant to kill her?' Sally shook her head as if to clear it. 'I'm all at sixes and sevens, Auntie! If her attacker didn't mean to kill her then why did he attack her at all?'

'Oh, I think he meant to kill her ... because of something she saw, but that something had nothing to do with Joseph Powell's murder.'

'You mean – she saw something else? Now that *would* be stretching coincidence too far.'

'I don't agree. The inspector believes she disturbed a thief. I am now of the same mind. It is the *type* of thief in which my problem lies.'

'What exactly do you mean, Auntie?'

'I am positive it was no casual, petty thief from the village. No, there is more to it than that.' Her brow was furrowed, her expression one of deep concentration. Why, she suddenly wondered, did she wish she could see what lay behind that beard the gardener wore? It certainly had nothing to do with any attempt to steal the silver, since he had permission to take just whatever he wanted from the house.

Sally interrupted her thoughts by saying, 'Are you implying, Auntie, that it was some sort of organized gang that was intent on the robbery?'

Louisa shook her head, her brow still deeply furrowed. An organized gang...

'A typical organized gang would never come here, in broad daylight, and walk into the house expecting to fill their bags with loot and remain undisturbed. Also, they'd have a car. No, there's some other explanation—'

'It must have been someone local, then,' broke in Sally to point out reasonably. 'It is well known how James lived, alone—'

Louisa raised a hand to stop her. Sally saw the sudden gleam enter her eyes and waited in a sort of breathless expectation. It was clear that her aunt had at last seen through the fog.

As the silence stretched, Sally at last blurted out, 'You've got it! You've solved the whole thing. I said you'd have that particular moment of enlightment, didn't I? Tell me. I can't wait another minute! What is this flash of insight?'

Louisa smiled faintly and to her niece's surprise shook her head.

'Sorry, love, to disappoint you, but I am very far from solving this crime.' An organized gang...? But not the kind that Sally meant.

'But not as far as you were a few moments ago,' was Sally's perceptive rejoinder.

'Something has come to you; I saw it in your eyes.'

'True, something has come to me. But a mere glimmer, Sally, not the flash you so optimistically assumed.'

'All right. Tell me about this glimmer. You have an idea who killed Mrs Smallman?'

'It's only an idea and, therefore, I'm not yet willing to take either you or the inspector into my confidence. All I can say with certainty is that the two murders are not connected in any way at all.'

'Not connected...' A sigh escaped Sally. 'In that case, there are two murderers at large.'

'And we have to find two motives.'

'Well, as it seems Mrs Smallman surprised an intruder, we can safely conclude there was a motive for her murder – but what motive could there be for Mr Powell's murder?'

Louisa laughed despite the frustration she felt.

'You are suddenly very interested in this situation. Maybe I shall need your help – be glad of it.'

But Sally shook her head. 'I am totally in the dark, Auntie. How little did I guess when I received that solicitor's letter that I'd find myself embroiled in a situation as baffling as this.'

'It will all come out in the end,' returned her aunt with more optimism than she felt. And she added, 'Shall we go over all we have learned up till now?'

Eagerly her niece agreed and Louisa began. 'I should first tell you of my own deductions. That is, certain things I find puzzling without having a clue as to why I am puzzled.' She paused a moment, making herself more comfortable on the thinly padded wooden seat that was all the arbour contained. 'On arrival and meeting with the Thorpes, I instantly read from their facial structure that both were sly, untrustworthy. I soon found myself thinking that their respective roles of butler and housekeeper covered up something else but not until a few moments ago did I even take a wild guess as to what that something was – no, Sally, I am not revealing anything more as I have not a shred of evidence, so I am going on to the next point, which is: why did Albert stare so intensely at you on our first meeting with him? It impressed you so strongly that you were embarrassed by it, true?'

'Yes. It felt as if he was searching into my very soul.'

'Just so. And now for point three: if Tessa was so devoted to James, she being his pet and not Albert's, why has she so quickly transferred her love and affection? Dogs are known to pine for a lost master or mistress for some time.'

'Yes, I agree. I never thought about it but as you say, Tessa is now devoted to Albert.' She added when her aunt did not immediately speak, 'Of course, you have to remember that Tessa would know Albert very well, and he did say he used sometimes to take her for walks.'

'True ... and yet...' Louisa gave a small sigh. 'We'll leave that and go on to the next puzzling factor. The will. Who signed as witnesses? Albert states emphatically that James never went out, never went through the gates. Albert himself could not have been a witness because he is a beneficiary. No solicitor came to the house. As you know from Eric Philpots himself the will and the letter containing the instructions arrived at his office right out of the blue. His firm had never acted for James, had never even heard of him.'

'How did he hear of them, I wonder?'

'The Yellow Pages; he just picked out a solicitor, and had Albert post the package to the firm he had chosen. I've asked Albert about this and he says he did in fact post the large envelope to the firm of solicitors of which Eric is a partner.'

'When was this?'

'That's another thing. I asked Philpots and he refused to say. I asked Albert and he was very vague, saying it was probably about two or three years ago, but I have the impression that it was more recent – in fact, very recent. However, let us leave that and go on to what we both know. We know that Joseph Powell was murdered and so also was Mrs Smallman. We could have difficulty in finding who pushed Powell from the top of the cliff, but I think we should be able to find the killer of Mrs Smallman. I shall expect the police to help with that. Now what else? We have found that all the beneficiaries did harm to James at one time or other.' Here she paused undecided. She looked at her niece and saw the cool pose of interest and decided to enlighten her. 'Sally, I have come to the conclusion that your mother was the one who jilted James—'

'My mother!'

'James was once in an amateur dramatic society and at the time your mother was also in the same society. You say you have a snapshot of her with a man who was not your father. I believe you have a photo of James Devlin.'

Bewildered, Sally just sat there, speechless for a long moment before saying unsteadily, 'This strengthens the idea that we were all brought here to – to be punished. But it still doesn't make sense because the man who wanted to punish us is dead.'

'As murder was obviously not his objective then what exactly did he have in mind when he brought to this house six people who, in his opinion – and his mind was warped, remember – had wronged him? Revenge of some kind, but what?'

'I expect we shall see the light when the will is read,' submitted Sally with a sigh of resignation, and Louisa nodded her head in agreement.

Before anything more could be said Tessa came bounding along, tail wagging, and Sally bent to stroke her.

'Oh, but you are a dear little dog!' Sally looked up to smile at Albert as he stood there in the familiar khaki overall and Wellington boots.

'A lovely evening,' he observed. 'Just the kind I like for a stroll. You get all the scents from the flowers and, if you're lucky, the song of the thrush up there in that oak tree.' He pointed and they looked up. 'A bad business, this murder,' he said, changing the subject. 'Do you think it was premeditated?'

Now why, thought Louisa, should he ask a question like that?

'No, I do not. Have you any theories, Albert?'

'I should imagine one would be in serious error by theorizing. I'm sure you'll agree, Mrs Hooke?'

'Unless one forms a theory there is nothing to work upon.'

'And you are working on this case, hoping to find the murderer?'

'I am certainly interested,' she replied. 'Murder especially encourages my powers of deduction to work overtime.'

'It is as I expected. You have made an intelligent guess as to why Mrs Smallman was murdered?'

'The inspector's conclusion is the feasible one.'

'Ah, yes, but is it your conclusion, Mrs Hooke?'

'You are very interested,' observed Louisa, wondering why she had the impression that her answer was important to him.

'It's an interesting situation.'

'Undoubtedly it is. As regards to your question, Albert, I am in agreement with the inspector that Mrs Smallman disturbed a robber.' She paused a moment but as he made no comment she went on, 'As you should know more than any of us here, there is a fortune in Georgian silver in the house – a temptation for anyone who might know of its existence.'

'True. James became interested when he bought this house. The owner had died; his heirs, a son and daughter, lived abroad, he in Australia – in Sydney – and the married daughter in South Africa. Neither actually wanted to come over but the daughter did make an effort. I am of the opinion that there had been some estrangement,' he inserted, for the moment diverting. 'However, she desired only to get rid of the property and return to her family. So she offered the entire contents to James on the day he came to view the house. He agreed and this mass of Georgian silver came into his hands – a collection which, I believe, took a lifetime to collect.'

'He was fortunate,' submitted Sally. 'It's beautiful, and must be worth a mint, as Auntie says.'

The old man nodded his head. Tessa was now on her haunches, but leaning heavily against his leg. Louisa stared at the dog and wondered why some elusive glimmer of light had come and gone in less time than it takes to blink an eyelid.

Louisa said, 'We were given to understand that you are at liberty to take anything you want from the house. Shall you take some of the silver?'

He paused. Louisa knew a strange tension in the air.

'I think I might take a couple of pieces,' he smiled at last. 'Did you notice the silver and cut-glass inkstand?'

'The one with the candleholder and snuffer as well as the inkpots? Oh, but it is beautiful!' Sally's eyes actually sparkled. 'It was used in Regency times to do the wax-seal thing, wasn't it?'

'That's right.' He looked at her and his smile reappeared. 'I've always liked it – although for myself, I don't know much about antiques of any kind. I shall take furniture to fix up my cottage, and it is probably valuable but for me it is just utility. I'll take just enough and no more.'

Louisa and Sally exchanged glances. Both were thinking the same thing. Here was his chance to acquire more money than he would ever need, and yet he was taking only what was necessary. And he had even been hesitating about the price of the cottage.

The Thorpes always left coffee out in the dining room so that anyone could help themselves during the evening. The glass percolator was bubbling when Louisa and Sally came in from the garden, so they each took a cup to the sitting room. The three men were there, in low armchairs; all stood up as the women entered.

'Do please sit down,' was Louisa's immediate and gracious request. 'It's a beautiful evening: I should have thought you gentlemen would have gone out for a stroll.'

'As a matter of fact,' said the doctor, 'that was our idea, but then we all began discussing the murder and so we're still here. I expect the air is a little damp and chill by this time.'

'Not noticeably so, but of course it's quite dark now.' She sat down on a small settee and Sally took possession of the space next to her. 'So you've been discussing the murder.' Louisa took a sip of her coffee, decided it was far too hot and put it down on a small table at her elbow.

'Naturally.' It was Hilliard who spoke and he added, 'We seem to be prisoners here. That policeman has dictated that none of us must leave.' His voice had a level edge as he added, 'Does he suppose any of us could commit murder?'

'In a case like this,' returned Louisa, 'everyone must stay for questioning. It happens to be routine procedure and there is no question of any of you being suspect. You might be required at the inquest – and perhaps that of Mr Powell as well.'

'You speak with an air of authority.' Hilliard looked resentfully at her. Ignoring his manner she asked if any of them had any ideas as to why Mrs Smallman was murdered.

It was Leonard Fulham who spoke.

'We've all agreed on a theory, yes. We think she walked in here and disturbed a marauder who was intent on stealing silver. We have decided he's a local, and this is for two reasons. Firstly, he'd realize he could be recognized, and so he grabbed the first handy weapon, the poker, and struck her a mortal blow. We can't say if he got away with any of the silver because, as you see, it's everywhere. I guess a good deal could go before it was missed.'

Louisa said quietly, 'And the second reason?'

'Only a local would know that the house

was unoccupied—'

'It wasn't unoccupied,' interposed Sally. 'There are nine of us living here, not counting the gardener.'

'But this wouldn't be generally known to, say, people who live a small distance outside the village. In fact, the villagers themselves probably didn't know there were six of us coming. The way James lived must have been known for miles around here, and when he died it would be taken for granted that the only person left was the gardener and he happens to spend almost his entire life outdoors. He was saying that even in wet weather he would be in one of the greenhouses. You can't keep everything secret and we feel sure that this would be known. So anyone bent on easy theft could come along and feel quite safe. All he had to do was make sure the gardener wasn't anywhere near the house itself. The fact that the front door was unlocked would seem to him to be nothing unusual as the gardener wouldn't bother to lock it when he was in the grounds. There was no need, not with those high wrought-iron gates always shut.'

'You're assuming that the locals all knew about the fortune in silver James had.'

'The gardener was chatting and mentioned that groceries were delivered twice weekly. So obviously the delivery lad would have noticed at least some of the treasure. The windows aren't covered with nets – and you only have to open the front door to see the long table absolutely cluttered with silver. Village gossip and all that—' Bernard shrugged expressively and spread his hands. 'It's the simple solution with which we're sure you'll agree, Mrs Hooke?'

She glanced at Sally and saw the lack of interest with which she regarded the verdict to which the men had come.

'The simple explanation is not always the correct one,' warned Louisa. 'You see, although this intruder you have – er – invented perhaps knew, or thought he knew, that the house was empty, he'd scarcely have come by daylight, in the middle of the afternoon. If he knew so much then he'd know that Albert slept away in the east wing and he'd obviously come at night when there would be no danger of being disturbed.'

'So you're throwing out our theory?' John Hilliard glared at her. 'We all now know that you consider yourself as something of a sleuth,' he added with a distinct sneer. 'So in that case you might be able to come up with another explanation?'

Before she could reply the doctor looked straight at her and asked if she was working with the police.

'I ask simply because the inspector was willing to have you in with him when he was doing the first interviews. Are you, in fact, a detective?'

She shook her head, saying she did not have the status of a detective. She was a private investigator, she told him.

'But,' she added, 'I am interested in crime. In America – Boston, where I lived – I often helped the police. I am intending to lend the inspector any powers I have. In other words, we are, in a way, working together.'

'So if that's the case, then perhaps you do happen to have come up with another explanation?'

'Not one that I would reveal, Mr Hilliard.'

'That can mean either that you have no real faith in it, or that you are being deliberately secretive.'

She looked directly at him.

'Mr Hilliard, I haven't said I have an explanation. However, I assure you I am working on it, as will be the inspector. Whatever ideas we eventually pool will probably come out at the inquest.'

Bernard Wilding's face wore a troubled frown as he said, 'Two deaths, Mrs Hooke. Two. One cannot help wondering if there will be a third.'

'A third?' There was an amused curve to her mouth. 'Isn't that a little too melodramatic, Mr Wilding? I'd not have expected such an idea to come from a level-headed man like you?'

He looked at her through narrowed eyes.

'You puzzle me greatly, Mrs Hooke,' he said. 'Forgive my saying so, but there is a sort of arrogant self-confidence about you which I find singularly vexing.'

She had to laugh.

'I imagine it is only politeness which prevents you from using a stronger word than vexing?'

'Perhaps,' he agreed but instantly added, 'I'm sorry, Mrs Hooke. There is no excuse for rudeness.'

'You were merely outspoken. It is a sure sign of honesty for one to say what one thinks. We shan't fall out over it, Mr Wilding. I have rather a thicker skin than most.'

'And a subtler sense of humour.'

'So I have been told on more than one occasion.' She added after a pause, 'I haven't altogether thrown out your theory, gentlemen. But shall we say, I have amended it?'

The doctor eyed her speculatively. 'But that is as far as you intend to go as regards taking us into your confidence?'

'I'm afraid so.'

'You can answer this, I suppose: are we to take it that you are of the opinion that Mrs Smallman did in fact surprise someone?'

She hesitated thoughtfully before answering. 'In my opinion the crime was not premediated.'

'Ah,' from Bernard. 'So she did surprise someone?'

'Perhaps.' She yawned, an exaggerated gesture. 'I'm tired.' She stood up and smiled at her niece. 'Stay if you want, Sally. It's only half past ten.'

'I'll come up with you.'

Goodnights were said but as they reached the door the raw tones of anger caused them to turn.

'It is to be hoped,' said John Hilliard, 'that all this will prove to be worth our while!'

Sally sat on the bed after taking her shoes off.

'Do you think those men are scared?'

'They're anxious, and I believe the two friends would leave if they were allowed, and let the legacy go hang.'

'But not Mr Hilliard?'

'He's far too interested in the money to want to leave.'

'So he at least isn't scared. Well, I guess they'd all be in a rare panic if they knew what we know.'

'That there were two murders, not one? Yes, no doubt they would be feeling a little more than apprehensive.'

Sally was at the window. She opened it to let in some cool, fresh air.

'The Thorpes,' she breathed and moved swiftly to one side. 'They're both out there and I'm sure there's another person with them.'

Louisa switched off the light before joining her. They both peered out into the darkness. Three figures could be seen, some considerable way from the house.

'It's not easy to say if two of them are the Thorpes or not.'

'Shall I run down and see if they are in the kitchen?'

'Yes, do that. Meanwhile I'm going out there. Whether it's the Thorpes or not there's something funny going on.' She reached for a dark blue knitted jacket. 'Make some feasible excuse – if the Thorpes are there. Say you have a headache and ask for some aspirins.'

'Supposing they are not in the kitchen? How will I know if they've gone to bed?'

'By knocking on their door, of course. Apologize for disturbing them but feign real pain and ask for the aspirins.'

By the time Louisa reached the garden the three shadowy figures were nowhere to be seen. She wandered around but there was no sign of them. She stopped to listen but there were no voices either. But suddenly she heard another sound ... the starting up of a car, and it seemed to come from the narrow lane running to the side of a copse which formed a windbreak for part of the gardens.

She herself was by the shrubbery and she moved into it. The Thorpes, making no sound, were moving towards the house, which they entered, by the back door. Louisa made her way to the front and was met by Sally as she entered the hall to say that the Thorpes weren't in the house.

'They are now—' She broke off as the phone rang. Picking up the receiver she heard a muffled, 'Can I speak to John Hilliard? It's urgent, I'm his son.'

'Hold on.' She told Sally to fetch John Hilliard. The receiver was lying by the phone ... She stared at it, eyes narrowed. That voice...? Something nagging at her brain? Her eyes moved as Hilliard appeared. Picking up the receiver she handed it to him. A clock chimed. Eleven. She watched his face closely, first having noticed the look of anxiety as he came into the hall. He feared bad news from home. Louisa was wide awake, an alert vitality about her as if she were ready to spring. Hilliard frowned at her but she made no move to afford him privacy. He listened. She saw his eyes dilate.

'Wh-what—? I – who are you?' His face was ghastly. Louisa controlled the impulse to snatch the receiver from his trembling fingers. 'I s-said wh-who—?' She did then take hold of the receiver.

'This is Louisa Hooke! Who is speaking?' The line went dead.

Slowly she replaced the receiver. John Hilliard looked as if he were on the verge of collapse as he stood there, his hands on the marble top of the console table supporting his sagging figure.

The chief inspector was of the opinion that it was a hoax.

'We get this sort of thing often.' He glanced at Louisa. 'You'll know, Mrs Hooke?' he said and she nodded in agreement. A hoax, perhaps, but not the ordinary type, as whoever made that call was in possession of considerable knowledge as to what was going on at the manor. And no ordinary villager could have this knowledge.

The chief inspector was perusing the message that John Hilliard had written down. Corlett read aloud:

'Two deaths. Who will be the next legatee to die? You. But not tonight so sleep well.'

Louisa listened, wishing with all her heart she could have taken a recording of the message. This nagging insistence which led to ... nothing but frustration. It was like the desperate effort one sometimes makes to recapture a dream, a dream that remains elusive except for tantalizing wisps which curl away to be lost in space. The chief inspector said, having watched her changing expression for a moment or two, 'You have an idea?'

'I agree it's a hoax – of some kind. But not the usual act of mischief of which you and I are familiar. Don't you realize, Inspector, that whoever made that call knows about the murder of Mrs Smallman, and the accident—'

'All the village knows,' he pointed out quietly.

'All the village doesn't know the names of the people staying here. And even if they did, how would anyone know Hilliard has a son?'

'Surmise,' was his casual rejoinder. 'Most men of that age have children.'

She shook her head.

'I'm not satisfied. However, I think I've convinced Hilliard that it wasn't anything to worry about, that it couldn't possibly be a serious threat.'

'He seems to accept that.' He smiled faintly. 'The promise of money is so strong that it appears to have overcome his initial fear.'

'Yes. He's the mercenary type.' Her voice was edged with contempt. 'He'll stay – unless of course he has another fright.'

'Well,' said Sally sitting on her bed and watching her aunt discard her jacket, 'what will happen next, I wonder?'

Her aunt looked at her.

'I believe you are enjoying all this.'

'I find it interesting, watching you work. How did you manage to bring the inspector out at this time of the night?'

'I didn't. It was Hilliard himself. However, it gave me the chance of telling him of the Thorpes' escapade and that there was a car in the vicinity.'

'What does it all mean, Auntie? What could the Thorpes have been doing? And was the presence of a car anything to do with their being out there, in the dark?'

'I feel sure the two were connected. As for what they had been doing out there, well, they could have been giving the person in the car some precious antiques.'

'The silver? You believe they were stealing some of it?'

'It's possible, but with the car gone we have no proof.'

'What did the inspector say?'

'He was keenly interested but without proof he can do nothing. He certainly cannot accuse them of stealing some of the silver.'

Six

Immediately after breakfast the following morning Louisa and Sally were out. The air was fresh after a shower of rain, the sun was climbing into a sky of cloudless blue.

'We'll drive slowly along the cliff road and find a suitable place to stop.' Louisa had her map and was studying it while Sally drove the car. They found a lay-by and pulled into it.

'I don't see how you can expect to discover anything.' Puzzled, Sally brought the car to a halt. 'We've decided it was murder, but what do you expect to find? And,' she added at once, 'we ought to be telling the inspector of our conclusions.'

Louisa shook her head. She folded up the map and tucked it into the glove box.

'Not yet. I want to take a good look around—'

'But you'll never find the place where he fell.'

'I'm hopeful, Sally.' She opened her door and stepped from the car. Before her was open terrain – the flat top of the cliff which eventually made an almost sheer drop to the sea. Sally was beside her; the breeze, soft and warm, caressed their faces and tossed Sally's hair. Louisa's was immune, protected by the severity of its style.

Sally said as they walked towards the edge, 'No matter what we find it isn't going to explain why he was murdered or who did it.'

Sending her a sideways glance her aunt replied, 'I did say it was going to be difficult, but nothing is beyond explanation.'

'Well, you've explained Mrs Smallman's death and hopefully the murderer will be brought to justice, so I can see a good reason for your optimism concerning Joseph Powell's murder.' Sally skipped to keep pace with her aunt. 'Have you any ideas ... clues?'

'At this moment, not a single idea,' admitted Louisa. 'We shall have to see what our investigations bring to light.'

'And should they reveal nothing?'

'Have faith, my child. I am optimistic about our little mission.'

Sally gave a tiny sigh. She fervently hoped that this would not prove to be an abortive venture, because her aunt had such high hopes, such confidence that she would leave this place with far more knowledge than when she came to it.

She said, a little hesitantly, 'You feel sure you can discover who murdered Mr Powell?'

'It will be difficult. This I have to admit.'

'But you're intending to have a good try?'

Louisa nodded. She increased her pace and to Sally it was an indication that her aunt would be obliged if she refrained from pursuing the present topic of conversation.

The narrow path which ran along the top of the cliff was eventually reached and Louisa slowed her pace. Sally was avidly interested as her aunt kept her eyes on the ground, stopping now and then to prod the earth or run a hand over the rough grass. The path was by no means dangerously close to the edge, but it ran through Sally's mind that there ought to be a rail since it could be a danger spot here, especially for children. She asked presently:

'What exactly is it you're looking for, Auntie?'

'The place where he fell. There is bound to be some indication.'

'Such as?'

'The ground having given way, or some loose stones. You don't slip off a cliff and leave nothing to show.' She glanced up. 'Imagine yourself slipping. You'd take with you some earth, or even grass. It would only be if you jumped that you'd do it cleanly.'

'Yes, I see what you mean. I'll have a look as well.' And in fact it was Sally who spotted the loosened earth and shouted triumphantly, 'It's here, Auntie! Very plain...' She tailed off, her eyes fixed on the area of grass close to the loosened earth. Her aunt came up to her. 'Look at that. Signs of a struggle?' Sally waited rather breathlessly for the verdict.

'Someone else was here,' murmured Louisa almost to herself. There was a hint of excitement in her manner. 'But no struggle. Now, I find that most strange. No sign of a struggle, but this area flattened...'

'No sign—?' Sally pointed. 'What about all this trodden-down grass? Several pairs of feet—'

'I wouldn't say several. One other person...' Louisa was down on her haunches, having brought out a large magnifying glass from her handbag. 'Yes, just two people, Sally.'

Sally shook her head in bewilderment.

'There must have been a struggle. No one could come upon another person by stealth, not up here where all is so open. There isn't one single tree or bush to be seen.'

Louisa straightened up and looked at her niece.

'Does nothing strike you about this?' she asked, then shook her head. 'No, it doesn't, obviously.'

'Tell me, Auntie?'

'It's simple. There is definitely a positive conclusion to be drawn this time. The person who was here with Joseph Powell was no stranger to him.'

'No!' Sally shook her head, more bewildered than ever. 'But who is there who would know him?'

Her aunt was examining the ground again.

'I'm hoping to discover whether the two people came together, or whether the murderer came on his own.'

'The murderer...' Sally shuddered. Icy fingers seemed to be running along her spine. How little she had known, on receiving that letter from Mr Philpots, just what was in store for her. Yet she was suddenly recalling her mother saying that her sister, Louisa, '... seems always to be involved in some crime or other.'

Sally glanced around. A young couple who had been strolling along had now turned and were retracing their steps. The sky was darkening, portent of a summer downpour. All seemed bleak, deserted. She opened her mouth to suggest they return to the car but her aunt was so completely absorbed in her examination of the ground that she held her tongue.

'It's difficult.' Louisa was shaking her head. 'You see, others have been up here – not many, but some. However, I can be almost sure that Joseph Powell came here alone and that the person who pushed him over this cliff was known to him. This is one point, Sally, on which I am positive, because I find no sign of a struggle.'

'But who?' Sally shook her head. 'We're not absolutely sure he was pushed.'

'You're forgetting Mrs Smallman's letter. She saw something happening here.'

'Yes.' A deep sigh escaped Sally. 'The only people who knew him are those of us living in the house.' She stopped rather shortly because her aunt was not listening.

'Yes, he was definitely pushed to his death. An experienced fell-walker would take no risks. Now, who could have done this murder?'

'I've just said the only people who knew him are those of us at the manor.'

Louisa was strangely silent and Sally refrained from disturbing her thoughts. They reached the car and got in. The drive back to the manor was a silent one and so Sally gave a jerk of surprise when her aunt said, answering the question Sally had put to her twenty minutes ago, 'That's the rub, Sally. Yes, we have only the people at the manor, and which of them would want to follow Joseph Powell up there and send him to his death?'

'There might be someone – an acquaintance from his past. It's not unusual for old acquaintances to bump into one another in the most unlikely places. That's why we have the expression "It's a small world".'

Louisa smiled.

'A good try, love, but I'm not impressed.'

'It *can't* be one of those three men.'

'No, I agree about that. John Hilliard's not

one of the world's most pleasant characters, but he's no murderer.' She paused and frowned. 'So that leaves the Thorpes, Mr Philpots, and Albert.'

'Albert!' with strong indignation. 'Albert wouldn't hurt a fly. He's gentle and kind and he loves animals. You'll never find vice in people who care about animals.'

'Gentle and kind people have been known to kill, as the inspector remarked.'

Sally brought the car to a standstill on the little patch at the side of the house which she had used since she arrived.

'Well, we didn't get far, did we?' she said, switching off the engine.

'I wouldn't say that. We know that Joseph was pushed off that cliff by someone he knew, and trusted. No struggle, which means he was taken by surprise. Someone he knew and trusted...' she repeated, her glance falling on Albert, who was walking along the shrubbery path with Tessa at his side.

The inspector, meanwhile, had reiterated his order that no one was to leave the manor. He would be questioning them all again. Also, they might have to attend one or even both inquests.

'Hilliard's still complaining that he's a prisoner here,' the doctor told Louisa, 'but he wouldn't leave even if he was allowed – not until after the will is read, that is. But I

186

suspect he'll make a fuss if he's kept longer than tomorrow.'

'Which he will be,' pronounced Louisa strongly. 'He might as well resign himself to obeying the inspector's orders.'

The doctor looked around.

'Sally not with you? You went for a drive? I noticed your car was gone from its slot.'

'We did have a drive out, yes,' was her non-committal reply. And then, 'Sally's gone to find Millie. She was talking of going back to Ireland until the time when she comes to live with me, but we're trying to persuade her to stay with Sally – as I am doing for the present as I mentioned. Sally has three bedrooms so there is no reason why Millie can't come back with us. We can call at Mrs Smallman's home and collect her things. It's not far out of our way.'

'The girl's found a good friend in you, Mrs Hooke.'

'And Sally. They're of an age so I feel sure they're going to be friends for a very long time.'

At that moment Sally popped her head around the door of the sitting room.

'We're going off for a walk, Auntie. We'll all meet for lunch.'

'And I'm going out into the garden. This weather, and that beauty, are there to be taken full advantage of.'

The air was cool and clear. The sun was out

again in all its glory, its heat rapidly taking up the moisture dropped in the heavy downpour that had come as they were driving home from their investigations of the cliff. Albert was pulling up some weeds from the bed of mixed annuals and Tessa was close beside him. Louisa thought she would have a female dog, since if this one was anything to go by they were as faithful as it was possible to be.

'Isn't it wonderful after a shower of rain?' The old man straightened up, patting the dog's head as he did so. 'Makes weeding a lot easier as well.'

'I'm surprised at the way you continue to care for the gardens here. In another few weeks all this beauty will be gone.'

'I shall not come back to look,' he admitted. 'However, as one gets older the work in a large garden becomes a chore – or so I am to gather from the gardening programmes on the television. So my small plot will mean that gardening will remain a pleasure.' The familiar brown overall, put on clean this morning, was smudged with wet soil. Following the direction of her eyes, he made a grimace. 'Sometimes I wonder why I bother to put on a clean overall every day.'

'It's how one is. I can't imagine you starting the day in a soiled overall.'

'No, I never do.' He went on to say that the cottage, being already vacant, could be occupied immediately the contract was signed.

'Which will be tomorrow afternoon,' he added.

'You will have to be at the reading of the will, though.'

'Yes, and I shall go to the estate agents' immediately afterwards. There's a train at—'

'We'll take you, Albert. We've to remain here so it'll be no trouble. In fact, we shall enjoy the ride. Millie will come too.'

'Thank you very much.' He looked at her with affection in his eyes. 'I've become suddenly rich...' He was talking to himself. 'It isn't money that makes you rich...' He was acting as if he had made a discovery— No, she decided. He was going over a discovery already made. Sally with her soft heart would understand. He had found friends, after so many long years when most of his days must have been spent in isolation, cut off, just as his employer was cut off. He was coming out of himself; he had gained confidence already. He was looking forward to his visits to Melcombe Porcorum, and to their visits to his cottage.

She asked him when he intended to make the move, adding that if it was in the very immediate future Sally wouldn't mind using her car to transport anything he was taking from the manor.

'The small antiques should not go in the furniture-removal van,' she advised. 'We'll help you to pack them and take them to the

189

cottage.'

'I was thinking of an immediate move,' he replied, but added that he ought to have the bathroom made first, in order to avoid the mess and upheaval while he was living there.

'Perhaps it would be advisable,' she agreed. 'But we'll come and give you some assistance even if it's after we've left here. Just give Sally a ring and say when you want us. Saturdays and Sundays are always free, but Sally works in an office during the week.'

'Yes, she said. An office is a nice place to work, I should imagine.'

'She likes it. They think a lot of her; she's earmarked as PA to the boss of a new department they're opening.'

He said nothing. His eyes were bright ... Why bright? Tears made one's eyes bright...

She changed the subject.

'Mrs Powell will be here this evening. She intended coming tomorrow, early, but Mr Philpots advised her not to leave it till then in case of accident, like the taxi breaking down, or there being traffic jams.'

'Could happen, which would make her late and she could miss the reading of the will.' His attention became focused on a bright green lizard which was sitting, motionless, on a stone.

Louisa said, watching his interest with the lizard, 'I wonder who will inherit Mrs Small-man's share? Millie seems to think she has a sister, but if not, I daresay some relative will turn up – a second cousin or other distant relation.'

'That's true,' he agreed.

'What do you think of these people, Albert? The two friends are all right, but the two who are dead were nothing to write home about. And then there's Mr Hilliard.'

'He was complaining to me that he is a prisoner here. And yet he didn't say he wanted to go home.'

'He's afraid,' stated Louisa. 'And yet, he doesn't want to go home and lose his inheritance.'

Albert stood thoughtfully, stroking his beard. He said at last, 'I suppose it's the two deaths that's made him afraid?'

She nodded her head, thinking about the threat received by Hilliard.

'The circumstances are rather chilling, one has to admit.'

He shrugged. 'The accident – well, similar accidents have occurred. And the business of Mrs Smallman's murder – she surprised an intruder, so the inspector thinks.' She said nothing and he went on, 'So he's afraid?' He glanced around to see where Tessa had gone. She was on the lawn chasing a wood pigeon. 'Fear is a very strange emotion, Mrs Hooke. It can take so many forms.'

'I agree. There is fear of death, of old age and eventual incapacity, fear of water, or thunder, and the very common fear of the dark.'

'You – I cannot imagine that you know what fear is, Mrs Hooke.'

She smiled at that and puckered her brow.

'I must admit,' she said presently, 'that I am not prone to fear but that doesn't say that I'm totally immune. For instance, were I faced with a lunatic with a loaded pistol I couldn't say I'd feel too happy.'

'No one would.' He glanced at the dog. 'You've been out for a drive,' he commented, changing the subject. 'I expected the rain to last longer but, fortunately, it came in just one heavy, and short, downpour.'

'We did go for a drive. I thought we'd take a walk along the cliff top. It's invigorating and cool, with the clean breeze coming in from the sea. No fouled air up there.' She was watching him closely. Where was he at the time Joseph Powell was being sent hurling down to his death? If only she could see what lay beneath that beard.

'The cliff top,' he murmured. 'Where Mr Powell met with the accident.' He shook his head. 'Strange things are happening, Mrs Hooke.'

She said quietly, still watching him with a keen and probing eye, 'You haven't spoken much about the two deaths.'

He shrugged his shoulders.

'I don't speak at all to the others. They

appear to regard me as an inferior – the three men, I mean, and even the Thorpes keep aloof. You and young Sally are the only ones I have any wish to converse with.' He paused as Tessa came to him and lifted a paw for him to take. It was a regular habit of hers, Louisa had noticed. 'I like Millie but she, too, keeps away.'

'She's shy, that is all. We shall bring her out, though, once we get her to Melcombe Porcorum. As you know, she's coming to work for me.'

'Lucky girl,' he smiled. There was a wistful quality in his voice as he added, 'You make a charming family, you and Sally. Millie will be very happy – which she couldn't have been with her previous employer.'

'Mrs Smallman ... One wonders what her husband was like. He, too, must surely have suffered at her hands.'

'Probably.' He looked at her. 'Makes one glad one never married. It's such one devil of a gamble, isn't it?'

'Like so many other things in life, yes, it's a gamble. But there are still some happy marriages. Mine was happy, Albert. And my only regret is that we never had children. It wasn't to be.'

'No. Such things are in the lap of the gods.' He bent to stroke the dog. 'Sally's parents – were they happy?' His voice seemed to catch.

'They remained together. I was away – I

believe I mentioned I'd been living in Boston – the US – for over thirty years. I saw Sally and her parents only once a year. We used to spend a month with them.' Had he noticed that her answer was noncommittal?

'And now you are to be living close to your niece. She'll be like your daughter.'

'She already is.' A softness entered her voice. He gave a sigh and reached up to pick a rose. She said curiously, 'Did you never think of marrying, Albert?'

He shook his head.

'Never. I wanted to be a gardener from when I was at school. I worked, and trained, in a nursery, a large concern, and was there for years. Then I went to work for a widowed lady. It was better because I was able to design the garden and do as I liked in it. There was a lot of repetition at the nursery and it could be boring without some scope for one's own ideas. The lady died and I went to James. Again I could do as I liked – alter things, redesign the layout.'

'And now it's to go under a bulldozer.'

'I'll have my little garden around the cottage. It'll be all my own, Mrs Hooke, and you have no idea what that will mean to me.'

'I think I have,' she returned with a smile. 'There is nothing like owning one's own home – the pride of possession. I hope you'll be very happy there, and of course you'll be visiting us. Sally has taken an especial liking to you – I don't know if you are aware of it, but she has.'

His blue eyes brightened in a strange, unfathomable way.

'She's a charming girl. Of course I shall be coming to see you both. I was wondering if I could afford a small car. I did drive once but James never had a car so I haven't driven since I left Mrs Riverton's employ. I used to drive her into town or to the cinema. She liked to go once a month.'

'I am sure you'll manage to buy a small car. But if it's to be a secondhand one then make sure you have someone reliable to look it over for you. You want to be safe.'

He nodded his head.

'I don't know if Tessa will take to a car. I believe it's best to let them begin as puppies or they might not take to it. If she doesn't like the car then of course I shan't have one.'

'Because you'd never go anywhere without her?'

'Never.' He seemed to Louisa to have stopped rather abruptly but she couldn't be sure. His next words were, 'You see, Mrs Hooke, she's mine now and I must regard her as family. James used to say that if you don't treat a dog as one of the family then you should never have one. He never fastened a dog up outside in all the time I knew him.'

'And quite right. I'm having a dog and he – or she – will be one of the family. Millie says she loves dogs so we have no problems there.'

He said, 'About the grave of Bess. If you feel – well, what I want to say is that you mustn't feel obliged to have it unless you really want to have it.'

She returned perceptively, 'You feel, now that you are definitely having the cottage, that you could have the grave yourself?'

'I could, of course, but I'm old, Mrs Hooke, and so in a few years the grave could be destroyed – by new owners of the cottage.'

'Yes, of course. So you still want me to have it?'

'Only if you are happy about it,' he said and she had to smile, because having in one's garden the grave of a dog one has never known could scarcely be an occasion for happiness. Still, she mused, her act would certainly give two other people happiness. And the grave was a thing of real beauty and would be admired, she felt sure – even though a fairly lengthy explanation would have to be proffered every time she had a visitor whom she might be showing around her garden. Albert was looking at his watch.

'You'll have to excuse me,' he said apologetically. 'I'm helping with the lunch – waiting on the tables. So I have to wash and change.'

She hesitated before remarking that he had taken to the job of butlering rather well, seeing that he had no previous experience.

Her piercing gaze held his; she was curious to know what his comment would be. He merely shrugged his shoulders and replied, 'm afraid my efforts are exceedingly amateurish, Mrs Hooke, since I know nothing about the special qualities required of the professional butler. I did occasionally wait upon James, if he happened to be off colour. Otherwise he usually wished to be left alone.' Unconsciously his voice dropped, to a low undertone.

Louisa stood watching his departing figure until it was lost to sight around a bend in the path. Tessa was close at his side.

Slowly she made her way back to the house, the most odd expression on her face. That voice ... She had heard it somewhere else...

The chief inspector, along with his assistant, Inspector Wright, was doing the rounds of the village, questioning all of its few inhabitants. He had invited Louisa to accompany them but she declined, feeling there was nothing to be gained. She now had a strong theory about Mrs Smallman's murder, and that did not include the possibility of the killer being anyone from the village.

Sally and Millie had chatted together over lunch, leaving Louisa contentedly busy with her own thoughts. When lunch was over, the girls said they were going for a walk.

'You're coming too, of course?' Sally said to her aunt, but Louisa shook her head.

'I have other things to think about,' she said. 'You two go off and explore the village.' And she added, 'If you happen to find yourself in conversation with any of the locals, and can in some subtle way slip in a comment about James Devlin, you might just be able to glean some information as to who he got to witness his will. Don't, whatever you do, ask any questions outright. I am of the opinion that he went to a solicitor, but when I questioned Albert about his employer having been out he said definitely that James never, ever left the manor.'

'Yet he must either have left or he had someone come to the house to sign the will.'

'Or,' murmured Louisa so softly that Sally only just caught her words, 'it was never signed at all.'

'What?' Sally stared at her. 'Mr Philpots has seen—'

'A letter which was with the will. All of us did manage to elicit that small item of information from our reticent friend. The letter contained the entire instructions and one of those was that the will must not be opened, by anyone, until the day for its reading, which of course is tomorrow.'

Sally stared at her aunt.

'You surely don't honestly believe that the will was never signed?' She spread her hands

198

in a little helpless gesture. 'It won't be legal; we'll have had all this for nothing.'

'Could be. But it's purely conjecture on my part and we do know that conjecture can be completely wrong, so we have to wait and see.'

'It will certainly be a blow for Mr Hilliard.' Sally's voice held the merest access of gratification and her aunt had to smile. The girl cared nothing for her own loss; she was actually looking forward to the possibility of the will not being legal, just to witness the reaction of the unlikeable John Hilliard.

Sally changed the subject then, to ask about this thinking her aunt had to do in preference to coming out for a walk in the sunshine.

'I'm endeavouring to slot a few things into place,' was the reply from Louisa.

'The moment of enlightenment will come to you in a flash,' returned her niece in tones of firm confidence but Louisa was shaking her head.

'No, not this time. Usually that does happen and in fact one moment of enlightenment might have occurred—'

'Might?' The tone of the interruption held puzzlement.

'Some flash of knowledge did come last night after I was in bed, but I haven't any proof that it's correct. All is coming slowly, and has to fit into the pattern. So much is still hazy.' She shook her head and a frown creased her brow. 'This case has so many conflicting circumstances,' she went on presently. 'Take for instance the theory of retribution. You yourself said you believed you had all been brought here for some form of punishment. Right. So we have the "accident" which you and I have now concluded was murder. We have a second murder—'

'Which so far is uncomplicated. Two gone, four to go.'

'Really, Sally—'

'I'm trying to be helpful.' But amazingly there was amusement in her eyes. 'Sorry, but you must admit that up to that point we could believe in the idea of retribution. Murder by proxy.'

'Except that we didn't accept that anyone would agree to commit six murders for someone who was dead.'

'OK, so we have a full stop at that point.'

Louisa said, looking straight at her niece, 'There could have perhaps been a person willing to commit the murders.' She paused significantly and Sally's manner changed as she waited for her aunt to continue. 'Albert,' was the brief and softly spoken word.

'He was with us when Mrs Smallman was killed.' There was a protest in Sally's voice. 'Nor did Albert kill Mr Powell. Albert is a good man, Auntie, a good, kind gentleman for whom I have already formed great respect. And I have a strange affection for him—' She broke off and for a long moment there was silence between them. She looked up at last. 'I feel he's becoming like an uncle, like someone who's been in the family for years.' She stopped again. Her aunt was nodding her head slowly and there was a most curious expression in her eyes. 'It's a silly idea, I know,' went on Sally with a little self-deprecating shrug, 'but he really does have a most attractive character.'

Louisa said, returning to Sally's first sentence, 'Yes, Albert has an alibi as regards Mrs Smallman's murder, but where was he at the time of Joseph's death? Sally, when I spoke just now of a moment of enlightenment I was not thinking of Albert. But when I was speaking to him earlier I did have a moment of enlightenment.' A pause and then, 'He had lowered his voice and I recognized it as – the voice I'd heard on the phone when John Hilliard was threatened. It was low and muffled, disguised, but definitely it was Albert who told John Hilliard that he would be the next to die.'

'No! No. I won't listen! Albert – you're mistaken, Auntie. Albert can't be the murderer!'

'I didn't say he was.'

'You implied – you've just told me it was he who threatened John Hilliard.'

'That is quite true, and I am not mistaken about that. However, this doesn't mean he

201

killed Joseph Powell, but if it had been his intention to kill you all, the fact that someone else killed Mrs Smallman would account for the stunned expression on his face when he heard of her murder.'

'Auntie, what are you really saying?'

'Just this: if he had planned to murder all six beneficiaries and someone killed one of them for him...' She tailed off, shrugging her shoulders.

Sally's eyes filled up.

'I can't believe he could hurt a fly – no, Auntie, there is some explanation. The voice – surely you could be mistaken?'

There was a plea in her words which made her aunt say quickly, 'Sally, dear, I agree with you that Albert is not a killer. But I do have to add that it was definitely him whom I heard asking for John Hilliard, he who told him he'd be the third to die.'

'The inspector said he believed it to be a hoax. Are you saying Albert would act in such a mischievious manner?'

'I know it doesn't sound like him as we have come to know him, but I haven't made a mistake. Sorry, dear Sally, but yes, Albert did act in that mischievous way.'

'I have to believe you,' came the reluctant rejoinder with a sigh of resignation. 'But I also know for sure there is some logical explanation and we shall come upon it.'

'We haven't much time.'

'No – very little, in fact, unless of course the inspector makes us stay until he is quite sure none of us is guilty of Mrs Smallman's murder.'

'He could very well do that; however, he is of the opinion that she came upon an intruder, remember.'

Sally merely nodded and a moment later she and Millie had gone off for their walk.

Louisa sat in the shady arbour, adding notes to those she had already made. She glanced back to previously written pages. Yes, there were a couple of clues ... If only she could see what lay beneath that beard...

She glanced up as the doctor was walking past the arched entrance to the tiny retreat. He stopped and smiled. She invited him to join her and he sat down, hitching up his trousers as he crossed his long legs. She saw his profile – strong, as was the jutting chin. Ears flattened to the head. A man dedicated to his profession, she thought – as she had from the very beginning. A man who, having taken the Hippocratic Oath, would observe it to the letter, in the dogmatic way in which it was first laid down.

He broke the silence, remarking on the beauty of the garden, and this small haven in particular.

'Yes, there's something about it,' she mused. 'I imagine James Devlin spent long hours here, with his books. I shall have to ask Albert.'

He glanced at the notebook on her lap.

'Still working on the mystery?' he observed and she nodded her head.

'You've lost your fear,' she said.

'Fear?' with a sudden lift of the straight dark brows. 'Fear is not the word I would use to describe my feelings, Mrs Hooke—'

'Sorry,' she interposed swiftly. 'You were apprehensive and it was natural after two deaths.'

He said, slanting her a glance, 'Have you reached any logical conclusions about the two deaths?'

'I suspect, Doctor, that you have convinced yourself now that there have been two murders, not only one.'

'You have to admit that that particular type of accident is rare, and for it to happen to one of the beneficiaries and be followed by the murder of another...' He spread his hands expressively. 'Well, one doesn't have to possess much of an imagination to connect the two.'

'And who,' she enquired, not without a hint of sarcasm, 'have you picked out as the murderer?'

Something in her tone caught his attention; he said perceptively, 'You *have* reached a conclusion. I believe you have made some most intelligent guesses, Mrs Hooke.' He was thinking about what her niece had said, that she had remarkable insight where crime was concerned.

'Correct, Doctor, but I'm not willing to divulge them just yet. I don't know enough about your benefactor...' She paused a moment, to warn him of her intention. 'I'm asking you, Doctor, to tell me of anything he might have said to you at the time you were treating him – or, I should say, rescuing him from something he had no wish to be rescued from.'

'You still believe he brooded over that?'

'He wanted to die; he wished to get away from people, because they had treated him badly. You came along and interfered with his plans for attaining the peace he craved. You brought him back into a world he hated. He never did again find that particular courage it takes to bring about one's own death, so he did the next best thing: he cut himself away from the human race, lived with only a gardener and his dogs. He loved gardens, or anything to do with nature; this much I have gathered without much trouble from Albert. As he didn't care for the heavier work in a garden, he employed another man, though even he was not too welcome, certainly he never became a companion to the man he employed. James Devlin could not have been happy, Doctor, and, therefore, it is reasonable to assume that he never ever forgave you for depriving him of the peace which he had planned for himself.' She flicked the pages of the notebook, becoming thoughtful for a space and then said, 'Tell me, Doctor, did James tell you the name of the woman who jilted him?'

His eyes became veiled. He said with a hint of indignation, 'Have you forgotten that I took the Hippocratic Oath, Mrs Hooke?'

'Indeed not. In fact, I was just thinking about it and I decided you would never break it. But I can assure you that it would help my investigation were that woman to be whom I think she is.'

'He did tell me – it was when he was rambling. But you will realize that I cannot reveal the lady's name.'

'She's probably dead by now.'

'It makes no difference.' His voice was firm. 'I'm still bound to silence.'

She said after a moment of considering, 'If you won't confide in me, Doctor, then I shall confide in you. I wonder if you have asked yourself why my niece should be here, when she never even met James Devlin?'

'I – we, Bernard and I – naturally discussed each one of the legatees and I admit we were puzzled as to why Sally was a beneficiary.'

'It's my belief,' she said, 'that Sally's mother was the girl who jilted James.' She sent him a sideways glance. 'My maiden name was Hilbury ... and of course my sister's was the same.'

He said, after a rather long interlude, 'So that explains another bit of the mystery.' He was far away in thought; she knew he was thinking of James, the young man, a man so devastated by his loss that he decided there was nothing left for him to live for. 'It explains why she is here and,' he added significantly, 'it strengthens the idea that retribution was James Devlin's aim.'

She passed that off impatiently. 'Don't bring that up, it confuses me.'

'Nevertheless, you agree with it. You know for sure, Mrs Hooke, that we were all brought here to be punished – murdered. The fact that two of us are dead surely points directly to this theory?'

'I did ask you a moment ago if you had picked out someone as the murderer. I'm asking you the same question again, Doctor?'

'We have wondered—' He stopped then went on, 'All this is in strict confidence?'

'Of course. I have already confided in you in the certain knowledge that this conversation will remain enclosed within your mind and mine, that you will not even repeat it to your friend.'

He nodded and then went on to say that the only person who might possibly have agreed to carry out James Devlin's wishes was the man who had lived with him for the last fourteen years.

'You must admit that Albert, too, has lived as a recluse, cutting himself off from people. He could have become strange, his mind affected – recluses aren't normal; you'll agree with that?'

'Yes, I agree that there is something abnormal about any person who deliberately cuts himself off from the rest of humanity.'

'Do you suppose that Albert could—?' The doctor shook his head. 'He was with you yesterday at the time Mrs Smallman was murdered.'

'Precisely. Apart from that, though, Sally and I have reached the unalterable conclusion that Albert isn't capable of murdering anyone.'

The doctor shrugged exasperatedly.

'I'd like to go home,' he said, veering away from the subject. 'And so would Bernard. However, it isn't long now and we have decided that if we remain alert and lock our bedroom doors we'll be safe enough.'

'I am sure you will be,' agreed Louisa firmly. 'There won't be any more deaths, of this I can assure you.'

'You can *assure* me?' He sent her a frowning glance.

'I'm confident, Doctor, that we are all perfectly safe. Do you suppose I would let my niece stay here if I thought for one moment she could be in any danger?'

'So you, too, are confused,' he was swift to

insert. 'First you say that we were brought here to be punished—'

'Correction, Doctor. I have never said any such thing.'

'But you have not denied it. Just now, when I mentioned it, you made no denial whatsoever.'

She hesitated. She liked the doctor – and his friend too. But ought she to confide? She said at length, 'As we have agreed this conversation will not go any further, I will tell you that at first, and after speaking to you all and making the discovery that all had done James Devlin an injury—' She lifted a hand. 'No, don't interrupt. We are assuming that as far as James was concerned, your interference with his plan was in fact an injury. So, as I was saying, after I had made this discovery, and certainly when one of the legatees met his death, I reached the conclusion that retribution was in fact the reason for your being here. But there was only one man who could have derived any satisfaction and that man is dead.'

'So how do you account for the two deaths?' He sounded impatient, she thought, and wasted no time in pointing out that the death of Joseph Powell *could* have been an accident and that the murder of Mrs Smallman had been committed by an intruder bent on theft.

'I think,' she added on a careful note, 'that

this latter must be left in the capable hands of the police.

'You do?' with a cold smile and a sceptical lift of the brows. 'Very well, Mrs Hooke, as you say, you intend to leave it all to the police to unravel.'

'Unravel? So you still believe there is a mystery?'

'Mrs Hooke,' he said with some asperity as he rose from his seat, 'I do possess average intelligence.' And on that parting shot he strode away in the direction of the house.

Louisa stared at his retreating back, a smile on her face. So he did not believe her? Well, she could hardly blame him.

She stayed in the arbour for another few minutes, her mind almost frantically active in its chase of some wisp of insight that had come and gone only to leave behind an access of frustration. There *had* been something during the conversation with the doctor, just as there had been something when she and Sally were talking to the gardener. Albert ... Again she asked herself where he was at the time Joseph Powell was sent to his death. But hadn't she and Sally decided most definitely that the old man could never harm anyone?

'And yet, I know from wide experience that benign and harmless-looking people can turn out to be ruthless killers.' She sighed heavily, and added to herself, 'But he definitely did not kill Mrs Smallman.'

'Talking to yourself, Auntie?' Sally was laughing softly as she stood there, looking down at Louisa. 'No flash of enlightenment yet, then?'

'Did you hear what I was saying?'

'No. I just arrived. It was just a mumble. Tell me.' She seated herself by her aunt. She wore a pretty cotton frock of pale blue trimmed with white on the collar and cuffs. In answer to her aunt's next question she said that Millie had gone to lie down. She was brighter but still affected by her employer's violent death.

'Tell me what you were saying to yourself,' she added after making herself comfortable.

'I have some strong clues regarding Mrs Smallman's death.'

'Yes; you told me that.'

'As for Powell...'

'No clues at all?'

'He knew the person who pushed him off that cliff. I'm sure of it, Sally. True, he wasn't a big man, but if he had been attacked by a stranger he'd have put up some sort of a fight.'

Sally said, 'Could it possibly be Mr Philpots?'

'That would certainly account for Powell's not putting up a struggle.'

'We haven't really thought of Mr Philpots,

have we? He had the opportunity to commit both murders.'

'And why should he?'

'Someone has to be guilty,' returned her niece reasonably.

'We have to find the motive, Sally. There has to be a motive, and Mr Philpots couldn't possibly have one. He never met James Devlin, and he never met any of the legatees till recently. No, we have to rule him out just as we've ruled out the three other men here.'

'And Albert,' stated Sally firmly.

'And Albert...' She let her voice tail off to silence. A sudden frown had appeared on her brow. To her right she saw him hoeing the rose bed.

'You haven't ruled out the Thorpes.' Sally eyed her aunt speculatively. 'Has your analytical brain figured out a possible motive in their case? You did say they were interested in "something else", if you remember?'

Louisa merely shrugged. Her whole concentration was fixed upon the gardener.

Seven

Millie's face wore a weak smile as she joined Sally and her aunt for lunch in the Blue Drawing Room. Mrs Thorpe would have set it out in the smaller sitting room but as an objection by Bernard Wilding was taken up both by the doctor and John Hilliard, she agreed – albeit with a sort of soured animosity – that perhaps the room where a murder had been committed was not the proper place in which to have lunch.

'How are you now, Millie?' The query came from the doctor, who looked at her with the eye of the professional.

'I feel better, thank you.' Her shyness was most apparent; she looked uncomfortable in the men's presence and Louisa wondered how in this day and age a young girl could be so completely shut off from company as she obviously had been while in the service of Mrs Smallman. This would all change in the very near future. Sally had friends; she would take the girl under her wing and bring her out.

'It has been a great shock to you,' said the

doctor gently. 'It will take a little time for you to recover fully.'

Millie merely nodded and he added after a pause, 'Mrs Hooke tells us you are going to live with her?'

'Yes, that's right.' A sudden light dispelled the film of anxiety which had affected Millie's eyes. 'I'm very much looking forward to that.' She sat down and Mrs Thorpe appeared with a tray on which there was the tea, sugar and milk. As she placed these on the table her eyes met those of Louisa and held for a long moment. Tension was in the air; Sally was vitally aware of it. She quite naturally recalled to mind what her aunt had said about the Thorpes being interested in something altogether different. Different from what? Her aunt had said quite firmly that they were not interested in any of the legatees. Sally drew a sharp breath; her aunt heard it and regarded her with a quizzical expression.

'I'm just baffled, that's all!' supplied Sally with a hint of asperity.

'We all are, my love.' Her gaze returned to the housekeeper but the woman was now serving the table at which sat the three men. Mr Philpots was absent, having said earlier that he had to return to the office but would be back at the manor in time for dinner.

The light meal was pleasant, with everyone, as if by common consent, avoiding the bizarre happenings of the past couple of days. Both Louisa and Sally were relieved that the conversation never once included anything that would upset Millie. And afterwards, when the meal was over, Sally suggested they take a drive round the countryside.

'You two go,' smiled her aunt. 'I have other things to do.'

Sally grimaced and said, 'Seeing that you aren't intending to take me into your confidence I shall welcome the chance of diverting my inquisitive mind from a frustrating state for which you, dear aunt, are entirely responsible!'

Louisa laughed. 'If you remember,' she said with mock reproach, 'you asked to be my partner. Up till now you haven't been much help.'

'Do you need help?' copying her aunt's manner.

'Never, my child, have I needed help more!'

'But you've solved one murder. You can't expect too much, now can you?'

'I haven't said I've solved Mrs Smallman's murder.'

'As good as, though. And as a matter of fact, I'm pretty sure in my own mind that you definitely have solved it. You know who the murderer is – and you won't tell me,' she added with a pout, but with an expression in her eyes which belied any resentment whatsoever.

'I won't tell you, or anyone else, until I have proof. At present I haven't one shred of proof. It's all a hunch, a conclusion reached simply because certain of the jigsaw fits, but—' She tilted her head. 'Although it fits, it does not necessarily match, if you can see what I mean?'

Sally nodded her head, suddenly serious. She glanced towards the door. Millie had gone to her room to collect her handbag. Sally said quietly, 'So you are going to spend the rest of this afternoon trying to find what really does match.' It was a statement and Louisa had to smile. This young niece of hers had such confidence in her. It was to be hoped she would not meet with a disappointment.

'Right, Sally, I am.' Her glance was sent towards the door. 'Here is Millie now. Enjoy your run out.'

The chief inspector phoned within five minutes of Sally's departure and asked for Louisa.

'For you, Mrs Hooke.' It was Mr Thorpe who held out the receiver to her. His eyes had an alert look and he made no move to leave the hall. In fact, he began to rearrange some silver tankards that were cluttered together on a massive silver tray.

She turned to him and said coldly, 'I'd like

privacy – if you don't mind?'

She saw the muscles of his jaw tighten but he did move away and she heard the clatter of crockery as he began to clear the tables.

'I'm glad I found you in, Mrs Hooke,' began the inspector. 'I wondered if you have discovered anything of value.'

'That's one way of putting it,' she returned with a hint of amusement. 'I have something, yes, but not one single shred of proof.'

'Well, any hunch of yours will be accepted by me as a bonus because I haven't collected one clue.'

'You and your men have questioned everyone in the village?'

'And the occupants of houses in the vicinity of the village. But everyone has an alibi.'

She said softly, a wary eye on the door of the drawing room, 'Have you no ideas of your own, Inspector? Not a suspect?'

'No. Have you?'

'Yes.' A slight pause and then, 'Shall you and I have a chat?'

'Oh certainly.' The eagerness in his tone brought a smile to her lips. She intended confiding in him certain conclusions she had reached, but she had a shrewd suspicion that, much as he professed to admire her skill, he would be reluctant to make an arrest on the somewhat unsubstantial information she would be giving him.

★ ★ ★

217

The chief inspector called for her and as she got into his car she looked up, and saw Mrs Thorpe at one of the landing windows.

'You are not going to think much of my – er – hunch, as you call it,' she said cheerfully. 'And I do want you to keep in mind that I haven't one shred of proof, nor can I see any chance of finding it.'

'Ah, but two minds are better than one, Mrs Hooke.' He drove along the avenue of trees and through the gates. 'They were closed when I came in so ought I to close them?' he asked, slowing down.

'I've noticed they are always kept closed – oh, here comes Albert; he'll close them.' In fact he was hurrying towards them across the wide expanse of grass which bordered the drive. He smiled and lifted a hand, telling them he would see to the gates.

'Thank you, Albert.' Louisa had opened the window and she called out to him.

'He's an oddball if ever there was one,' commented the chief inspector as they drove away from the manor. 'The villagers don't seem to know him at all.'

'He was a recluse as well as his employer, but he is more – normal now, if you know what I mean?'

'No, I don't, as a matter of fact.' He turned into a narrow lane and Louisa saw a small stone bridge in front of them.

'On the first afternoon he was reticent –

polite but withdrawn. Then Sally and I seemed to draw him out. He changed rather dramatically...' She tailed off, thinking about it. 'Yes,' she mused, 'there was a marked – very marked – change in the man. He has become our friend.'

'In such a short time?'

She nodded her head. Why, she asked herself, did her mind persistently toss back to her the picture of Albert standing by Sally's car, shaking his head in bewilderment. He had seemed stunned by the news of Mrs Smallman's murder. And why should she have even entertained the idea that the woman's death had occurred at the wrong time and under the wrong circumstances? And the murder committed by the wrong person?

All this would fit only if, as she had mentioned to Sally, Albert had meant to murder Mrs Smallman himself. This brought her back to the possibility of his having agreed to murder all the six beneficiaries, fulfilling a promise made to James Devlin.

'The whole thing's crazy. Sally's right: he couldn't hurt a fly.'

'What did you say?' Corlett was slowing down to take the narrow road over the bridge.

'It was nothing of importance.' But it was important; it was vitally important.

Corlett brought the car to a stop after

crossing the bridge.

'A pretty spot, don't you think? The river has cut off a meander at some stage in its history and so we have this charming little oxbow lake.' He turned to her. 'Tell me how far you have progressed, Mrs Hooke?'

She began slowly, affording herself time to think about just how much she should tell. However, she did feel that the time had come for the police to be put in possession of most of her suspicions.

When she had finished he just sat in silence, pondering what he had been told. Contrary to her expectations he was obviously accepting her ideas. She saw his eyes narrow and his lips purse. He said at length, 'Although I cannot make an arrest, I am persuaded that, whatever else, I have to consider all this seriously, Mrs Hooke. As you know, I have a high regard for your particular finely developed instinct. You are famous for that and for this gift of physiognomy.'

'Yes. I do believe one can learn a great deal from the study of a person's features.'

'And you have studied the features of every person at the manor.' It was a statement; he had taken the obvious for granted.

She said thoughtfully, 'All except one, Inspector. Albert's...'

'Ah, yes.' He gave a light laugh. 'The beard has you at a disadvantage.'

'It has me beaten,' she corrected. 'I have to

admit that although both Sally and I have taken a great liking to the man, I would very much like to see what lies beneath that luxurious beard.'

Mrs Powell arrived at half past three, and so she was invited to join Louisa, Sally and Millie for afternoon tea. She was sallow, but Louisa decided this was her natural colour. Her eyes, dark brown and faintly almond-shaped, moved rather more than was normal. She was about sixty years of age, surmised Louisa – or maybe slightly less. A non-descript type, yet, paradoxically, she gave the impression of depth in her thinking capacity. The long, slightly bent nose spelled a certain weakness in her character: she could be dominated by the stronger will of her hus-band. But despite this the firm mouth spelled strength. Louisa's final analysis was that when she had been in her husband's pre-sence she was submissive, but in his absence she was very capable of self-command and resolve. She would be able to make a decision, thought Louisa, and keep to it.

To make a decision and keep to it...

Sally was talking to her in gentle, soothing tones.

'How are you feeling now, Mrs Powell? You look better than you did on Friday.'

'I do feel a little better, but—' She looked at Louisa. 'Mr Philpots told me there had been a murder – yesterday. The lady who had her maid with her.' She showed no sign of shock and Sally felt that because her own tragedy was still so new, the fact of another death almost slid over her head.

'Yes,' said Louisa. 'And this is Millie, the maid you are talking about.'

'Oh!' She looked apologetically at the girl. 'I'm sorry. I had no idea. You must be feeling terrible.'

Millie nodded her head. 'It was a dreadful shock. I was in the laundry, at the back –' she pointed vaguely – 'ironing her dress for dinner—' She broke off, shuddering. 'Mrs Thorpe came and – and told me...'

'Try not to think about it, Millie.' Louisa nodded to Sally, indicating she should pour the tea. 'Try to eat something, dear,' she said persuasively to Millie. 'You'll feel better if you do, believe me.'

Sally was thinking: how dreadful, two people here who are affected by deaths. She sipped her tea, her eyes wandering from one to the other ... and suddenly she was staggered to realize that, of the two, Millie was by far the more upset.

Louisa was talking quietly to Amy, asking again about her late husband's expertise at fell-walking.

'He's been doing it for years – not so much lately because he is—' She stopped and bit her lip. 'He was in a club when he was younger. Since he left the club he's gone out on his own, and mostly it was walking rather than actual climbing – something he did in his youth.'

'But he was an expert at one time?'

'Oh, yes. It was his hobby before he met me.'

'Do you walk a lot, Amy?'

'I've been with him sometimes, but he never had much patience. I was too slow and I was also afraid if the ground was rough.'

'Are you afraid of heights at all?'

Sally, suddenly alert, saw that her aunt's eyes were narrowed and intent as they fixed those of the other woman. She saw Amy's gaze drop, saw a faint flush suffuse her cheeks.

'Of heights?' Amy now feigned surprise. 'Why do you ask? No, not particularly. I don't like them but I've walked on them, with Joe.' She paused. 'Why do you ask?' she queried again.

Louisa paused, darting a glance at her niece. Sally's eyes held that particular sparkle of expectancy. Louisa decided this was not the place for the questions she wished to ask Amy, so she shrugged and replied carelessly,

'No particular reason,' and she smiled on seeing the look of disappointment on her niece's face.

Albert was moving about, serving sandwiches and cakes while Mrs Thorpe was watching him. The three men were chatting together but now and then one of them would cast a glance in Amy's direction. Discussing her loss, and feeling sorry for her, concluded Louisa.

Albert brought the cakes to their table.

'Try one of these,' he said to Millie. 'You must eat, young lady.' He smiled down at her but then his eyes moved to Amy. Abruptly he swung away to go to the sideboard to get another plate of cakes to carry to the table occupied by the three men. Albert's swift move away from their table sent something into Louisa's brain only to be lost on the instant. What had happened to make her nerves tingle like this? She worked her brain furiously to recapture a flash of light, frustratingly aware that an answer to many questions had been within her grasp, then vanished before she could seize it.

Her eyes followed the gardener then came back to rest on Amy's face. The woman seemed shaken, her hand unsteady as she picked up her fork.

Sally said something to her and she answered in a low voice. Louisa distinctly felt something electric in the air but with a sigh of resignation she diverted her thoughts and joined in the conversation going on at her table.

Albert approached again to offer her one of the hot scones he had just carried, on a silver tray, from the kitchen along with jam and cream.

'For you, Mrs Hooke?'

'Just a scone and jam, please, Albert. No cream.'

He served her then went to the others but as Amy was eating a cake he never offered her the scones but went over to serve the three men. Louisa leant back in her chair, aware of Mrs Thorpe hovering in the background, her brooding presence marked by the severity of her dress and her matching black hair scraped away from forehead and ears. Louisa ate mechanically, having fallen silent, her mind again grappling to find what had evaded her yet again.

Earlier she had decided to have a talk with Amy and she said smilingly, when tea was finished, 'I'd like to have a chat with you when we leave here. Sally and Millie can go for a walk.'

'We are going for another run in the car,' Sally informed her.

'Then we shall all meet later.'

Louisa naturally chose the arbour and when she and Amy were settled she turned to her and said conversationally:

'I'm glad to see you look much better today than you did on Friday.'

'Yes. Well, life has to go on.'

'For some. But not so for Mrs Smallman.'

'It is awful that she was murdered.'

'She sent me a note which I received after she was dead. It referred to your husband.'

'To Joe?' Amy looked perplexed. 'What do you mean?'

'Apparently she had taken a taxi drive and this took her to the road running alongside the plateau which ended in the cliff from which your husband – er – fell...' She ended slowly and with her eyes never leaving her companion's face; she saw it lose colour, noticed the twitching of the thin white hands. 'The note held the implication that someone was with your husband and—'

'I don't understand,' broke in Amy with more loss of colour. 'Are you saying my Joe was meeting someone up there? But that's absurd.'

'I don't believe the meeting was pre-arranged, if that is what you are asking.' She paused a moment and when she spoke again it was to say she had doubts about Amy's husband's death being the result of an accident, and there was a significance in her words that made Amy look at her quickly.

'Just what are you trying to say?' Apart from her loss of colour Amy had full possession of her control.

'I am keenly interested in mysteries, Amy, and I feel there is some mystery about your husband's death. I am what is termed an amateur sleuth; I have decided to look into the circumstances of your husband's death.'

She was watching the other woman closely but saw no sign of anxiety in her demeanour.

'If you are suspecting murder, Mrs Hooke, then you have to admit that there is no one here who would want to kill him. He didn't know any of these people.'

'I went up to the cliff and found the place from where your husband fell. There was evidence of another person being there with him, but no sign of a struggle.'

Amy was still cool and showing no sign of strain. Louisa had to admire her self-control, her firm determination not to give herself away.

'If there was another person and that person made an attempt to push Joe off the cliff then Joe would have put up a fight, so if your idea is correct there must have been a struggle.'

Louisa was intrigued by the woman's mentality, by the sheer perfection of her outward calm, and her fearlessness when she must know what her questioner was getting at. Louisa felt a white lie would not come amiss at this point in the conversation.

'Mrs Smallman's note said that the person she saw with your husband on the cliff was a woman.'

'That is impossible. This Mrs Smallman – where was she? You can't see much from a taxi on a road that is hundreds of yards away.'

'You know it?' The words were almost shot

at her.

Amy paused as if to get a grip on herself. Then she answered in a steady voice, 'I asked my driver to take me along the cliff road before coming here. Joe had told me he was taking a stroll along the cliffs and I suddenly wanted to see what it was like. I saw it only from the car. It was lonely, not one person walking. I guess it isn't a popular walking place, but the view's spectacular.'

'You were there today?'

'Yes. I've said so. It was before I came here.'

'You didn't want to go to the edge of the cliff?'

'No—' The woman shuddered. 'I couldn't have brought myself to do that – not to go to where my husband fell.' She looked at Louisa and asked curiously, 'If you are so interested in crime, then why aren't you investigating Mrs Smallman's murder?'

'The police are in charge of the case. You see, that is definitely murder whereas there is no proof that your husband's death was anything other than an accident.'

'But you yourself have doubts.' Amy's voice was now gruff, as if she had something stuck in her throat.

'I do, yes.' Her eyes were hard, brittle. Louisa was asking herself just what she was expecting from this conversation with Amy Powell. She recalled the strange look that fixed both pairs of eyes as Amy and the gardener stared at one another. She assumed an air of only mild interest as she said, 'James Devlin's gardener wasn't with him at the time you and your husband were associated with him – over the inheritance, I mean?'

'No. James was quite poor at the time. He was living in what he called a combined room – which means the bed and everything else is in the one room – in an apartment house. He never took to Joe but he seemed to like me, at first that was, and he and I chatted once when we had lunch together while Joe was doing something else. James mentioned having sold his house, the one his parents had left him, in order to go into partnership with someone, but it hadn't worked out and James was left with so little that he couldn't even raise a deposit so he could get a mortgage.'

'But then he became comparatively rich?'

'He could afford to live in the small stately home which he and Joe had inherited.'

'Because of course there was money as well as the property?'

'Not much actual cash, but plenty of valuables in the house which, under the terms of the will, had to be sold and the money shared equally—' She stopped abruptly and a tinge of colour crept into her pallid cheeks. 'I can't talk about what Joe did to James. It's over and done with; they are both dead...' Her voice trailed and for a long moment there was silence except for the song of the thrush in the branches overhead. Again, for some incomprehensible reason, Louisa felt the air highly charged. 'All I want now is to forget and to live in peace.'

'Amy – can I be very outspoken with you?'

'Well – er – of course.'

'Were you happy with your husband? I ask simply because of the impression I have that all was not right between you.'

Amy swallowed convulsively, as if her throat were tied up in knots.

'You're asking me to be – be disloyal to Joe—' She seemed to choke and brought out a handkerchief to dab her eyes.

Feigning grief ... as an afterthought. Louisa's mouth curved with a sort of grim amusement.

'I'm sorry if my question upset you,' she said at length. 'I did have a reason, I assure you.'

Amy looked at her with an inscrutable expression. She said, after a moment of considering, 'I suppose you were bound to guess. Well, he was never a good, kind husband, Mrs Hooke. We lived together rather because it had become a habit – married couples often do stay together for that reason only.'

'I agree.'

'It was never quite right between us. He was a gambler and he was dishonest.' She paused, any assumed grief having been forgotten, then continued, 'He really did upset me over that business of the paintings. He could have taken one and told James. Then James would have claimed the other. James had had several dirty tricks done to him and then this, I thought. Joe never did admit he'd been dishonest. He was always envious, and angry, that James had come off best after all. And Joe always blamed me because it was James and not us who had the house and lands. Well, it was my fault; I said I didn't like the house and wouldn't live in it, but that was only because I felt it only fair to let James have it. He wanted it but I know he'd not have argued or made any objection if we had insisted we should have it. He was a mild man...' Her voice trailed away to silence and she was a long way off for a while. Louisa gave a small cough, which brought Amy back to the present. She had been playing absently with the handkerchief in her lap but now she glanced up. 'Yes, a mild man, Mrs Hooke, and a kind one. He was an ardent lover of animals and birds. He once said that if ever a human being did him an injury again he'd cut himself off from them entirely. That was when I felt sure he knew about the paintings. He did cut himself off, so I expect he did have that final dirty trick done to him.'

That final dirty trick ... Louisa's thoughts naturally flew to the shooting of Bess, and to the scorn with which Mrs Smallman had treated the distraught owner. That was the last straw: James had cut himself off – apart from the gardener whom he needed because he loved a garden and seeing things grow. But even with the gardener he could not bring himself to form a friendship, with the result that Albert had been a recluse too, though probably not from choice. Still, he had had a contented life; he seemed satisfied with what had been his lot.

Amy was speaking again, asking Louisa what were her intentions.

'I mean,' she continued, 'how shall you go about investigating Joe's death? Even if you do suspect he was – was pushed, how could you prove it?' She was looking around and remarked before an answer to her question could come, 'The flowers in this garden are magnificent.'

Louisa nodded. The summer blooms were at the height of their glory, and especially the roses which grew in profusion up and around the little arbour. Their perfume was filling the air, and in the tall tree the thrush was still singing.

'How could I prove it?' Louisa gave a small sigh. 'It would be most difficult, although,' she added, watching Amy closely, 'in my time I have solved cases equally as difficult as this.'

Amy said, 'I'm sure it was an accident. Joe wasn't infallible; he could make a mistake, I suppose.'

Louisa hesitated a moment and then, slowly and with a certain emphasis, 'I may as well be honest with you, Amy. I intend to try to discover whether or not your husband's death was an accident ... or if he was murdered.'

Amy shifted uneasily on her seat.

'You haven't very much time. You'll not be here much longer.'

'I can stay on as long as I like.'

'Yes – of course. But not here, in this house.'

'There are hotels in Dorchester.'

Amy nodded.

'You have some clues? I mean, has something happened since I left here?' Her eyes were lowered, her hands tightly clasped and not quite steady.

'Mrs Smallman's note happened.' Louisa subjected her to a penetrating stare and at last Amy raised her eyes. But she seemed lost for something to say and Louisa added with slow deliberation, 'You hired a car and driver, but you do drive; I remember your saying so.'

'Oh, yes, I do drive but, somehow, I cannot bring myself to drive here.'

'How long did it take your driver to get from your home to the manor?'

'Two and a quarter hours, roughly?'

'So, if you had decided to drive yourself

you'd have done the journey in just over two hours. What I'm saying is, that you'd not find it at all difficult?'

'Er – n-no, I wouldn't.' She was uneasy but fighting to appear calm. She did not like the trend of the conversation, thought Louisa grimly. Then suddenly Amy lifted her shoulders and looked her questioner straight in the eye. 'Is there some purpose in what you are asking me, Mrs Hooke?' she asked forthrightly, and Louisa could have smiled, for here was a challenge ... a daring one.

She said, without much expression, 'I am sure you know my reasons for the questions, Amy,' and she added as Amy rose to leave, 'Your calmness does you credit, considering your recent bereavement.' Calm on the surface, thought Louisa, but disturbed by fear while tenaciously holding on to a certain confidence which was fairly strong within her.

'Shall I wear the blue again? This one's too fussy, don't you think?' Sally held up the peach-coloured dress with its lace frills and low neckline. 'No, it isn't suitable at all.' She swung round to hang it back in the wardrobe. 'The blue it is. I have also to think of Millie; she doesn't have anything at all smart.'

'She will have.' Louisa was stretched out on her bed, hands clasped behind her head.

'You'll soon bring her out. I'm looking forward to the metamorphosis.'

'It's going to be fun – for us both.' Her aunt had lapsed into thought and Sally asked, not for the first time, 'Have you made up your mind, Auntie?'

'About Amy Powell?' She flicked her niece a glance. 'I've no proof, as she herself pointed out.'

'Do you suppose she knew that you had guessed?'

'I'm sure of it. She seemed to be waiting at one moment for the denouement.'

'For you to accuse her outright?'

Louisa nodded absently. Amy had managed an amazing control while answering questions as to her driving and the time it took to drive to the manor.

'You see, I can't accuse her outright without some evidence.'

'You've said you are sure she drove over here on Friday afternoon. She had heard her husband say he was going for a walk along the cliffs. She had thought it all out, deciding that any money he inherited would be wasted at the bookmaker's or whoever else he gambled with. She wasn't happy and never had been so she had nothing to lose—' Sally turned. 'But so much to gain, Auntie, such a lot to gain.'

Louisa nodded her head.

'She's a clever woman, although I suspect

235

her husband had no knowledge of how smart she really was. Her manner's misleading but her facial contours are not.'

'To you, no, they are not. But to anyone who hadn't studied physiognomy she would appear a timid, diffident person.'

'She planned the murder of her husband well; there are no flaws. He had told her of his plans for the walk and she was probably there long before he arrived, just to make sure, since she would never ever have another chance like that.' Louisa looked at her niece and grimaced. 'She's going to get away with it, Sally – yes, she planned the perfect crime.'

'She's getting away with it only because the witness is dead,' Sally was quick to point out.

'It's debatable as to whether or not Mrs Smallman would have actually been able to recognize the person who pushed him off the cliff. She could be sure it was a woman, but the road is rather a long way away from the cliff.'

'But if Mrs Smallman had said she saw a woman there then obviously Mrs Powell would be questioned and she would have had to admit that she was not at home.'

'Perhaps.' Louisa became thoughtful for a moment, then nodded her head. 'Yes, she would have been found out; she must have stopped for petrol. However, with the only witness so conveniently murdered, our Amy is sitting pretty.'

'She gets the legacy.' Sally stood before the mirror. The blue dress suited her, and it was formal enough without being too fussy. She turned. 'I know it is awful of me but I feel she deserves the break. Her life cannot have been happy in any way at all with a man like that.'

'You agree with murder going unpunished?'

'Of course not ... but this case is different.'

'Murder is murder. If Amy was so unhappy there is always easy divorce.'

Sally hesitated for a moment and then, 'Well, I have to say I would not feel good were she to be arrested and jailed for life.' There was a note of defiance in Sally's voice and Louisa had to laugh. A stickler as she was for justice being done, she failed to understand her own sympathy with a woman whom she felt sure had sent her husband to his death.

After a while she asked Sally if she had noticed anything strange at the table at teatime.

'Strange?' frowned Sally. 'In what way strange?'

'I could not help thinking that there was something between Albert and Amy – a most, most odd sort of look, a momentary fixation of their eyes. I had the impression that their faces were familiar to one another.'

Sally's frown deepened.

'You mean – they know each other?'

'I felt there was an instant of recognition but then Albert moved away.'

'Did you ask Amy when you were speaking with her?'

'I asked if Albert was with James Devlin at the time she and her husband knew James. She said no.'

'Then you must have imagined it.'

Louisa shook her head.

'No, Sally, I did not imagine it. Those two—' She stopped abruptly, her eyes opening to their fullest extent. 'Good God, I've been as blind as a bat! Clever, you say? No, I am not clever at all.'

'What are you saying, Auntie? You've solved two murders, found the killers. Of course you're clever, brilliant, in fact.'

Her aunt was so deep in thought that Sally doubted if she had heard her flattering remark.

'Yes,' murmured Louisa slowly. 'Blind, totally unsuspecting.' She looked at Sally but went on talking to herself. 'How could I have missed—? But there was an excuse. That beard had me foxed, unable to read his features—'

'Auntie!' broke in Sally with swift comprehension. 'The moment of enlightenment has come!'

'Oh, yes, Sally – and about time too.'

'You spoke just now of the beard. You meant Albert? Has the solving of the mystery something to do with Albert?'

'It has everything to do with Albert.' She sighed heavily. 'And you are not going to like what I have to say.' She paused, and another sigh issued from her lips. 'It has to be said, my love. Albert brought you six here to be murdered— No, let me say a little more first. This revelation that has just come to me – and I have to say it was helped by my conviction that Amy and Albert had recognized one another – explains so much that has been puzzling me and causing me so much frustration. For instance, if Albert had brought you here to murder you all, it would explain his manner of shocked disbelief on learning that someone else had done a killing, a killing he himself had planned to do. The murder of Mrs Smallman.'

'Auntie, what are you saying? Why should Albert...?' Her breath caught; she swallowed as if something were blocking her throat. 'Albert is – is James Devlin? You are saying he – he changed places with— Oh, it's too impossible! Too fantastic! Albert is gentle and kind – we've said so several times. No ... but you never would make a mistake like that.' She looked at her aunt through misted eyes. 'Would you?' She added on a tiny sob, 'You have always wanted to see what was behind that beard.'

Louisa reached out to take her hand and pat it gently.

'Sally, dear, I am just as upset as you, but the situation is not so bad at all. We have decided that Albert is no killer, and my discovery has not altered that. But he originally meant to kill you all—'

'He couldn't kill anyone!'

'That's just it. His intended revenge turned sour on him when he realized he couldn't harm any of you. That embittered recluse was in reality the kind, animal-loving gentleman we have come to know and taken to our hearts as a friend.'

'But why?' Sally spread her hands. 'I can hardly imagine him even thinking he could commit six murders – six! The whole thing's crazy!'

'Let us go over all the facts –' Louisa glanced at her wristwatch – 'we have a few minutes to spare. Now, sit down and listen – listen to one of the most fantastic stories you will ever hear. You have this young man, James Devlin. He lives with his parents – the mother he adores – and they have a nice home and he is engaged to be married. All is rosy, the future looking as if it will run according to plan. But suddenly the father runs off with a younger woman, which leads to the mother's suicide. A month later his fiancée breaks off the engagement. What is left for this young man whose future looked so perfect only a few months ago? He tries to build a new life so he sells the house left to him by his mother and puts the money into the business of John Hilliard. They are partners; he works all hours in an effort to forget. Then he is thrown out by the man he trusted and so he decides to take his own life. He is saved by two men whom he instantly hates with a black venom as they have intruded into his life and prevented him from leaving a world which no longer holds anything for him.

'However, he recovers and again the future begins to look more pleasant when he is left a share, along with a distant cousin, in a small stately home and its contents. But once again he is robbed; Joseph Powell takes two very valuable paintings and sells them at Sotheby's, pocketing the proceeds. Also, as if that were not enough, Powell robs him again by a confidence trick over the value of the house.' Louisa paused a moment but Sally remained silent, impatient for her aunt to continue. 'James won after all, though, as the estate came under a compulsory order for its sale; the motorway was to run through it. We know what happened, that the deal made James into a wealthy man. But he was embittered, and in the main I guess he kept himself to himself. But he did have a friend, Jack Smallman. He and his wife became regular visitors to the house, where James kept a manservant. One day his guest was out shooting pigeons and accidentally shot James' pet dog. We know what happened, and how Mrs Smallman treated the matter. She and her husband were ordered off and told never to set foot in the place again. This was the final straw and James decided to cut himself off completely. After all, he could scarcely be blamed for mistrusting his fellow men. Albert came to him – I rather think he sacked the manservant, wanting to be entirely alone in the house.' Again Louisa stopped and this time Sally spoke.

'I do see all this, Auntie, but it doesn't explain what he had in mind when he made his will.'

'As I have just said, he meant to murder all who had done him a dirty trick— No, don't interrupt yet. You are going to say that you, personally, had not hurt him. Well, his mind was warped – I am sure he will admit this.'

'Admit? He's supposed to be dead – every-one here thinks he's dead. How is he going to get out of this mess he's got himself into?'

'Let us leave that for the moment. He was a man with an embittered heart and a warped mind and for many years – probably from the day his dog died – he harboured this obsession to get even, to punish them all. And those who had escaped by death would be represented by someone near and dear to them.'

'But that was a crazy idea.' Sally spread her hands in a little helpless gesture. 'I still don't understand any of it!'

'You will. Concentrate and try to fill in the missing bits – they are there, Sally, they just need picking up and putting into place in the jigsaw. To continue: you and Mrs Smallman were invited down here simply because your mother and Mr Smallman were dead and so unable to come and be punished.' She paused on hearing Tessa barking below the window. She smiled faintly. 'She's protesting because she knows she's to be fastened up while Albert helps with the dinner.'

'It's because she is never away from him.' Sally moved to the window and looked down. 'She's a real pet, isn't she? And,' she added as the thought came to her, 'she was always *his* dog.'

'Of course.' Louisa waited until her niece had resumed her seat on the chair by the dressing table. 'You just heard me talk about Albert's beard. It has always puzzled me, even though I had no suspicion of what it hid. Amy recognized him in spite of it, and she must have had a severe shock, which she hid most successfully.'

'That phone call to Mr Hilliard – you said it was Albert who made it.'

'Yes, it was, and why? Because Albert couldn't resist this one small bit of satisfaction that he would derive from putting fear into the man who had treated him so badly over the partnership.'

'As Albert is James he owns all this.' Sally

spoke slowly, dazedly. 'Why was he pretending he might not have enough to buy the cottage?'

'That was for effect, as most of his behaviour is; he has to be convincing as the gardener, the role he has adopted – he was once an actor, remember.'

'Will he really leave here and live in that cottage?'

'I rather think he has no wish to keep this huge place on now that he has lost his gardener.' Louisa hesitated a moment and then, 'I never mentioned it to you, dear, but I rang Mrs Millsom while you and Millie were out; she has decided to sell me the cottage but only if I buy the half-acre paddock adjoining.'

'Paddock? I didn't know there was a paddock.'

'It seems there is, and I shall have to buy it if I want the cottage. I thought I might offer it to Albert. He might prefer to live close to us instead of settling so far away,'

Sally's eyes glowed. She could hardly keep still for excitement.

'That'll be wonderful! The four of us – we'll be a family. Oh, Auntie, it's great that Mrs Millsom has decided to sell her cottage to you, and even better that we can have Albert living close as well.'

'Don't take it for granted that Albert will accept the offer of the land; he seemed to be very keen on the cottage he showed us.'

'Oh, that,' returned Sally with a dismissive shrug of her shoulders. 'He was content because it is a charming property, but given the chance of living in Melcombe Porcorum with us he'll not hesitate to change his mind. He can build a bungalow and still have a garden.'

Louisa smiled and returned her thoughts to what they were going over before the diversion. She was quiet for a moment, thinking of James Devlin's desire for revenge. Had he really believed he could carry out the mass murder? It was amusing in the light of what they knew about him, in his role of Albert the gardener. Undoubtedly his mind had become warped during those twenty years of loneliness in the isolation which was his choice. When the gardener died and he saw his chance of revenge, he had not stopped to think but had changed places, with this idea of revenge in mind. The obsession had triumphed over the subconscious awareness that he was incapable of killing or in fact, as Sally would say, incapable of hurting a fly.

Yes, it was amusing. But how long was he intending to be Albert Forsythe?

'We shall have fun at Albert's expense,' she told Sally at last. 'After dinner we shall invite him to have a chat with us.'

'He'll be so embarrassed at being exposed. Isn't there some other way, Auntie, than just telling him outright that you know what he has been up to?'

'Frankly, I don't think he'll be too embarrassed. You see, he has an inkling that I have guessed.'

'He has?' frowned Sally in some doubt. 'Are you sure?'

'I feel fairly sure,' replied Louisa, nodding her head.

Sally thought of this, but decided not to comment. Her aunt would handle Albert in her own particular way, whether or not he had a suspicion that she knew of his masquerade. She said after a while, 'Are you going to watch the Thorpes tonight, as you said, and am I to watch as well?'

'I have a better idea, and I shall need your help to carry it out.'

'My help,' said Sally eagerly, 'in what way?'

'Tomorrow, the Thorpes will be in the kitchen for most of the morning – washing up the breakfast dishes and then preparing the lunch. I want you to hang about, in the hall and sitting room, but with your eye always on the kitchen door. Should either of them come out you must talk to them, loudly, so I can hear and get away to one of our bedrooms.'

'What are you going to be doing?'

'Just wandering around,' was the casual rejoinder and with that Sally knew she had, for the present, to be satisfied.

The chief inspector was listening carefully to what Louisa was telling him.

'How many boxes do you say are packed and ready for removal?'

'Eight, and also two suitcases. All contain silver. I found them in one of the spare bed-rooms underneath one of the sheets which had been thrown over the furniture.'

He looked at her perceptively.

'You obviously expected to find – well, what you actually did find.' A statement and Louisa nodded her head. 'They'll have been doing this since the first day they were here, I reckon.'

'Probably. If so, they will already have removed thousands of pounds' worth of antique silver. It is obviously their trade; they are professional thieves.'

'It's clever, the way people like them get into these houses, through a domestic agency.'

'And with forged references.'

'Exactly.' He paused a moment, consider-ing. 'We'll catch them red-handed tonight.' He paused again then asked Louisa if she had reached any other conclusions about the Thorpes.

'You're asking if I still believe one of them to be the murderer of Mrs Smallman? Un-doubtedly, Inspector, it was one of them. They must have been packing silver from one of the sideboard cupboards into a box when she walked in and, knowing her, she would instantly ask what they were doing and I guess actually accused them of stealing. I rather think it was Mrs Thorpe but don't ask me why. Mrs Smallman was foolish in turning her back on the woman.'

'How are we going to pin the murder on her?' He shook his head doubtfully.

Louisa smiled to herself before saying, not quite without a hint of smug satisfaction, 'My reading of her facial bone structure and contours tells me that she would be likely to break down under intensive questioning. Get her without her husband and she'll weaken. She'll bluster and deny it for a time but ... yes, Chief Inspector, I can guarantee she'll give you the confession necessary for a conviction.' She thought ruefully of Sally's saying the credit would be his.

'Mrs Hooke, no wonder you are famous. Your powers of deduction coupled with that fantastic gift put you right at the top as a detective.'

'I like to call myself a private investigator,' she began then added with a laugh, 'but no matter so long as success is achieved.'

Eight

As it was an hour until dinner Louisa and Sally were taking a stroll in the garden, enjoying the cool of the early evening after a day of rather more heat than that to which they were used.

'Auntie,' murmured Sally after a long silence, 'you really are a wonder. You've cleared up the whole thing, solved the mystery, and all in less than four days.'

Louisa smiled enigmatically.

'I had a lot of luck,' was her modest rejoinder.

'Well, I suppose all efforts are in some way supported by luck. But in this case it has been far more your genius, plus that incredible accuracy in reading a person's character from his or her features. I feel so proud of my clever aunt.'

Louisa laughed, turning her head to look at her niece and thinking how fortunate she was to have made the decision to come to England and make a home close to such a charming young lady.

She said at last, thoughtfully, 'There were

several coincidences in this case which helped, in a way.'

'The coincidence that Mrs Smallman
should have seen Mr Powell pushed off that
cliff and then being murdered herself before
she could speak to you.'

'Yes, that certainly was a coincidence.'
Louisa paused in thought. 'I have given the
chief inspector all he needs to arrest the
Thorpes. I'd bank on it being her rather than
him but we shan't know yet as he isn't
intending to make an arrest until after the
reading of the will.'

'But there can't be a will. Albert isn't dead
... er, I mean James isn't—' She frowned
impatiently. 'I am so confused!'

Again her aunt laughed.

'I have to admit that I myself am a bit
puzzled. Will James carry this farce right to
the end and let us all gather to hear Philpots
tell us there is no will because the testator
isn't dead?'

For a long moment Sally was deep in
thought.

'Mrs Powell is in for a terrible disappointment.'

'She knows James and Albert are one and
the same.' After a moment of contemplation
Louisa added, 'She's committed murder for
nothing.' Louisa wondered how she felt
about that.

'Good Lord – yes!'

'And Hilliard has a disappointment in store, too.'

'James has a lot to gloat about.' Sally stopped abruptly. 'You know, I can never call him James. He'll always be Albert to me.'

'He won't mind. After dinner we shall seek him out and have a chat.'

'Do you honestly believe he meant to kill us all?'

'*He* believed he could, but both you and I know he just couldn't keep to his resolve. When he made it he was unstable—'

'He has never seemed unstable,' broke in Sally with a frown.

'Not now.' Louisa looked at her for a moment in silence. 'I feel sure that you and I have influenced his thinking. Until he met us he was harbouring this grudge, and this urge for revenge, having decided once and for all – and, I might say, irrationally and dogmatically – that everyone was against him, that no human being was worth knowing, that only animals knew what faith and loyalty was. But then he met and got to know you and me and he changed completely. He is looking forward to a new life, a good life, with new friends whom he knows care about him. He'll meet people in our village and gradually he'll find himself being healed of this malady which has been affecting him for so long.'

'I still find it impossible to see him even

contemplating all those murders.' Sally shook her head. 'How was he intending to do these evil deeds? What method had he in mind? Was he intending to shoot us? I can't imagine him even holding a gun, much less pulling the trigger. It's so absurd it is laughable.' And she did laugh, to have her aunt join in.

'I shall very much enjoy our little chat with him.' Louisa had a hint of mischief sparkling in her eyes. 'I shall have fun at his expense first. He deserves it!'

Millie seemed much better as she joined Louisa and Sally at their table. Albert drew out her chair for her and she gave him a smile.

'Enjoy your meal,' he said, bowing slightly to Louisa. Amy came and joined them, her pallid face showing signs of strain as she met Louisa's gaze. Sally watched her swallow convulsively, then put a handkerchief to her lips.

'Some wine?' from Louisa who picked up the bottle from the cooler, Albert being busy serving the three men and the Thorpes were somewhere at the back. Eric Philpots came into the room, immaculately dressed, and joined the three being attended to by the gardener, sprucely attired in grey slacks, blazer-style jacket and white shirt. 'Did you have a rest this afternoon?' enquired Louisa as she poured the wine.

Amy nodded and answered unsmilingly, 'I lay down on the bed but – but my mind was going round and round.'

'It is understandable that you are not quite yourself,' speciously from Louisa. 'However, I am sure your state of mind is only temporary and very soon you will be feeling much happier. Your inheritance will be some compensation.'

Sally frowned darkly at her and was about to change the subject when John Hilliard spoke.

'The last evening we shall all be gathered here. In a few hours we shall know how much we have inherited.' He looked pleased with himself and Louisa could not resist the temptation to say, with a sideways glance at Albert, 'No one has been able to discover who signed the will...' and she added more slowly, and emphatically, 'Perhaps it was never signed at all.' She gave Albert a smile to which he responded but there was a very strange expression in his eyes.

'What!' John Hilliard glared at Louisa across the space separating their tables. 'What a nonsensical thing to say! If it had not been signed it would be invalid. Any fool knows that.'

Louisa made no response to that. She had noticed the doctor and his friend exchange glances. Albert had come to the table and she spoke to him softly.

'What do you think, Albert? Shall James be laughing at us all tomorrow morning, laughing from the – er – grave?'

He looked at her from beneath bushy grey brows and replied in a whisper, 'We shall have to wait and see, Mrs Hooke.' He poured wine into Sally's glass, then topped up Louisa's. With a little bow he moved over to the sideboard where, on a silver salver just brought in by Thorpe, stood a beautiful Minton soup tureen and matching server. Louisa watched him intently; he stood for a moment before picking up the bowl. When he turned, his eyes moved to meet hers.

Leonard and Bernard were deep in thought. Louisa was enjoying herself as she noticed the expressions of John Hilliard and of Amy. She said, 'What do you think, Amy? You knew James. Did he strike you as a man who would play that sort of a practical joke on his friends?'

'Friends,' intervened Bernard quietly. 'You have given us to understand that James regarded us as his enemies.'

'Look here,' interrupted Philpots, 'just what is this conversation all about? I feel some subtle undertone, as if the topic under discussion has a veil around it.'

'A very excellent way of putting it,' applauded Louisa. 'Tell me, Mr Philpots, don't you suspect something dramatic will be presented to us tomorrow morning?'

'You have suggested the will wasn't signed. Is that what you really think?'

Louisa paused, while Sally waited in a sort of breathless expectancy, her whole attention with her aunt.

'What I think,' replied Louisa in a slow and quiet voice, 'is that there isn't a will at all.'

Sally gasped. Although she had suspected something outspoken by her aunt, she was unprepared for this. Her eyes flew to Albert; he was regarding Louisa through narrowed eyes, while Amy seemed to shrink into herself, her face pale, her expression one of resignation. If, as her aunt had declared, Amy had recognized James, then she already knew there would be no legacy.

A general murmur followed Louisa's words. John Hilliard rose from his chair in an angry gesture, then sat down again. The two friends spoke to one another before Leonard asked in a calm untroubled voice, 'Do you know something which we don't, Mrs Hooke?'

'I have to admit I do.' She looked at Amy. 'But there are others who are also in the picture—'

'Picture? What picture!' exploded Hilliard, twisting in his chair to face Louisa's table. 'Stop talking in riddles, woman, and come out with it!'

'Mr Hilliard, please control your tongue.'

Philpots subjected him to a glance of censure. 'Your rudeness surprises me.'

Hilliard's face turned an ugly crimson but he refrained from making any response. Louisa was still looking at Amy, waiting for an answer to her interrupted question. Words trembled on Amy's lips but all that came forth was, 'May I have some more wine, please?'

Louisa smiled. Albert was there to pour Amy some wine. Sally drew a long breath and felt she would never again find herself in an atmosphere so thickly charged with so many human vibrations.

The doctor was the first to break the uneasy silence that had followed Amy's prosaic request.

'You were not serious, Mrs Hooke, just now when you suggested there might not be a will at all?'

'I happen to have the will in my possession,' broke in Eric Philpots before Louisa could answer. She said, again with that enigmatic smile, 'You have what is probably a bulky envelope, sealed and with the instructions that it must not be opened until Monday. But you will have to admit that your envelope need not contain a will ... er ... the last will and testament of one James Devlin?'

The air was electric now with all eyes turned upon Louisa.

Sally whispered into her ear, 'Auntie, is this

the time for the denouement? You surely wouldn't embarrass Albert before all these people?'

'There is no way to hide James Devlin's mischievous behaviour. But you are right; you and I shall tackle him alone, later – after dinner is over.' She looked at Eric Philpots and added on a note of self-deprecation, 'It was just a thought which I ought not to have voiced. Forget it,' she ended lightly but although everyone resumed their eating there was a certain gloom that, having descended on the company, seemed set to remain throughout the meal.

'Albert, shall we be seeing you outside later this evening?' Louisa spoke to him as they passed on their way to the drawing room, where coffee and liqueurs were to be served as usual.

'I shall be there, in the arbour, in about an hour.' He was totally cool, although he stared right into Louisa's eyes and shook his head in a sort of rueful gesture. He added sotto voce, 'Shall you still want me for your friend, I wonder?'

Impulsively Sally touched his hand. Her reassuring smile told him all he wanted to know.

A few minutes later, as she and her aunt were sitting at a small table for two, Millie having excused herself to go to her room for a handkerchief, Sally said to her aunt on a note of urgency, 'Albert remains our friend, doesn't he? I mean, he's still the same man we've learned to love?'

'Love, Sally!' exclaimed Louisa in some surprise, and a hint of colour touched Sally's cheeks. 'Love is rather strong, isn't it? You've only known him for a few days.'

'It's so strange,' admitted Sally, 'but I really do believe I love the old man. He seems to have become like my – my father...' She stared at her aunt in wonderment. 'He could have been my father,' she breathed as the idea registered. 'If only Mother hadn't jilted him.'

'We're not one hundred per cent sure she did jilt him,' Louisa felt obliged to remind her.

'It all fits, Auntie. Oh, yes, I am sure, very sure, that it was Mother who jilted him.' She lapsed into silence; Louisa saw her flick a finger across her eyes.

'You would have liked to have a potential killer for a father?'

'He is not a potential killer! Albert was an idiot ever to have embarked on this crazy plan of revenge. He must have known, deep down, that he would never be able to carry it out.'

Louisa nodded, her attention caught momentarily by the upright figure of Albert as he passed the door, carrying a loaded tray to the kitchen.

'I have to agree. But I am of the firm belief that it was only in his subconscious that he knew he would never be able to carry it out. Consciously he was a man obsessed by the desire for retribution; he had implanted in his mind the fact that these people weren't fit to live – we've all said something like that about someone at some time or another,' she added before going on: 'He had decided they were unfit to live because they had done him an injury – each and every one of them. Even the doctor and his friend had been cursed for their interference in his plan to die. All these years the desire had grown and become a festering, malicious growth within him. The man we know today, Sally, is not the man who changed places with his gardener. He has been transformed by his association with you and me; he has also realized that Bernard Wilding and Leonard Fulham are decent, upright men who did only what was the right thing at the time. As for Powell and Mrs Smallman – well, they met their deaths, if it is any consolation to him – which I do not think it is. I'm sure his whole outlook has changed, due to you and me. As I said before, he's beginning to live again; he's looking forward to life instead of harbouring that morbid wish to be dead.'

'It's a wonderful thing we've done for him.' Sally's big eyes were shining as she added eagerly, 'We must persuade him to forget that cottage and buy the paddock. He can build to his own liking – and he can have Bess's grave on his own land.' She gave a little contented laugh. 'We shall make him really happy and he'll soon forget the past. He *must* be persuaded, Auntie.'

'I don't think he'll need much persuading,' Louisa assured her.

'Whatever happens tomorrow morning this visit hasn't been wasted.'

Nine

Although Millie came and joined Louisa and Sally for coffee, she stayed only a few minutes.

'I feel so tired.' She looked apologetically at her friends in turn. 'I think I'll go to bed.'

'You're still in shock, Millie, dear,' from Louisa with a troubled frown. 'Yes, go and rest and tomorrow you are sure to feel better.'

'Yes – goodnight, then.'

'That young lady would benefit from a week's holiday by the sea,' observed Louisa when she had gone. 'Maybe you can arrange it? You were saying you had some days holiday owing to you.'

'Yes, I have. It's a good idea. We could go to Bournemouth.'

'Even Bridport would be a treat for her. I guess she's never moved far from that woman's house in the five years she's been working for her—' She broke off as Amy, having left the room, passed the window.

Albert had left the room only seconds ago...

Sally was about to open a conversation when, noticing her aunt's expression, she asked if anything was the matter.

'Er – no...' But she was still preoccupied.

'Excuse me, ladies and gentlemen.' John Hilliard was also leaving. 'I think I'll take a stroll before the light fails.'

'You're restless, Auntie.' Sally looked ruefully at her. 'As everything's solved you can't be concentrating on the mystery.'

'Those two – Amy and Albert. I have a feeling they have arranged to meet, some-where in the grounds.'

Sally frowned.

'What makes you think that?'

'They left within seconds of one another.'

'Amy told me she is thinking of going home tonight.'

'Tonight? At this hour? When did she tell you this?'

'Just before we came in here.' Sally glanced at the tall grandfather clock in the corner of the room. 'It's only nine o'clock; she'll be home well before midnight.'

'I wonder where they are?' Louisa murmured, so quietly that her niece did not catch the words.

'What did you say, Auntie?' And, before a reply could be made she was adding, 'You seem worried. Is anything wrong?'

Louisa snapped out of her preoccupation and gave a light laugh.

'What would I be worried about, my love?'

'You tell me,' challenged Sally looking her straight in the eye.

'Well, as I said, I feel those two have arranged to meet.'

'Auntie, you are not suggesting Amy and Albert are – well – smitten with one another?'

'Of course not.' Louisa shook her head. 'Nevertheless, I have this hunch.'

Sally shrugged her shoulders.

'Well, if they have arranged to meet, perhaps Amy wanted to tell Albert she was sorry for what her husband did.'

Louisa smiled faintly, nodding her head.

'Maybe you are right,' was all she said, but Sally knew she was glad when, on glancing at her watch, she could say it was time for their appointment with Albert.

It was as they were walking slowly along the path leading to the arbour that they noticed something dark against the high yew hedge, on the other side of which was a garden seat.

Their puzzlement lasted only a few moments and then Louisa said with a frown, 'Hilliard. What's he doing, crouched down by the hedge?'

'Must be looking at something on the ground,' was Sally's casual reply.

'Studying nature, you mean?' Louisa's tone was sceptical. 'He is more likely to be assessing the value of the property, though not in a position like that. I wonder what he's up to?'

'We'll soon find out,' replied Sally as they drew closer to where, still so intent with what was occupying him, John Hilliard had no idea of their approach.

He gave a start on hearing Louisa's voice, and he flushed darkly.

'What is it that you find so interesting, Mr Hilliard? May we share in the entertainment?'

Straightening up, he shrugged his shoulders, adopting a casual mien, but both Sally and her aunt knew instinctively that he was annoyed, even angry, at the interruption.

'It is nothing of importance. I was watching a spider that had a moth in its web.' The exchange of glances between the two women was not lost on him and he said shortly, 'What exactly were you suspecting me of doing, Mrs Hooke?'

It was her turn to shrug her shoulders. She strongly suspected he had been eavesdropping ... on Albert and Amy, but as the hedge was about four feet deep and very high she had no means of seeing if anyone was occupying the seat on the other side.

'It just seemed strange, seeing you crouching there,' she answered with a faint smile. 'You're interested in nature it would seem.'

'Not particularly, but my eye caught the web and the moth's wings fluttering.' He seemed reluctant to leave, a circumstance most puzzling to Louisa. His whole manner was one of guarding something. Sally was moving on and although her aunt would have preferred to stay until Hilliard had moved away, she resignedly followed her niece.

'I'm far from satisfied with his explanation,' she mused and turned her head ... just in time to see him reach into the hedge and bring out something so small that there was no possibility of her identifying the object as he slipped it into his jacket pocket.

She said nothing to Sally and they strolled on again towards the arbour, but neither Albert nor Amy were anywhere to be seen. Nor did he keep the appointment.

'Something's wrong,' Louisa was saying some half an hour later as she and Sally left the arbour to take a final stroll in the fading light of the summer evening. 'I'd very much like to know if Amy and Albert were on the other side of that hedge.'

Sally looked sharply at her. 'You think he was listening?'

'I'm sure of it – well, no, not certain until I have asked Albert if he was with Amy on that seat.' She glanced at her niece. 'You do realize that if those two did happen to be chatting, then she would have been calling him James, not Albert.'

'Oh, Lord, yes! And so if John Hilliard was listening...'

'Just so,' returned Louisa through tight lips. 'That Hilliard's a wily old bird; he was definitely up to no good. A spider's web,' she added scornfully. 'I saw no web, did you?'

'No – but I wasn't looking.'

'Nor was he. I do wish we knew where Albert is.'

'He usually takes Tessa for a walk about this time.'

There was no sign of him and eventually they were back in the house, and as it was only ten o'clock Sally suggested they have a cup of coffee before going to bed.

They filled their cups from the percolator in the small drawing room and took them into the larger room, where the four men were seated in low armchairs, chatting together. Eric Philpots soon left them, saying he must be making his regular phone call to his wife.

Of the three men left two were relaxed and at ease but John Hilliard, Louisa noticed, seemed to be in a state of excited emotion, his eyes too bright and with a faraway look in their depths.

The doctor said, glancing across the room at Louisa, 'Did you two ladies enjoy your walk?'

'It was perfect,' from Sally with her bright smile. 'The air is so pure round here, so fresh and clean.'

'Very different from our town air,' observed Bernard, but he added at once, 'I live in the country, though, and so does Leonard, and Mrs Hooke has spoken of your delightful cottage, Sally.'

'It's thatched, and black and white – as are many of the cottages in Melcombe Porcorum. It's a real old-world village – well, little more than a hamlet because we do not have even a corner shop or post office, only the village pub, which was at one time a coaching inn where travellers to London stopped to change or rest their horses.'

'It sounds idyllic.' Bernard glanced at John Hilliard then at Louisa as if to ask if there was anything wrong with the man as he was so silent and thoughtful, obviously not wanting to join in any conversation.

Louisa said, 'Did you go far, after we had spoken to you?' She looked straight at him so he was obliged to answer her.

'No, not very far. I am not one of your long-distance walker fanatics. A short stroll is quite enough for me.' He seemed to resent having to talk, seemed as if he needed to think, deeply, about something. In fact, he avoided further obligation to join in the conversation by rising from his chair and bidding them all goodnight.

Louisa knew that neither of the friends would comment but she was by no means loath to do so.

'There's something on that man's mind. Sally and I met him out there, in the garden, and he was supposedly studying nature by watching a spider with its prey, a moth.'

'A spider and a...' Leonard tailed off and laughed. 'I cannot imagine John being interested in nature. Are you sure?'

'Not in the least but that was his explanation for having his face in the yew hedge.'

Sally had to laugh and say, 'Not exactly in the hedge, Auntie. He was just bent down, looking at something.'

'Just what was he doing?' asked Bernard curiously.

'That,' replied Louisa drawing a deep breath, 'is what I would like to know. I suppose you two gentlemen will think me meddlesome just because, with something very strange going on out there, I want to know what it was.'

Bernard shook his head.

'No, Mrs Hooke, we would not consider you meddlesome, not now that we know you and your brilliant expertise in the field of crime. You have a gift and that gift is a rare one. So when you say something strange is going on we too are curious. Just what is on your mind?'

She paused, again sighing deeply. 'You must admit it is not normal for a man like John Hilliard, whom we now know to be of the aloof, rather aristocratic type, to be bent down close to a thick green hedge and, when questioned, to say he was watching a spider.'

'No,' declared Leonard emphatically, 'no, it cannot be considered the normal behaviour of John Hilliard as we have come to know him.' He pursed his lips, thoughtfully reflecting, 'I remember our first meeting him and thinking he was a man with a superiority complex, an unbending personality, a man who, aware all the time of his success in life, felt he had earned himself the right to be looked up to, and he always acted accordingly, in that superior manner.'

'You have described him perfectly, and it does not in any way accord with his behaviour out there this evening.'

After a small silence Bernard spoke, to ask Louisa if she had any ideas about the behaviour she mentioned and which, he added with a hint of amusement, seemed to be troubling her quite a lot.

'If you really want to know,' she replied seriously, 'I think he was eavesdropping.'

'Eavesdropping?' with a frown of puzzlement. 'On whom?'

'The two people whom I know were out there, Mr Wilding, were Albert and Mrs Powell. You may not have noticed but they left the dining room within seconds of one another.'

Bernard's frown of puzzlement deepened.

'Do the two know one another?'

She realized she had to be careful as it would only complicate matters if, at this stage, she revealed that Albert was in fact James Devlin.

'I could have been jumping to conclusions in thinking the two would meet up and talk out there. I would like to come back to John Hilliard.' She looked at Bernard Wilding. 'When he came in here, after his walk, did he say anything?'

'Only something about its being a pleasantly cool evening.'

'I see ... And his manner? Anything unusual about that?'

'No...' It was Leonard who spoke. 'Wait a minute—' He turned to his friend. 'He seemed a bit agitated, excited – certainly he was not in his cool, self-disciplined state of mind. You'll agree, Bernard?'

The other nodded his head.

'I agree, yes. And he was fidgeting with something in his pocket. I had the idea that had we two not been here he'd have brought it out, whatever it was, and – well – examined it—' He broke off, shrugging. 'I had the impression that he wanted to look at it but would do so only in private.'

Louisa was nodding slowly.

'When we'd left him, standing there by the hedge, I looked back and it was to see him reach into the hedge and take something which he put into his jacket pocket.' She looked at the two men in turn. 'What would he be taking out of the hedge that would fit into his pocket?'

'Well,' interposed Bernard thoughtfully, 'I would say it was something he himself had put there.'

'Yes,' agreed Sally brightly, 'for otherwise he'd not have known it was there.'

'Unless someone else had put it there and he saw them.'

'No,' returned Louisa firmly. 'That isn't feasible.' She paused in thought. 'If, as I strongly suspected, he was listening to a conversation going on on the other side of the hedge, then what would he be likely to put in that hedge?' Again she looked at each of her listeners in turn. 'Surely you have an idea?'

Both shook their heads, looking blank.

Louisa said quietly and with some amusement, 'I know that if I wanted so much to learn what someone else was talking about, I'd record the conversation, were that possible, of course.'

'By God, you've hit on it!' Bernard slapped

270

his knee. 'And Hilliard does have a small recorder, the type used when one wants to memorize things; it acts as a notebook but is much more easy to use. He carries it about with him. I saw it a couple of times in his hand.'

Louisa was nodding, satisfied that this was the answer. Hilliard listened, then, as the conversation became interesting, he simply slipped his recorder into the yew hedge, making sure it was wedged on a branch in the thickly-growing foliage.

'He has heard something to his advantage,' she murmured almost to herself. 'How am I to discover what it was?' She leant back in her chair, sipping her coffee, her wide, intelligent brow creased in a frown of annoyance; she was vexed with herself for not following Amy and Albert when she had suspected they would meet up, and talk.

What of? Louisa had guessed that Amy liked James Devlin a lot and on her own admission would have liked to have him for a friend. But, she had added, James wanted nothing to do with either Joseph Powell or his wife because, maintained Amy, he had known of the theft of the paintings.

Aware that the two men were looking somewhat expectantly at her, she wondered just how much they had guessed, what had been the outcome of their discussions on the situation here, and its relationship to the happenings of the past. She decided to tell them that John Hilliard was the man with whom James had been in partnership and she added in conclusion, 'Did you yourselves guess at this?'

'We did wonder where John Hilliard came into the picture,' returned Bernard, 'but no, we never actually suspected he was the man.' He paused and it was his friend who resumed with: 'So James had a very strong grudge against him.' He looked at Louisa. 'That threatening phone call which Corlett put down to a hoax – it might almost have come from James himself.'

Louisa lowered her head to hide her smile. Sally interposed with a sigh, opening her mouth to blurt out that it *was* James who had made the call when, just in time, she caught the flash of warning in her aunt's eye and stopped herself, blushing hotly.

Louisa said swiftly, 'I wonder, if I asked Mr Hilliard what it was he took from the hedge, would he tell me?'

Leonard shook his head at once. 'By nature he's a secretive man.'

'Well, he's not going to be secretive over that small object, which I have decided is a recorder, because I intend to tell the inspector about it and I am sure he will demand an explanation.'

Louisa was up very early the following

morning, hoping she would see Albert before he went into the house to help with the breakfast. But he was nowhere about, nor was the dog, so she concluded he was away somewhere in the fields, taking Tessa for her usual first walk of the day.

Reaching the arbour, she sat down, her active mind recapturing the dramatic happenings of the previous night.

Corlett was at the house, while two of his men kept watch on the front and back entrances. Just as Louisa had predicted, the Thorpes carried out the boxes of silver and the suitcases. She was with the inspector as he came towards the loaded car when it was about to be driven away. The arrests were made and a short while later she and the inspector were alone in the drawing room. It was after midnight and Sally, too sleepy to stay up, reluctantly went to bed.

'Well,' said Corlett with a satisfied air, 'that is a good night's work, and I have you to thank.'

She smiled faintly but said on a rather sharp note, 'You didn't charge Mrs Thorpe with murder.'

'No.' He gave a small sigh before adding apologetically, 'I didn't have a shred of evidence – oh, I know you are convinced she did it, and although I value your clever deductions and the results of them, I cannot charge her without at least some evidence of

her guilt.' He looked at her. 'You do understand?'

'Yes, as a matter of fact, I do.'

'You feel sure she would confess, break
down under pressure, but, if you will forgive
me, that's mere conjecture on your part.'

She laughed lightly. 'I forgive you. I would
feel the same were I in your position – that is,
I'd be most reluctant to make a charge on
conclusions reached by an amateur like me.'

'You might regard yourself as an amateur,
Mrs Hooke, but your reputation puts you
right at the top where the solving of crimes is
concerned.' He paused a moment as if undecided as to what he was about to say. Then
he spoke in a low but firm tone of voice, 'I
have wondered about the other death, that of
Joseph Powell, and am now asking you if you
still regard it as an accident?'

The question, so unexpected, gave Louisa a
jolt; she instantly thought of Amy, fairly
confident that she would get away with her
husband's murder.

'Apparently, Inspector, you've had second
thoughts—'

'I asked you a question, Mrs Hooke. Please
give me an answer.'

She shrugged resignedly. 'I do have other
ideas, yes.' She noted his change of expression, knew he intended asking her outright if
she believed Joseph Powell was murdered.
She had felt a certain sympathy with Amy,

274

but it was not as strong as that of Sally who had said she would not feel happy at seeing Amy jailed for life. A sigh escaped Louisa. Amy had undoubtedly had a hard and frustrating life with Joseph. But, after all, murder was murder. 'I think the answer you are wanting is, yes, I do believe Joseph Powell was murdered.'

He leant back in his chair, an air of complete satisfaction about him.

'I have been up to have a look at that cliff walk.' He looked at her significantly. 'I suspect you have, also?'

She nodded at once and said yes, she had been up there with Sally.

'Tell me, Inspector, when, and how, did you become suspicious?'

'It was when I heard someone remark that Joseph Powell was an experienced fell-walker. In his youth he was also a mountain-climber. Did you know that?'

Louisa nodded her head.

'Yes, I had heard it mentioned.' She paused a moment and then, 'Like you, Inspector, I decided to take a look at that cliff path because an experienced fell-walker would – one would expect – be most unlikely to fall. It wasn't as if he were an old man.' She looked at him. 'You came to the same conclusion?'

'Correct. And, like you, Mrs Hooke, I discovered that there had been another person there, with him. I say this with confidence because you would have examined the place thoroughly.'

'And found, again like you, Inspector, that as there was no sign of a struggle, the other person was known to him.'

He said, in a faintly accusing tone of voice, 'You suspected murder but never confided in me. I thought we were working together.'

'I had my reasons,' she returned. 'It has always been my policy never to put my findings with the police until I have some proof. The case of Mrs Thorpe was an exception as I was, and am, positive of her guilt.'

He nodded his head. 'As you are so sure, I must accept that she is guilty. But, as I have said, without one small shred of evidence I am unable to charge her. However, we do have her in custody, which leaves me time for further investigation. But now, of course, I have two murders on my hands.' He went on to ask if she would work with him. 'Your help would be invaluable, Mrs Hooke.'

This, she decided, was the time to reveal more of what she had kept to herself. Slowly she unzipped her handbag and withdrew an envelope which she handed to the inspector.

'You had better read this,' she said. It was Mrs Smallman's letter.

There was a small silence as he read the single sheet he had taken from the envelope. His changing expression was a study both of interest and accusation.

'You withheld this?' He shook his head. 'But why?'

'As I have just told you, Inspector, I prefer to have proof before I hand my discoveries over to the police.'

'There is no excuse for your keeping this from me.'

'Perhaps you are right. I felt at the time that it would only complicate matters. I hope you are not going to hold it against me?'

'No, but I am now entitled to your help.'

'Of course, and you shall have it.'

He tapped the letter which he had folded up again.

'Proof that Powell was in fact murdered. And,' he added significantly, 'it throws doubt on your conviction of Mrs Thorpe's guilt. In fact,' he went on thoughtfully, 'it would seem Mrs Smallman was murdered because of what she had seen up there. Surely you have to agree?'

'No, I can't agree. Mrs Smallman's murder was not premeditated. I still believe she came upon Mrs Thorpe – or perhaps her husband – taking silver from the sideboard cup-board—'

She was stopped by a roughly spoken inter-ruption.

'This time, my idea makes more sense than yours. It is without doubt that Mrs Small-man was killed because of what she saw.'

'I can understand how you feel, as I felt the same at first. But my instinct now tells me otherwise.' She had half a mind to tell him that it was Amy who had pushed Joseph Powell off that cliff but somehow she was unable to do so. However, she could not underrate the inspector's powers; he was a clever man, an experienced detective, and Louisa felt sure it was more than likely he would pursue this murder and very soon have Amy as his number one suspect.

'You puzzle me greatly, Mrs Hooke,' she heard him say into the silence. 'This letter throws an entirely different light on the whole situation, you must surely agree about that?'

'Mrs Smallman would be unable to see anyone well enough to recognize them. Her taxi was parked in the lay-by – or I should imagine – and from there it is impossible to see a face clearly. She saw someone push Powell, but she could never say who that someone was and, therefore, she was not murdered by that person.'

The inspector drew an impatient breath. He said with some asperity, 'You have your theory and I have mine. We shall see who is right.' He paused a moment, and then, 'With this new evidence, which points to someone other than Mrs Thorpe as Mrs Smallman's murderer, I am keeping everyone here at least until after the inquest, which is on

Thursday.'

'You mean, we all have to stay?'

'That is exactly what I mean,' he answered implacably. 'There is a murderer at large hereabouts and until I have him safely in custody no one leaves this house.'

As none of the four men staying at the manor had witnessed the activities of the previous night, it was with some considerable surprise that they came into the dining room to find Sally and Millie laying the tables. Albert was nowhere to be seen. Corlett entered the room and seemed to be in a hurry. He said briefly that the Thorpes had left the manor, that there was a murderer still at large and ended by the announcement that no one must leave without his permission.

'But surely,' said Leonard in his quiet, cultured voice, 'none of us is a suspect?'

The inspector looked directly at him. 'No one is suspected, as yet. But the murderer is obviously not far from here, and until he is under arrest I am sorry, but everyone must stay.'

Leonard spoke. 'As Joseph Powell's death does not now appear to be an accident, we are to assume both murders have been committed by the same person?' He seemed to be considering this. He frowned and his eyes went to meet Louisa's and he knew she was thinking of the conversation in which he had told her he believed Powell's death to have been murder. 'Are you now saying that Joseph Powell's fall was, in fact, no fall at all, but that someone pushed him off that cliff?'

'Yes, I do believe he was sent to his death by someone's deliberate act and so, I repeat: no one leaves here without my permission.' He looked up as Amy came into the room, followed closely by Millie carrying a silver tray on which were several racks containing toast. These she placed on the tables and went out again. Amy sat down and Louisa felt she would soon be regretting her change of mind about leaving the previous night. For she had intended leaving, according to what Sally had said. Now, though, she could not leave ... But what of her husband's funeral?

Louisa said close to her ear, 'You obviously came in just too late to hear what the inspector was saying. He has said none of us can leave—' She broke off as the inspector began to speak again.

'Mr Philpots, being a solicitor doesn't give you privileges. You will stay here, with everybody else.'

'Stay?' Amy went pale. 'Why have we to stay?' Although she had spoken quietly to Louisa, Corlett heard and, turning to her, said distinctly, 'I have reached the conclusion that your husband, Mrs Powell, did not fall accidentally off that cliff, but he was sent to his death by the same person who murdered

Mrs Smallman.' He looked piercingly at her, his large face set in formidable lines. 'In view of this no one is allowed to leave. I shall be questioning you all again during the afternoon. This morning, I am told, is when James Devlin's will is to be read.'

Amy was white now and her lips moved spasmodically. Louisa was sorry for her, doubtful if her former calm and cool demeanour, which held against Louisa's questioning, would be maintained when she was questioned by the inspector.

Amy, however, at present, made a swift recovery and her voice was steady as she asked if she was not to be allowed to go home for her husband's funeral.

'It's tomorrow,' she ended, looking up at him expectantly.

He was thoughtful for a moment and then, 'You can go but be back here by the evening.'

'Thank you.'

Giving her a keen, penetrating glance, the inspector left the room, saying he would be back shortly. At once three of the men began to speak, while Eric Philpots, an angry expression on his face, listened, with a glance now and then in Louisa's direction. She had to smile, aware that he was considering her at least partly to blame for what was happening.

'Mrs Hooke,' said the doctor, obviously of the same mind as the solicitor, 'I expect you know all about this latest development, so perhaps you will share your knowledge with us?'

'I can add little to what information you have been given by Chief Inspector Corlett—'

'Nonsense!' interrupted John Hilliard. 'Are you saying you don't know why the Thorpes are not here, to serve us?'

'Ah – no, I do know about them, and I don't think the inspector will mind if I tell you that late last night – or,' she amended, 'early this morning – Mr and Mrs Thorpe were caught stealing a large amount of silver, and were arrested. For anything else you want to know, well, you must ask Inspector Corlett.' Her eyes were on John Hilliard who, despite his anger, seemed well satisfied with himself ... smug, in fact. She pursed her lips. Just what was that disagreeable man up to?

Bernard Wilding, taking no notice of her fixed absorption with John Hilliard, asked her curiously, 'Perhaps you'd tell us if you had any hand in the apprehension of those two? Leonard and I have seen you watching them, and it was obvious that you had an interest in them. Have you suspected them from the beginning?'

She paused a moment, then nodded her head. 'I believe you gentlemen know by now that I am keenly observant.' Again she paused, smiling faintly. 'I am usually able to spot a criminal when I see one. Those two are professional thieves and I imagine jewellery is what they specialize in, having established an outlet. However, they obviously came to hear of the fortune in Georgian silver just lying about in this house, and decided to spend a few profitable days here. Mr Philpots was fooled by their excellent references.'

'Forged?' from the doctor.

'Undoubtedly.'

'Last night ... they didn't get away with any of the silver, but had they already stolen some?'

'The inspector and I believe so,' she replied.

'You have admitted, though tacitly, that you've helped bring those criminals to justice.' Bernard Wilding sent her a wry glance. 'I believe we have a genius in our midst. So perhaps you have some ideas as to who the murderer is?'

'The solving of that problem,' she returned with a firm and final inflection, 'is the concern of the police.' Her eyes moved to meet those of Amy. The woman lowered her head and Sally, sensing something electric in the air, inserted a bright and smiling apology for the delay in the arrival of the meal, then added, 'I hope you will all enjoy your breakfast, which is coming along at once – and please, if you find the cooking excellent, give all your praise to Millie!'

* * *

'Where,' Louisa was asking her niece an hour later, 'is Albert?' Sally shook her head, troubled. 'I looked around the grounds as you asked me, but both he and Tessa are missing.'

'The will is to be read in about half an hour.'

'You intended talking to him, didn't you? I mean, you were intending to find out from him what his intentions were and what he was going to do about the fiasco of the will.'

'Yes, that was my intention, and I had expected our talk to have taken place last evening but –' she spread her hands – 'he never kept the appointment.'

'You said you thought he was with Amy. Why don't we talk to her?'

'I already have, at breakfast. She admits she was with him and they were on that seat by the yew hedge. But she and Albert went their separate ways at about ten o'clock and she has not seen him since.'

She and Sally were in the drawing room, where they had all been asked to gather by the solicitor, but as yet the others had not arrived.

'Did she tell you what they talked about?' Sally thought what a strange situation it was. A gathering of the legatees to hear a will read which she and her aunt knew to be invalid, presupposing a will existed at all. Amy, also, knew there would be no legacy for her.

'Old times.' Louisa spoke into Sally's musings and she lifted her head to meet her aunt's gaze. 'It was easy to see that Amy had liked James Devlin all those years ago. When I say liked, I mean liked him a lot.'

'And he? Were her feelings reciprocated?'

'No, James was too disgusted because, according to Amy, he knew of the theft of the paintings by her husband. He had no time for either of them. But last evening they chatted amicably, it seems, and parted on good terms.'

'I wonder why Amy didn't go home last night, as she had intended?'

'She told me about her change of mind. She felt too tired for such a long journey, and decided to leave today, but I expect she regrets her change of mind.'

'In view of what we know, that she killed her husband, do you really expect her to come back after his funeral?'

'Oh, yes, she'll come back. I have an idea that in spite of her anxiety she believes that she can stand up to any questions put to her by the inspector.'

'But she knows he's out to find the murderer.'

Louisa nodded. 'But she also knows of the inspector's conviction that both murders were committed by the same person, and she can quite confidently assume he cannot possibly connect her with the killing of Mrs

Smallman because she wasn't here at the time.' Although she was saying this, Louisa strongly suspected that the inspector would not be long before he realized there were two murderers, not one.

'You said she'd committed the perfect crime, and it would seem that she has.'

Louisa changed the subject to ask Sally if she had rung her office to let her boss know that she had to remain here for the time being.

'Yes, I rang while you were at breakfast. He was understanding, very nice about it but could not contain his curiosity so I had to give him a brief outline of what has been happening.'

Louisa laughed. 'You'll be plied with questions from everyone in the office when you get back.'

'I wish it was all over and we were back home, and looking forward to Millie and Albert coming to live in our village.' She paused and a frown creased her brow. 'I feel so anxious. I think I'll go and see if I can find Albert. He can't have forgotten he's expected to be here—' She broke off as Eric Philpots put in an appearance and, glancing round the room, looked with some impatience at Louisa.

'Where are the others?' he asked.

'We're early. They'll be here.' She paused a moment and then, 'Have you seen Albert this morning?'

'No, but he is aware he must be present at the reading of the will. I expect he's out with his dog – but he's cutting it a bit fine. I was out there just now and he was nowhere about.' He seemed only faintly perturbed but Louisa, and Sally also, were very anxious.

'Come,' said Louisa rising, 'we'll do as you suggest and go and try to find him.'

'Don't go too far,' the solicitor called after them as they left the room. 'I said eleven o'clock. I want this business over and done with.'

'There isn't any hurry,' Louisa reminded him over her shoulder. 'You can't leave, remember.'

'That is something I'm hardly likely to forget,' he snapped and, following her from the room, said he would try to get someone from the village to come and see to the meals. 'If not,' he added, 'will you ladies oblige?'

'We won't make any promises,' retorted Louisa swiftly. And she ended with, 'There is a cosy little cafe just outside the village and Sally and I, and Millie, might just take all our meals out. So you gentlemen might have to fend for yourselves!'

Ten

The people sitting round the large table which had been brought into the drawing room were the doctor and his friend, Sally and her aunt, Amy, John Hilliard and Eric Philpots, who was at the head looking important as he fingered the long white envelope he held between his fingers.

'We shall have to conduct this without one of the beneficiaries,' he said unnecessarily. 'Albert Forsythe has gone off somewhere with his dog and obviously forgotten where he should be at this time.' His voice was low and drawling. He sounded bored and Sally wondered how many times in his life he had found himself in this situation. She glanced around, wondering about Amy, what she was thinking, expecting? She knew there would be no legacy for anyone, simply because James Devlin was not dead. The others ... Bernard Wilding, whom she liked a lot and whom she knew for sure would not feel the anger and disappointment which John Hilliard would be feeling a few minutes from now. John was looking so pleased, so exultant

... Sally's thoughts trailed. She could not understand why the word exultant came into her mind. Yet it was as if he had some secret triumph ... over whom? She turned to whisper her impression to her aunt and was surprised to hear her whisper back, 'Exactly the impression I have. That man is so cocksure of himself. Of course, he's expecting a healthy legacy so his confident air could be owing to that.'

'But it isn't,' declared Sally with conviction and her aunt nodded her head.

'I agree,' she replied briefly.

Sally looked across the table at Dr Leonard Fulham. His face was a little more tanned than when he first came. He and Bernard had spent a great deal of time out of doors, enjoying the gardens and the long walks through the village and the country lanes beyond it. He smiled at her and she responded. How would he react to what was in store for him within the next few minutes? She rather thought he would accept with good grace, and maybe a little access of amusement. Certainly it would not rancour, as it surely would with John Hilliard.

'Ladies and gentlemen,' droned the voice of the lawyer, 'we shall begin by my opening the envelope containing the will.'

Sally whispered to her aunt, 'I want to laugh!'

'I agree it is rather funny.' Her eyes went to

the man with the paper-knife and they all watched as he slit the envelope and withdrew the thick wad of papers. Slowly he opened them out as total silence reigned in the large, elegant room.

One paper was spread out, and then another. A general gasp was heard when at last the final blank sheet of white paper lay on the table.

Louisa often wondered, afterwards, how she had kept her laughter from bursting forth. It was just as she had thought: there was no will.

'My God,' murmured Bernard, turning to Louisa, 'you were right. How did you guess?'

'I wasn't by any means sure. But it seemed, somehow, to be a fitting end to this business.'

John Hilliard staggered everyone by shrugging resignedly and saying with an air of one who has won, not lost, 'So that is that.' He met Amy's eyes, and stared steadily into them. 'Old Devlin's had the laugh on us.' He rose from his chair, preparing to leave the room. 'Will there be any lunch for us?' he enquired of the lawyer.

'I phoned the cafe mentioned by Mrs Hooke. They're delivering some light cooked snacks at half past twelve. It's a bit early for lunch but the inspector wants to begin interviewing the first one of you at half past one.'

'And who is the first one?' John Hilliard

wanted to know.

'I have no idea,' abruptly as Philpots himself rose from his chair, 'not being in his confidence.'

When these two men had left the room Bernard Wilding turned to Louisa.

'With your exceptional powers of deduction, what do you make of John Hilliard's reaction?'

'I'm as puzzled as you. That man is an enigma.'

'Indeed. We all expected a wrathful outburst, but instead he seemed – well, maybe it's a strong word, but – jubilant.'

'Certainly very happy with himself.'

'Auntie,' said Sally butting in, 'I'm terribly worried about Albert. He knew he had to be here and I'm sure Mr Philpots was mistaken in thinking he forgot.'

'Maybe he knew there was no will,' suggested the doctor.

Louisa lowered her head to hide her expression. She was usually able without effort to control her feelings but with her knowledge of all the deception she felt prudence was her best policy. The doctor especially had a sharp sense of observation and she was not in the mood for answering any questions he might be tempted to ask her. She rose and excused herself.

'Sally and I must go and find Albert,' she said as she walked to the door.

'Oh, I expect he's out there, refilling the bird feeders or pulling the dead heads off roses, with his pet dog sitting there beside him.'

'I sincerely hope so,' returned Louisa, but there was no optimism in her tone.

'How does one know where to look?' Sally was saying helplessly a quarter of an hour later. 'He just isn't here, Auntie.' Her voice quivered and she was close to tears. 'I'm so frightened. I feel sure something's happened to him.'

'I'm inclined to agree with you.' Louisa was thinking of John Hilliard and of his behaviour last evening. And what of his behaviour today, on hearing he was not to come by the money he had expected? Instead of anger, disappointment, he was happy, elated, not just complacent like the other two men, but totally satisfied with his lot.

Last evening ... Louisa stopped in her tracks, thoughtfully silent. Sally turned, stopped, then came slowly back to her.

'What is it, Auntie?' she quivered. 'Have you any ideas as to where he can be?'

Regretfully Louisa shook her head. 'Sorry, love, but I'm as much in the dark as you. Albert seems to have vanished, and Tessa with him.'

'We ought to tell the inspector.'

'He isn't a missing person yet.'

'Still, I shall feel a bit better if he knows. He

wants to interview Albert as well as everyone else, remember, so he'll not treat his absence lightly.'

'It's so unlike him, to break a promise – and he did promise to meet me.'

'What time is the inspector to be here?'

'About one, I expect, since he's said his first interview is to be at half past.' She became thoughtful. 'He'll want me to be present at these interviews, so perhaps we ought to collect Millie, have a bite of lunch at the cafe and then you can take Millie off for a drive, or perhaps a walk. How does that sound to you?'

'All right – but what about these snacks that are to be delivered?'

Louisa shrugged dismissively.

'I'm not keen on hot food that has travelled. No, let us go to the cafe.'

Sally nodded absently. She was on edge, her whole mind on Albert and prefering to have a thorough search of the grounds, especially the wooded parts where, should he have fallen, he might lie for hours, or even days. She said quiveringly, 'Auntie – aren't you very anxious about Albert?'

'Yes, of course, but I am not, like you, imagining him lying helpless in some remote spot. He has the dog with him and I am almost a hundred per cent sure that if he told Tessa to leave him and go back home she would obey him.'

'Yes, I believe you're right. If he were in some trouble he'd be sure to send Tessa back here.'

'He's safe enough,' decided Louisa with confidence. 'But where on earth can he be?'

Chief Inspector Corlett was told of the disappearance of the gardener. Louisa, who had been waiting for him in the drawing room, where he had said the interviews would be conducted, saw him frown darkly as she told him this latest piece of news.

'Sounds fishy. Do you suppose he could have had something to be afraid of? And now he's done a bunk, as the saying goes?' He was seated at a table, a sheaf of papers before him. Louisa studied him silently for a moment, noting the firm square chin and other strong facial features, such as the high cheekbones and broad forehead from where the greying hair was receding.

'Albert was with Sally and me when Mrs Smallman was murdered,' she reminded him at length.

'But not when Powell met his death.'

'You have said you believe both murders were committed by one and the same person.' This second reminder resulted in a shake of his head and a rather wry expression entering his eyes.

'Having slept on this business, I have had a change of opinion. I now feel sure we have two murderers.'

'You are of my mind, that Mrs Thorpe – or maybe her husband – killed Mrs Smallman?'

'Yes, I feel sure you are right, but, as I said, there is no evidence to make a charge. However, we shall perhaps discover something during these interviews.' He sent her a keen, penetrating glance. 'Have you any preference as to who we shall have in here first?'

She nodded at once and said she would like John Hilliard.

'I have something to tell you about him,' she continued. 'Last evening Sally and I, taking an after-dinner stroll, saw John Hilliard stooped by the yew hedge. He was eavesdropping on Albert and Mrs Powell, who were sitting on the other side of the hedge. John seemed ill at ease on seeing us and after we had left him he took something from among the foliage and slipped it into his pocket.'

'That sounds suspicious,' he said in some puzzlement. 'Have you any idea what it was?'

'I can't be sure, of course, but I have a strong suspicion it was a small recorder he carries about with him.'

'He – you're saying he not only listened to those two, but actually made a recording of what he heard?'

'Yes, that is exactly what I'm saying, Inspector.'

'Then let us have him in.' He turned to the

constable who was by the door. 'You heard? Let us have John Hilliard in.'

Louisa thought that to say he came in with a swagger might be an exaggeration but there was no doubt about the air of confidence surrounding him as with a glance of indifference for Louisa he gave his attention to the policeman sitting there, at the table, Corlett's keen eyes taking in the immaculate attire of the man, the manicured fingernails, the gleaming black leather shoes.

'Sit down, Mr Hilliard,' invited the inspector, his eyes moving fleetingly to the constable who was now once again standing by the closed door. 'You are here to answer some questions—'

'I've already told you all I know,' broke in John Hilliard rudely. 'I resent being questioned a second time.'

'Nevertheless, you will tell me again where you were last Saturday between three and five o'clock in the afternoon?'

John Hilliard gave an impatient sigh and then, brusquely, 'I took a walk into the village. I needed stamps and called at the post office. I had a cup of tea at the cafe and came back. The police doctor was just leaving. It would be about five o'clock.' Every word was clipped. John Hilliard made no attempt to hide his impatience. 'If there's nothing else—'

'There is.' The inspector looked hard at

him, rubbing his chin thoughtfully. 'Last evening you took something from that high yew hedge. Would you mind telling me what it was?'

Hilliard's eyes suddenly flashed fire. 'I do mind! It's damned impertinence to ask. My actions have nothing to do with your murder case!' He rose from his chair. 'And now, if you've quite finished—'

'I have not finished. Sit down. I will tell you when you are free to go.'

Hilliard glared at him, then transferred his gaze to Louisa. 'You obviously had a little snoop after leaving me last night. Want to know what I took from the hedge, do you? Well, I assure you both it was my own property!'

'I am not doubting it,' from Corlett calmly. 'Is there some reason for your secrecy, sir? You have something to hide?'

'I do not!' spluttered Hilliard. 'But I refuse to answer questions that are totally irrelevant to your enquiries. And now, I demand to be allowed to leave or, otherwise, I shall be in touch with my lawyer.'

'You may go,' decided the inspector but added, 'You know you are not at liberty to leave this house until I am satisfied with your alibi. It has to be checked.'

'Phew!' he exclaimed when the man had gone. 'A nasty piece of work if ever there was one.'

'We didn't get much satisfaction. I would very much like to know for sure if it was a recorder, and if so, I would like to know what is on it.'

The inspector frowned and seemed to regard the matter as trivial. 'I don't expect you would be much wiser if you did get hold of the tape and play it.'

Get hold of it...

It had to be in Hilliard's room, as he would hardly carry it about with him the whole time. Maybe an opportunity would present itself later, should Hilliard take a walk again this evening...

Bernard Wilding came into the room and sat down at the table, opposite to the inspector. He talked in a slow, modulated tone of voice, answering the questions put to him without any sign of resentment or impatience. The inspector was only doing his job, Louisa could almost hear him saying to himself. There were smiles on both sides of the table when eventually Bernard was told he was free to go.

Dr Fulham's interview went on similiarly friendly lines. He had nothing to add to what he had already told the inspector. But as he rose to leave he asked Louisa if John Hilliard had said anything about his activities of the previous evening.

'We didn't get a thing out of him,' she answered with a grimace.

'You know,' he said with a thoughtful expression, 'I am inclined to believe that there is something very interesting on that recorder.'

'I am certainly in agreement about that.' Louisa paused as he began to move to the door. 'I can't help wondering if Albert's disappearance has something to do with it.'

'Could be.' The doctor stared at her. 'Seems very odd that only a few hours after John Hilliard recorded Albert's conversation with Mrs Powell, Albert is not to be found.'

The inspector glanced up sharply. 'You're right. There is something odd about that business, very odd—' He broke off then added irritably, 'Damn it – we don't know if it was a recorder!'

The doctor shrugged and turned. The constable opened the door for him.

Corlett did not have Eric Philpots in but he sent for Amy.

She entered with a confident air and a smile for Louisa. She might manage not to give anything away, thought Louisa, leaning back in the armchair which she had taken in preference to one of the high-backed dining chairs drawn up to the table.

'Mrs Powell,' began the inspector, 'you know why you are here. I need from you a few answers—'

'I wasn't here when Mrs Smallman was killed. You know that, Inspector.' There was a hint of rebuke in her tone which he chose to ignore.

'I have no intention of asking you anything about that lady's demise,' was his abrupt response. 'What I am asking you concerns the death of your husband. Tell me, were you happy together?'

She gave a start. Obviously she had not expected a question like that.

'We got along, had our ups and downs as most married couples have.'

She was calm and met his keen and narrowed gaze unflinchingly. And then, as if she had suddenly remembered the conversation she had had with Louisa Hooke when she had admitted that Joe was not a good husband, 'Of course, Inspector, we had disagreements, and even quarrels, but in the main we were – well – compatible.'

'You know of course about the note written by Mrs Smallman and delivered to Mrs Hooke?'

'Yes, Mrs Hooke did mention it.'

'Your husband was not alone up there, on the cliff.' He was watching Amy closely, his strong, clear-cut features immobile, expressionless. A man with an exceptionally alert mind and, as she stared at his set face, Louisa had a strong impression that he now had a suspicion, albeit only a faint one, that this woman whose manner was one of total complacency could in fact be involved in her husband's death.

But she also knew that without an atom of proof, he would remain restrained in his questioning of her, and in fact he let the matter drop and abruptly changed the subject, asking her if she had seen Albert this morning.

'No—' She was clearly surprised by the question. 'He wasn't helping with the breakfast, as he usually does.'

'He is missing, seems to have vanished – he and his dog.' He still held her gaze and suddenly Louisa sensed a nervous tension in the movement of a muscle at the side of her throat.

'He can't be missing...' She looked across at Louisa. 'What can have happened? He can't have gone far, not with taking Tessa with him.' She had gone a little pale and she seemed to be swallowing convulsively. 'I was with him last evening, as you know, Mrs Hooke.' She shook her head bewilderedly. 'When you asked me, at breakfast, about him and I said I hadn't seen him, I—' She paused a moment, shrugging. 'I did not attach any importance to it. You showed no sign of anxiety,' she reminded her on a final note.

'At that time he hadn't really been missed – I mean, he hadn't been gone long, but now he has been missing for at least six hours.'

'When you were with him last evening, Mrs Powell, did he seem strange in any way –

301

nervous, unsettled?'

'No, not at all.'

'What did you talk about?'

'The past,' was her brief reply, and he sent her a hard look.

'Is that all?'

Before Amy could answer Louisa was asking, 'Did Albert confide anything to you – anything that might have surprised you—

'Or given you any inkling that he meant to disappear?'

'No – why should he want to disappear?'

'That,' replied the inspector with faint sarcasm, 'is what we are trying to find out.'

Louisa with her keen perception saw something in Amy's manner which the policeman had obviously missed.

'You answered Inspector Corlett's question but not mine,' she said slowly and distinctively. 'I asked if he confided anything to you.' She knew that Amy would not answer so she did not pursue it. However, she was saving the question and at the first opportunity she would get Amy on her own and put it to her again.

The opportunity came much later and was provided by Amy Powell herself. She was about to use the telephone in the hall when she spotted Louisa and Sally passing the open front door. Millie was a little way behind, having stopped, and Amy, watching her bent figure, came to the conclusion that she was taking a stone from her sandal. Amy went up to Louisa and asked if she could spare a moment as she had something to say to her. Louisa said an instant yes, and, glancing to where Millie was now standing still, hesitant as if afraid she might be intruding if she rejoined her two friends, told Sally to go off with the girl and they would all meet up in half an hour, which would be teatime and the sandwiches and cakes would have arrived from the cafe.

'I expect this request has something to do with the question I put to you, when you were being interviewed by Dectective Chief Inspector Corlett?'

Amy nodded, glancing round to ensure they had complete privacy.

'We were talking about the reason for our being here – that is, why and how it came to happen at all. You will hardly believe it but James Devlin plotted to kill all the beneficiaries—'

'He told you this?' broke in Louisa swiftly.

'Albert told me – er – Albert knew of – of the plan...' She tailed off disjointedly, and bit her lip.

'Amy,' said Louisa gently, 'shall we cut the subterfuge and come out into the open?' She looked her straight in the eyes. 'We both know that James Devlin and Albert Forsythe are one and the same.'

'You knew? How long...'

'From the moment I saw you recognize James Devlin.'

'When we were having dinner.' She drew a deep breath. 'You have amazing powers of perception. You're so quick at grasping things.'

'Anyone can keep their eyes open.'

'No one else noticed – or did they?'

'Those at other tables would not notice. No, I don't think anyone else has guessed.' She paused a moment and then, 'Are you going to tell me everything now, Amy? I mean – everything?'

Amy licked her lips. There was a heavy frown on her brow but no sign of any serious anxiety. An optimist, undoubtedly. She had killed her husband and was confident of getting away with it. However, Louisa was not as concerned about that as she was about learning more of what had transpired last evening.

She said she felt that what had been discussed between Amy and Albert had a strong bearing on his disappearance.

'I cannot see that,' said Amy a bit stiffly. She was already regretting having decided to confide, Louisa thought.

'Tell me more of what he said his intentions were,' Louisa encouraged her. 'He must have said why the beneficiaries were to be murdered.'

'Oh, yes, he did give a reason,' replied Amy but in a low voice, a voice of indecision, and in fact she suddenly changed her attitude completely and said without further preamble that she ought not to be talking about what had been said by James Devlin in confidence.

'But – you must tell me more,' insisted Louisa urgently. 'It's very important—'

'No! I've changed my mind,' and without another word she had turned and was almost running in her haste to get away from Louisa.

As arranged, Louisa met her niece and Millie for afternoon tea. Eric Philpots was there, sharing a table with the three other men. A waitress from the cafe was waiting on them, having brought in from the kitchen trays of sandwiches, scones and fancy cakes. Already there was a supply of these on the table shared by Louisa and her niece, Millie having offered to help the waitress by bringing in the pots of tea. Amy had not put in an appearance.

'How did it go?' was Sally's eager question. 'Did you get anything out of Amy?'

'Very little,' Louise admitted with a sigh. 'She had originally intended to tell me everything but suddenly she changed her mind and refused to be questioned. She went off in quite a rush.'

'So you know nothing of what is on the recorder?'

'No, but when Hilliard takes his usual predinner stroll I'm going to his room and if luck is with me I'll find that recorder.'

'And take it?' breathed Sally eagerly, making her aunt laugh.

'You obviously don't mind having a thief in the family.'

'Like you, I want to know what was so important to Mr Hilliard that made him record it.'

Louisa nodded and said tautly, 'I don't have the link but I'm convinced that Albert's disappearance is connected with what's on that recorder.'

True to her word Louisa went to Hilliard's bedroom as soon as she saw him leave the house. But though she made a thorough search the recorder was not to be found and she concluded he had it in his pocket, its contents obviously of value to him.

'I have to speak with Amy again,' she told Sally when they met once more. 'Millie will be joining us in a few minutes and so I want you to take her off somewhere.'

'Of course ... do you expect any better luck this time – with Amy, I mean?'

'She's aware that I know she killed her husband,' returned Louisa slowly and significantly. 'Is aware also that I haven't as yet told the police of my conviction. I am going to ask her to play ball with me.'

'To confide, or else...?'

'I shall do it adroitly, but she'll get the message.'

'Well, good luck. I can't wait to find out what her talk with Albert was about.'

Louisa found Amy Powell in the small drawing room, looking very comfortable and serene as she sat on a low armchair by the window. She had an open book on her knee but she was gazing through a side window, taking in the view of sunlit lawn with its scattering of flowering trees, and beyond them the low foothills cutting into the clear blue sky. She gave a start as Louisa entered and hastily picking up her book she smiled and said she was just going.

'No,' said Louisa in response to this instantly made decision. 'You and I have to talk.' She advanced further into the room and stood by a chair, ready to take possession of it.

'I'm not talking about Albert, if that's what you've come here for,' Amy almost snapped and Louisa's mouth tightened.

'I was thinking you might like to change your mind, Amy, in view of – well, certain suspicions I have regarding your husband's death.'

Although Amy went pale she sidestepped the challenge as she said, 'I doubt if you would benefit from knowing what James

Devlin and I were talking about.'

'Try me,' invited Louisa briefly.

'It was very private – in strict confidence,' began Amy and would have added to that but Louisa intervened with: 'You originally intended telling me everything about that chat. What made you reconsider and run off like that?'

'I realized I'd be betraying a confidence—' She broke off, shaking her head emphatically. 'No, it is far too private. I've said too much already,' and she added testily, 'Don't you find it wearisome, having to stay here? I know I do.'

An exasperated sigh escaped Louisa.

'It is too late for further evasion,' she said, trying to be patient. She paused, but when there was no sign of Amy's weakening Louisa decided to play what she hoped would be a trump card. 'I believe your chat with James Devlin was overheard and could even have been recorded.'

This had its effect. The colour drained from Amy Powell's face.

'Overheard – oh, my God!'

Louisa had not known what to expect but the strength of Amy's reaction took her by surprise. Her eyes narrowed.

'Now,' she said evenly, 'perhaps you are willing to talk?'

To her surprise Amy was shaking her head. White now, and thoroughly shaken, she rose from the chair and made for the door.

'I have to speak with James—' She swung round. 'Who – who was it who listened?'

'Aren't you going to tell me what was said between you and James?'

'I can't,' she choked. 'I want to know who was listening to us?'

'That I am not willing to disclose— Amy!' But the woman was gone and when Louisa reached the door it was to see Amy running up the stairs and a few seconds later she heard her bedroom door bang shut.

Eleven

Inspector Corlett, having reconsidered his initial conviction that he was looking for only one murderer, intended to waste no more time on speculation, but to subject Mrs Thorpe to some intensive questioning. This he decided to do in his own office, so that Louisa could be present. It was an invitation which she eagerly accepted.

'You believed almost from the first that one or other of the Thorpes was guilty of Mrs Smallman's murder?' The inspector was seated behind a large partner desk with Louisa sitting opposite, Mrs Thorpe not yet having been brought in.

'It was a hunch. I often have them.'

'And they are usually right.' He gave her a wry smile. 'I ought to have taken more notice of you. However, as I still have no proof and am sure that I shall never be able to get any, I'm conducting the interview here. You're convinced that if it is she who is the murderer and not her husband, she'll crack under pressure; so we shall see. I felt somehow that your presence would undermine her confidence, in which case she is more likely to make a blunder.'

'And give herself away.' Louisa was nodding thoughtfully. 'If she realizes the danger of her position she'll probably put the blame on her husband.'

'I've thought of that and, yes, it is a possibility.'

Louisa asked how long before Mrs Thorpe was to be brought in and when he said she would be here in five minutes, Louisa knew she had time to pass on some of her suspicions regarding the disappearance of the gardener.

'He's obviously running away from something,' she continued, having broached the subject, 'and I believe the reason is to do with the wily John Hilliard, a man I would not trust any further than I could see him.' She looked straight at the inspector and added, 'He once robbed James Devlin and I am of the opinion that his intention is to rob him again—'

'Devlin,' frowned the detective, shaking his head. 'Aren't you getting mixed up? Devlin's dead.'

A small silence ensued and it was plain that Corlett was becoming impatient.

'Inspector, I have to tell you that James Devlin is very much alive.' She went on to explain and to give him her own opinion.

He looked staggered and she had to smile as she read his thoughts, and it was this reading which made her say with a hint of amusement, 'I don't think he's committed any crime that you can charge him with, but then, I don't really know if it is a crime to bury someone in a wrong name and then to assume that person's identity.'

'But why did he do it?' snapped the inspector irritably. 'More complications! Will this business ever be cleared up?'

'The important thing at the moment is for you to get a confession from one of the Thorpes—'

'I agree about that, but where is Albert – Devlin? Has he been in trouble with the police at any time, do you know?'

Louisa could not fail to notice the eagerness about him and she was swift to say, 'I can tell you quite definitely that he has never been in any trouble with the police – and I can also warn you against suspecting him of

Joseph Powell's murder.'

'You seem very sure. Does this mean,' he added after a short pause, 'that you know who the murderer is?'

Louisa hesitated. This was a question she could well have done without. She decided in favour of prevarication.

'I have absolutely no concrete proof that my conclusion is correct, and so, Inspector, you will understand my inability to give a truthful answer to your query.'

His mouth tightened; he said bluntly, 'You know but won't tell. As I have previously reminded you, we are supposed to be working together on this case.'

'I'm sorry if I can't be of any help regarding Joseph Powell's death—'

'If you're trying to tell me it might not be murder, but the accident everyone believed it was, then you're wasting your time.'

She said after some consideration, 'If at any time I feel that keeping my ideas to myself will not serve, then I promise to be entirely open with you and tell you what I have deduced.'

Was he mollified? His set and frosty expression told her nothing.

'I shall have to be satisfied with that,' was all he said and the next moment Mrs Thorpe was brought in. Her mouth was tight, her eyes glinting with anger. But to Louisa's experienced eye there was about her an uneasiness which was not part of her usual makeup. She was a professional thief and along with her husband they made the perfect team. Louisa deduced that she could be thorough in her planning, keeping a cool head. But that was only theft. She had not expected to become involved in the far more serious crime of murder. She had been driven to it, had acted on the spur of the moment, without thought – or the truth was she had had no time to think. Exposure was facing her ... unless she acted swiftly. And this she did, and instantly her cool returned and she was able to wipe her fingerprints from the murder weapon.

But now, at this moment, she was showing signs of concern, even of fear, so if the inspector should recognize this and play on it...

His voice was brusque as he asked her again about finding the body. She straightened up and told him curtly that she had already said all there was to say; she could add no more.

'I am of the opinion that you can add a great deal more.' He looked directly at her. 'Perhaps you would like to have a lawyer present? We can get you one—'

'Why should I need a lawyer?' Already there was a huskiness in her voice. 'You had better explain.'

'I am enquiring about Mrs Smallman's

murder. This interview has nothing to do with the charge of robbery and I rather think you knew before you entered this room that it is the murder we shall be talking about.'

So, thought Louisa, suppressing the smile that rose to her lips, Mrs Thorpe had already guessed at the nature of these questions and that was why she had been nervous.

The woman said tautly, 'What has the murder to do with me?'

'I am of the opinion that you committed it,' he told her bluntly and much of the colour left her cheeks.

'I had nothing to do with it—'

'Mrs Smallman caught you taking silver either from the sideboard cupboard or from the large cabinet, which was also filled with silver. Mrs Smallman walked in—'

'Rubbish,' Mrs Thorpe spluttered, 'this is pure speculation and not what happened! She was lying there when I entered the room and I saw she was dead – that is, she looked dead to me.'

Ignoring the interruption, Corlett continued, 'Mrs Smallman walked in and surprised you. Knowing her, we are of the opinion that she would tackle you and accuse you and in fact, let you know that it was her intention to expose you.' He paused but Mrs Thorpe did not speak and he went on, 'She must have turned her back – probably she was already walking to the door – and you picked up the poker, the only available weapon, and hit her on the head with it.'

'None of this is – is true...' She glared at Louisa. 'I suppose it's you who's put this absurd idea into the inspector's head. Well, it isn't what happened. Mrs Smallman was lying there when I went into the room. I told only the truth.'

But Louisa was shaking her head.

'It is not the truth. I guessed at the beginning that the murder was not committed by anyone from outside. It was impossible that anyone could have entered, in full daylight and in the middle of the afternoon, with the intention of collecting silver and putting it into bags – no, all this would take time and no would-be thief would take the risk. He'd come at night. The only people to my mind who would steal the silver were you and your husband. You're professional jewel thieves; you get into houses like this and it is easy for you to collect jewellery, it being comparatively small. You heard of this hoard of valuable Georgian silver and decided it was well worth your time and effort, but silver, being more bulky, could not be picked up and put in your pocket. It had to be packed and packing took time. You were either packing silver into a box when Mrs Smallman surprised you, or you were getting it together ready for – perhaps – packing later on.'

'No, it isn't what happened!' The woman was weakening rapidly and the inspector took full advantage of this, almost shouting as again he accused her of the murder.

'It – it wasn't m-me,' she cried vehemently. 'It was – was my husband...'

It was an hour later that Louisa, having congratulated the inspector on gaining a confession from Mrs Thorpe, decided on a plan of action, and once back at the manor she sought out her niece, who was with Millie in the arbour, and told her she wanted her to take her for a drive.

'Millie, dear,' she added turning to her, 'it isn't the sort of ride we can take you on, so you will find yourself something to do. We shall not be too long, but this is very private business.'

Millie smiled and said it was all right. She understood and would have a quiet read until their return.

'Auntie,' Sally said as she and Louisa walked to the car, 'what is this? you're being very mysterious.'

'Am I – yes, I suppose I am.' She opened the passenger door of the car and looked at Sally from over the top of it. 'We are going to have a talk with Albert—' She broke off abruptly and gave a light laugh at her niece's expression. 'Yes, I think I know where to find him,' she added as she got into the car.

'But how?' Sally just stood there, by the car, and stared at her aunt. 'You know where he is?'

'I said I think I know. I'm not sure, but I have an idea we shall find him at the cottage he was intending to buy.'

'At the cottage?' frowned Sally, now sliding into the driver's seat. 'Why should he go there—? Auntie, this is all too puzzling! How do you know – I mean, what makes you think he might be at the cottage?'

'Let's drive and I'll talk as we go along. I have reached some conclusions,' she began as Sally drove through the gates, 'but I may be wrong—'

'I doubt it,' from Sally, not without a hint of pique. 'I guess you've known all along where Albert is.'

'No, I haven't. It's only since I saw the whole picture clearly, the pieces having fallen into place. I believe Albert ran away because, once again, he wanted to be alone, to get away from people, away from the rest of the world, to be alone with his dog.'

'But why? Why should he want to resume that life of loneliness? It can't be true, Auntie. Albert wouldn't want to get away from you and me.'

'Frankly, I don't think we were in his mind when he fled to the cottage. However,' she added, settling herself back, as she intended to enjoy the ride along country lanes and leafy avenues, 'as I am not one hundred per cent sure of my facts we'll wait until we get there and see if Albert has taken up residence.'

'He can't take up residence,' Sally was quick to point out. 'He was intending living near to us and so he cancelled – he didn't even get as far as paying a deposit. He can't just, well, squat in the cottage.'

'I believe it's only temporary. He knew where the key was and also knew no one would be there, in that lonely place. Of course, there could be another viewer come along but he was willing to risk that.'

Sally drove with speed, impatient to get to the cottage. Never, she thought, had she been so anxious about anyone. She had not been able to forget that Albert could have been her father had not her mother jilted him, and she knew an affection for him so strong that it was akin to love. So his welfare was her concern and if he thought for one moment he was going to cut himself off again he would have her to contend with.

Reaching the lane leading to the cottage she slackened speed and then slid gently to a stop outside the little wooden gate. No sign either of Albert or the dog. Louisa and Sally walked up the narrow little path to the front door. It was ajar and Sally made no hesitation about pushing it open and walking into the small square hall. Louisa followed, calling Albert's name, but there was no response. But once in the living room and able to see through the window, they saw Albert in the garden, with Tessa sitting contentedly beside him.

'I want to cry...' Sally gave a little cough, to hide her emotions. 'He's so – so – lonely.'

'Not for long,' determinedly from Louisa. 'Don't upset yourself, love. We'll be taking Albert back with us.'

Going to the back door, she opened it and called to the old man. Startled, he looked up, then rose, wiping his hands on a handkerchief he'd taken from the pocket of his khaki overall. Louisa said quietly as he came towards the door, 'Just what is the idea? You've had Sally and me in a panic.' Which wasn't true of course but Louisa added for good measure, 'Especially Sally here. She's been so worried that she wanted to have you listed as a missing person.' A trifle sheepishly he said he was very sorry but he had to disappear, to get right away from the manor and 'certain people in it'.

'I think I know one of those people, Albert, but the other? You have me puzzled there.' She had backed away from the door and a minute later the three were in the living room, sitting on the old sofa left behind by the previous owner. Sally saw at once that this was where Albert had been sleeping and tears came to her eyes.

'Albert,' she said before her aunt could speak, 'why have you run from us? We love you and care and yet you went away without a word—' She shook her head, and a tear fell on to her cheek. 'Whatever your problem is you're going to let Auntie and me solve it, and you're not staying here another night, on your own.' Tessa, having been ignored, put a paw on to her lap and gave a soft, sharp bark. Sally smiled then and stroked Tessa's head.

'I think,' began Louisa briskly, 'that you'd better tell us everything leading up to this absurd flight. I say absurd because you are not going to be allowed to resume the life of a recluse. Nothing's changed regarding the plans we've all discussed. You are coming to live close to me and Sally. With Millie there'll be four of us, and we're a family. Now, I want to know the reason for your sudden wish to get away from your beautiful home.'

At this he smiled faintly. 'How long have you known I am James Devlin?'

'Since the moment when Amy Powell recognized you at the dinner table...' She tailed off but after a small silence asked if anything was the matter.

He shook his head but then said in an expressionless voice, 'She is the other one you've just mentioned.'

'Amy? I see...' Louisa did not see. Her natural process of reasoning had failed her this time as she would not have suspected

Albert to have been running away from Amy. What had she done to him, she asked Albert, and for a while he was deep in thought.

'She hasn't done anything; it's just that I don't like her.'

Louisa shrugged. 'Well, tell us why you came here, to be all on your own?'

'I suppose you're going to insist,' he observed wryly.

'You suppose correctly,' came in Sally with a firm inflection. 'Since we intend to take you back we have to know what you have to fear at the manor.'

'It was the evening when Amy Powell recognized me. We met outside and talked; at first it was only about the past and she apologized for her husband – er, maybe you didn't know—'

'About the paintings he stole? Yes, we do know about that. So, what else did you talk about?'

'It became more confidential. Amy asked me why I had brought the six people here and I told her the truth, that I intended to murder them all...' He tailed off because neither Louisa nor Sally could refrain from smiling. He waited and then went on, 'She asked me how I intended doing it and I had to admit I hadn't really any concrete plans. I said Albert had weed killer in one of the sheds. It was silly of me even to have thought of such a thing as—'

'Mass murder?' with a lift of Louisa's eyebrows. 'Darned silly. Sally was right: you couldn't hurt a fly.'

'Nevertheless,' he mused, 'I had harboured a grudge, a hatred even, for those who had done me injuries and all those years I'd wondered what I'd do if ever the chance came for me to get even.'

'And when Albert died you felt the chance had come.'

He nodded but changed the subject. 'As I was saying, Amy and I talked a lot and she mentioned that you had told her you suspected her husband had been pushed from that cliff.' He was fingering his beard and Louisa wondered if it were real or just glued on.

'I don't see why anything you've told us should have made you want to run away,' she said, but with a strange inflection that made Sally think she was not being quite honest. 'However, do continue.'

'Here comes the important part, and you will soon see that I cannot possibly return to my home. I'd be arrested for murder.' He went on to tell them of the act of John Hilliard in recording what had been said between him and Amy.

'He came to me very early – it was only half past six in the morning and I was watering a couple of borders as it had been so hot as you know and some of the annuals were wilting.

John came to me and without beating about the bush told me of the recording and in fact played some of it to me. He said he was going to edit it and if I didn't do as he asked he'd give the edited tape to the inspector.'

'The recording,' breathed Louisa. 'I guessed he had recorded your conversation because I saw him take something from the hedge. So tell us – and carefully – just what was on the tape?'

'When Amy spoke about you telling her you thought someone had pushed Joseph off the cliff, I said I hoped that no one would think I pushed him off.' He looked at Louisa and then at Sally. 'Perhaps you can see how that would sound if all was edited out except my saying the words "I pushed him off"?'

'Go on,' urged Louisa tautly. 'What else had Hilliard to say?'

'He heard me say I invited the six here with the intention of killing them all.'

Louisa drew a breath. Sally suspected she was in a rare fury.

'There's more, obviously.'

'He was in a very nasty mood, saying I had fooled them all over the legacies. He said he would make a bargain with me. He wanted the house and contents made over to him – as a gift. I was to say in a letter that he had once befriended me and now I wanted to repay him.'

A deep silence followed before Sally

breathed the one word, 'Blackmail.'

'He said he had been led by me into believing he had a substantial legacy and he wasn't letting me make a fool of him.' The old man glanced at Louisa and sighed as he added hopelessly, 'If only he hadn't listened he'd never have known I am James Devlin and the idea of blackmail would of course never have entered his mind.' Another deep sigh and then, 'So you see, I have to escape from him for a while, so I have time to think, but he'll win in the end.'

'Obviously you haven't written the letter he asked for?'

The old man shook his head. 'No, but either I write it or have to be on the run for the rest of my life.' He glanced at each of them in turn. 'You don't seem very troubled about my plight,' he added on another hopeless note.

Ignoring that Louisa said, watching him curiously, 'You've just told us that if you return to the manor you'll be arrested for murder. That,' she chided sternly, 'was an exaggeration. The real situation is that when you return you'll be faced again with John Hilliard and his threat. But do you suppose he actually wants to give the recording to the police?' She shook her head and sent him a penetrating glance. 'I assume he offered you the tape in exchange for the letter he wants?'

'Yes, that's right.' He was fingering his

beard again and, noticing Louisa's expression, he half smiled and said it was not real, but something he had kept since his acting days. And when she said she would like to see him without it he nodded his head and promised to get rid of it.

Louisa returned to the more important subject of Albert's flight.

'The situation as I see it is that John Hilliard believes he's dealing with the old James Devlin, the one whom he so easily robbed. He has no idea you have someone behind you now, that you are not, as he believes, totally alone – and vulnerable. He can't have edited the recording yet as it isn't likely he has the requirements with him, and so we shall run it as it was originally heard. Another thing is that you have to know I told Mrs Powell that your talk with her was recorded and she seemed to panic and said she had to speak with you.'

There was a long pause before the old man decided just how to frame his words.

'Amy Powell acted strangely at the end of our talk,' he said at last. 'She seemed to be afraid of something and although I cannot recall her saying anything concrete I had the impression that she regarded you as her enemy, and I felt you knew something about her which she was afraid of your revealing.'

Louisa said smoothly, 'And you have your own idea about what it might be?'

He nodded, after a slight pause.

'You're clever, Mrs Hooke, a private investigator, I heard you saying. I believe you discovered Joseph Powell was murdered and you know who his murderer is.'

Louisa and Sally exchanged glances. She said interrogatively, her eyes now fixed on his face, 'Do you believe he was murdered?'

'Yes, I do.'

'By whom?'

He looked straight at her.

'By the same person as you yourself believe has murdered him.'

Faintly she smiled. 'Just why would you agree with my conclusion?' she asked.

'Mainly because of her strangeness when talking about you. As I said, I had this strong conviction that she was afraid of you and she whispered something to herself like: "If it comes to a showdown I now have a way out."'

'You heard this – distinctly?'

He shook his head. 'Not distinctly. She wasn't intending to say it to me; she was murmuring to herself, her eyes staring into space. I felt she had forgotten I was there at all. She spoke as if from a great distance.'

Louisa asked Sally if she could understand what they were talking about.

'Of course. Amy Powell. You both believe she killed her husband.'

'Anything else?'

'Well – I have been wondering why Albert said he didn't like her. After all, he has no proof that she's a murderess.'

'Albert,' said Louisa looking at him, 'can you answer that?'

'We're all talking very frankly so I suppose I must tell you that I had the impression that Amy Powell will shift the blame if you do happen to accuse her of murder.'

Even before he had finished speaking Louisa was nodding her head.

'Shift it to you? You told her that your original intention was to kill the six who had done you an injury. She knew you well enough to be sure you'd own up to this if questioned and so it would quite naturally be you whom the police would seize upon and not her. So that is why you ran away from her.'

He shrugged and said it was John Hilliard mainly whom he had wanted to avoid, at least for a while until he could collect himself and think clearly.

'But I soon admitted to myself that there was nothing I could do and so became resigned to giving in to his demands.'

Louisa could not help smiling.

'You give in too easily, Albert—' She stopped. 'I shall call you Albert until you get rid of that beard,' she told him. But Sally came in and with a little sigh said she did not think she could call him anything else but

Albert, at which he smiled affectionately and said he would not mind at all.

Louisa became brisk and businesslike. 'We're all in this together, and Sally and I are taking you back to the manor, where all will be sorted out, and to our satisfaction.'

'About Amy,' began Sally in a tone of distress. 'Will she – I mean...?'

Her aunt looked steadily at her. 'I tacitly agreed to keep silent about my convictions but, Sally, if Amy is intending to make an attempt to shift those convictions to Albert...!' She tailed off, with a question in the eyes that looked steadily into those of her niece.

'No, she shall not!' declared Sally on the instant. 'You might have had some stupid intentions at first, Albert, but Auntie and I know you well by now and we care about you. No one is ever going to hurt you again.'

He was touched and for a long moment incapable of speech. But at length he did manage to say, 'I've been so fortunate in finding friends like you. I little guessed when I embarked on this puerile escapade that this would be the outcome.' He paused and looked at Louisa. 'You seem very sure of putting everything right for me, but John does have that recording and intends to use it as a weapon.'

'It would be an effective weapon only if it were edited. As it stands, I guess its contents would not be damaging to you in the least. You agree?'

'Oh, yes – but once edited—'

'I shall insist on the inspector obtaining that recording, as it is. I mean, without its being edited. Now, we must make haste if this business is to be cleared up without further delay.'

Albert said with a rather sheepish grin, 'Shall I see if I can get this thing off now, or wait?'

'As you were once an actor, I think a little theatrical touch would not come amiss. I suggest you effect the change in your appearance when we get there. I shall enjoy the reaction of the doctor and his friend, to say nothing of the poker-faced Mr Philpots.'

Albert was very quiet for the entire journey back to the manor and Louisa concluded that although he had a certain amount of faith in her ability to rescue him from what he himself had decided was a most dangerous situation, he did not see how she could force John Hilliard to give up the tape. But he had reckoned without the help she expected to have from the police.

Leaving Albert with Sally in the garden, Louisa went straight to the telephone in the hall and rang the inspector.

'Blackmail!' exclaimed Corlett. 'Murder, theft, an unlawful interment and now –

blackmail. Anything else you have to offer me?' he added sarcastically. 'No embezzlement, drug pushing or maybe one of those men is a forger?'

Ignoring all this Louisa asked the inspector to come over to the manor as soon as possible.

'I want you to bring a search warrant. John Hilliard's weapon for this blackmail attempt is the recording I mentioned.'

'Ah. So it was important after all.'

'Is important,' she corrected. 'But we have to get it now and by taking him by surprise. He's intending editing it and once he does this the whole content is changed.'

'I see. The tape as it is, I am assuming, is not damning but, edited, it can be.'

'Exactly. And if we don't take Hilliard by surprise he'll hide the recorder away and you will never see it again until it is edited.'

'I can't see that he'll be in any great hurry to edit it,' mused the inspector after a few moments' thought. 'He can tell Albert it's been edited.'

'Yes, but simple as Albert is, I don't think he's so gullible as to accept Hilliard's word. No, I am sure only the edited version, played to him, would be effective.' Louisa stopped, then added impatiently, 'Inspector, please come at once.'

'Yes, I'll come at once. You're lucky to find me here—'

'I know you're staying at the Red Lion—'

'But I was intending leaving later today.'

'Well, you can't leave,' was all she said and replaced the receiver on its hook.

Twelve

The first thing the inspector said to Louisa was in the way of an apology.

'My sarcasm was out of place. I just felt that this case had so many offshoots it would never end.'

'I know how you feel, Inspector. Don't worry; I'm not one to take offence easily.'

'You've been of such invaluable help...' He paused, looking at her interrogatingly. 'This latest? I suggested you and I have a few minutes' talk before bringing in the others. You say Albert – or James Devlin – is with your niece, in the garden?'

'I told Sally to keep him out there until I had explained it all to you. The situation is this: we must have the tape, that is our first priority. You have the warrant?'

'Of course – as a matter of fact I've had a warrant to search all rooms but chose not to use it. But it can now be used to search Hilliard's room.'

'You see, James assumed his conversation with Mrs Powell was private, confidential. He'd never suspect it was being recorded.' She went on and talked for ten minutes, and at the end of this the inspector had every detail of James Devlin's past injuries and his desire for revenge. He knew of the part played by John Hilliard when he had deliberately and heartlessly robbed a man whom he knew was so weighed down with grief and despair he would be unlikely to fight back and claim what was his right.

'And here ... John Hilliard spoke of this house and its resale value once it was renovated. He spoke as if he would be interested in buying it.'

'But then saw an easier way to achieve his aim.' Corlett's voice was grim.

'And cheaper.'

'By blackmail.' The inspector's grey eyes narrowed. 'Next to murder, blackmail is the most heinous of crimes.'

'I agree.' She paused reflectively. 'I never liked John Hilliard from the moment I met him but, somehow, I could not see him committing an actual criminal offence.'

'He had already robbed James Devlin,' the inspector reminded her.

'Yes, but it was in a much more subtle way.'

'I see what you mean.' Corlett pursed his lips. 'This attempt – it's a rather clumsy procedure, don't you think?'

'Undoubtedly it's clumsy, but you have to remember that he thinks he's dealing with an old man, alone in the world, a man who even when much younger hadn't the strength in him to fight back, to demand a return of his money. John Hilliard is pretty confident of his power over James but unfortunately for him Sally and I have befriended James and will protect him.'

'You want Hilliard charged?'

'I don't think James will agree to that. In total contradiction to his intention of being revenged on the six who came here, James Devlin is a mild, sensitive man who could never hurt anyone. No, I feel sure he'll let Hilliard go and in fact the shame which will result from his attempt at blackmail, plus the loss of a legacy he'd believed to be substantial, will be punishment in plenty to a man like him, and it's my belief that James will let it go at that.'

'You're probably right. You know Devlin better than I, so I have to take your word that he's a harmless, benign old man – and to my mind, a bit simple.'

A flicker of amusement crossed Louisa's face.

'He appears to be simple,' she agreed, but went on, 'I rather think, though, that he prefers retreat to attack. It's easier for him to run away, bury his head in the sand, hence his living all those years as a recluse. No human being was troubling him; he was protecting himself in his little cyst of loneliness. I can understand but perhaps you cannot?'

'No, I can't fully understand a mind that has no wish to open itself to what is around it. But then,' he added with a rueful smile, 'you know the man much better than I do.'

'So what is your intention now, Inspector? Have you a man ready to search for that recorder?'

He nodded at once and said yes, a sergeant would be searching John Hilliard's room immediately they had him in here for questioning. He added tentatively, after a small hesitation, 'I want to question Mrs Powell again. I had decided to do this today in any case, before I left for London.'

'You obviously have your reason. Something has transpired?'

'Has come to my mind would better explain my decision to investigate that lady further. I suppose you know that with many murders where the victim is married, it is the spouse who's the guilty one?'

She nodded and said shrewdly, 'You obviously believe she had the opportunity.'

'I have been making enquiries as to how long it would take her to drive here from her home. I was also dwelling on what you said that, should it become necessary – or words to that effect – you'd tell me what your own conclusions were. This meant that you had reached a conclusion and as there is no one else who would want to rid the world of Powell...' Tailing off significantly, he shrugged his broad shoulders.

Louisa was reflecting on Amy's intention of trying to throw suspicion on James should her own position become one for anxiety.

While out with Sally in the garden, James Devlin came to a decision. He made an excuse, left her and went to the bedroom he had occupied. Fifteen minutes later he emerged – without the beard. Intending to join Sally again, he was just passing the door of the small drawing room when it opened and he came face to face with the man coming out.

'Good God!' Leonard Fulham looked for a moment as if he was in shock after seeing a ghost. 'What – how—?' Again he broke off, staring blankly at the man who, without his beard, was easily recognized. 'James ... Devlin...' He shook his head, slowly, from side to side. The atmosphere was electric, but he soon managed to pull himself together, his brain working overtime as he tried to fathom out what had happened.

'Yes,' came the mildly spoken word at last. 'It is I, James Devlin, the man whose life you saved. Sorry if I startled you, but I didn't expect to meet you yet—'

'Startled,' broke in Leonard, not without a

hint of anger, 'you gave me one hell of a shock!'

'I guess so. I'm sorry,' he said again, his eyes going past the tall, upright figure of the doctor to the man behind him who on hearing voices had come to the door. And for a moment Bernard Wilding stood transfixed, dazed by the sight of what for a split second appeared to be an apparition. His lips moved but no sound came.

'What the devil is going on here?' It was the doctor who broke the silence. 'Your voice—Albert! What's the idea of this hoax?'

'It's a long story,' came the masculine voice edged with a hint of amusement, and the doctor swung round.

'You've been in on this masquerade from the start.' He glowered at Louisa, who could scarcely suppress laughter at the expression on the two men's faces – one of anger and the other of a sort of baffled disbelief.

'Not by any means,' returned Louisa shaking her head. 'Albert had us all fooled. But in order for you to be put in the picture I suggest you ask the inspector if you might be in when he talks to Mr Hilliard, which will be in a few minutes' in the drawing room.' She pointed to the room behind her. 'He's there now – the inspector, I mean. And now, please excuse me. I have something to discuss with Albert before we all go in to see the inspector.'

'You know,' began James hesitantly as he and Louisa were walking away from the two friends, 'I feel John Hilliard will deny he ever tried to blackmail me. If so, the inspector will naturally think it is more mischief on my part. He'll not believe me, I'm sure of it.'

'Let us wait and see,' suggested Louisa practically. 'Ah, here comes Sally. We have to find Mr Philpots now; it's only courtesy to let him in on what is going on.'

She turned to the man beside her and shook her head. What a web of complications he had woven on venturing on such a ridiculous scheme. Yes, she thought remembering the inspector's statement that he was simple, there was a simplicity about him, but this did not mean he was lacking in brain power. He just liked, and was satisfied with, the simple things of life: things that grow, animals and birds and Nature. Humans of this world had done him many injuries – some people, she mused, were prone to being the object of fraud and malice – and in consequence he had cut contact with his fellow men and become a recluse. He had taken in lost dogs, had supported the Home of Rest for Horses, the charity that had one of its branches in beautiful open country bordering the village of Hazeldene. James Devlin was one of those who can be described as 'the salt of the earth' she thought, and it was so sad he had had such a raw deal. But now...

She said quietly, 'Everything is still the same. The plans – I mean, you will be building yourself a bungalow in the paddock I mentioned. And so you will be living not only close to me but only five minutes walk from Sally's lovely thatched cottage. You will have a happy life from now on. As Sally said, we're a family – you know of course that Sally and I are taking Millie back with us. She will stay with Sally until I am settled in my new home and then she is to come to live with me, not as a servant as she was with her last employer but, as I said, one of the family.'

'She has been lucky too,' he said in a husky tone. 'I only hope that your optimism is not misplaced.'

'John Hilliard cannot harm you. That tape is to be found any moment now, though Hilliard doesn't know it. A warrant to search his room will produce the recording as it is – unedited.'

The people gathered in the drawing room were the two friends, James Devlin, Eric Philpots, John Hilliard, Louisa and her niece, Amy Powell, and, of course, the chief inspector.

Having been told that a search was being made of his room, John Hilliard exploded in an angry outburst as he demanded to know by what right his room was being searched.

'And what exactly are you looking for?' he

ended with a glowering look at the inspector.

'The recording you made of a conversation between Mrs Powell and James Devlin, the man we have hitherto known as Albert Forsythe, the gardener.'

John Hilliard's colour receded somewhat but his bombastic manner remained.

'You'll be sorry you've done this,' he said to James through gritted teeth. 'And you—' He turned to Louisa. 'You've had a hand in this, poking your nose into things right from the beginning.'

She merely smiled, her attention with Amy Powell, whose calm would have seemed to be unimpaired had it not been for the nervous employment of her hands as they plucked at her skirt, pressing it between her fingernails to make tiny creases. Louisa sensed that despite her general air of cool confidence her heart was beating overtime.

John Hilliard had heard the inspector saying that it was not necessary for the two friends and Eric Philpots to remain but they could do so if they wished, at which Hilliard almost shouted: 'I do not happen to want them to stay! In fact, I demand that they leave since this is a private matter.' He looked at the inspector. 'As using a tape recorder is not a criminal offence I assume there is no charge to be made against me.'

'The charge will depend on how you meant to use what was recorded.' The inspector's keen grey eyes fixed those of John Hilliard. 'If you intended to blackmail Mr Devlin then quite naturally there will be a charge.'

Louisa's glance shot to James Devlin's face and she saw the slight shake of his head, unnoticed by anyone else in the room.

'Blackmail!' exploded John Hilliard. 'No such thing! I would never stoop to such conduct!'

'But you once did rob Mr Devlin,' the inspector reminded him. 'You took everything he had and left him practically destitute. In view of this it would not appear to be unreasonable to consider you capable of trying to rob him a second time.'

The doctor and Bernard exchanged glances. They had made no move to leave, as requested by John Hilliard, and so interested were they in the proceedings that neither had any intention of leaving, nor had Eric Philpots.

The door opened and the sergeant entered with the small recorder, which he handed to the inspector, who looked around the company to indicate his intention and to request complete silence. The tape was played, the start of which was a question by Amy who asked why James had brought the six people to his home.

'I intended to kill them all,' was the answer.

'But – why – and how?'

'Why? Because of their injuries to me. John

Hilliard robbed me; so did your husband. He stole two very valuable paintings, sold them and kept the proceeds. He also swindled me over the value of the house we inherited. I wanted revenge. He wasn't fit to live.'

'So you knew it all. I suspected all the time that you weren't as blind as Joseph said you were.' A pause and then, 'Why did you bring Sally here? She hadn't done you an injury.'

'I'd rather not say what my grudge was – in fact, it wasn't against Sally at all. Then there was Mrs Smallman, who was brought instead of her husband who was dead. She herself had behaved badly to me. As for the doctor and his friend, well, they fought to bring me back to life when I had decided to die, to find peace away from a world I had come to hate. I know now I was mistaken in that particular grudge. They only acted as honourable people would act.'

'I asked you how you intended killing them all?'

A long pause before James spoke.

'Albert had said he'd bought some weed killer. I thought I'd use that.' So casual. Louisa, catching the inspector's eyes, saw only amusement in them. She guessed he was saving a question until the end of the recording.

The next part of the recording included that where Amy spoke about Louisa's conviction that someone pushed Joseph Powell off

341

the cliff and then the words from James, 'Well, I hope she isn't thinking that I pushed him off the cliff.'

At this the inspector looked straight at John Hilliard and when the recorder was switched off he said at once, 'You were intending to edit that recording.' The inspector leant back in his chair and regarded John Hilliard through narrowed eyes. 'Perhaps you can give me some indication of the parts you intended cutting out – or perhaps the parts being left in?'

'I refuse to answer such an absurd question!'

'You never meant to edit it? Is that why you consider my question absurd?'

John Hilliard shook his head and said wrathfully, 'What I intended doing with that recording is my own business—'

'If blackmail was intended then it becomes my business,' broke in Corlett in his usual quiet voice. 'I understand from Mrs Hooke, who is acting for Mr Devlin, that you threatened to edit the tape, leaving in what could only be damning evidence that Mr Devlin meant to murder six people and that in fact he did murder one of them. You offered to hand over the recording if he would give you this house, land and in fact, everything he owned—' The inspector broke off as gasps came from where the two friends were sitting by the long low window.

'This is unbelievable!' from Bernard. He regarded John Hilliard with contempt. 'Mrs Hooke, is this true?'

'You can ask James.' She looked at him, aware of his discomfiture. 'Tell the inspector why you went away,' she encouraged with a smile.

It was some moments before he replied, and then it was with a sigh of resignation.

'John Hilliard did threaten me. He wanted me to write a letter making him a gift of this property. I was to say the gift was for his once befriending me, and now I wanted to repay him.'

'That's a lie!' But the vehemence in John Hilliard's voice faded. He saw the contempt on the inspector's face as he said slowly, 'My guess is that, after editing, all that would remain of one particular sentence would be: "I pushed him off the cliff."'

Hilliard stared at the inspector in silence for a long moment and then said, coldly, 'I am thinking I would be well advised to refuse to answer any of your questions until I have my lawyer present.' His teeth snapped together. 'And that is final!'

Chief Inspector Corlett said, 'Why did you record that conversation? You must have had some objective.'

'I have said – it is final.'

After nodding in acceptance the inspector told him that the tape would be retained by the police and without affording him time to make a protest he turned to James Devlin and said, 'Tell me, Mr Devlin, just how did you intend administering the poison – the weed killer?'

Louisa could not help saying that he had no intention of ever poisoning anyone.

'I hadn't thought it out – not at the time, that is.'

'You left it a bit late,' returned the inspector with some amusement.

The older man was frowning in thought. He seemed far away, on his own again, and his words were scarcely audible.

'I think at the back of my mind I was getting a great deal of satisfaction from imagining their faces on learning that the legacy they'd all anticipated was not going to come to them.'

Louisa was nodding her head.

'I had an idea it was that.' She paused. 'And have you had a great deal of satisfaction?'

'Well ... er...' Louisa wondered if he regretted having taken off the beard: it would have hidden the rather sheepish grin appearing on his face. 'No,' he admitted, 'I haven't, because the two who would have felt it most are dead –' he glanced around before adding – 'and there are three of you who wouldn't have been bothered in the least.' His eyes came to rest on John Hilliard's flushed, angry face. 'And you, John – well, I have learned such a lot in the past four days that I now know there is no place in one's life for grudges, and so I am forgetting about the threats you made. Your disappointment at going back to your lovely home empty-handed is compensation enough for me.' He looked from Louisa to her niece and a smile touched the full, sensitive lips. 'Having found gold, I have no further interest in the dross.'

It was some time later that Louisa found herself alone with the inspector.

'Did you question Mrs Powell' she asked curiously.

'I didn't question her,' he admitted. 'We did have a chat, though.'

Louisa was not surprised by his answer.

'You felt there would be nothing to be gained by questions as to how long it would take to drive here.' Louisa was nodding thoughtfully. 'She's a smart one – smarter than one would at first assume after having had conversation with her.'

'You, like me, know she has planned the perfect murder?'

'I'm not sure I believe in a perfect murder. But there are those which have been so well thought out that much work – and a good slice of luck – would be needed to be success-ful in pinning the crime on its perpetrator.' She glanced at him and paused. 'I expect you have guessed that she didn't stop at any filling station?'

He smiled faintly.

'Like me, you have decided she carried spare petrol with her.'

'In the boot, yes. Another thing about Mrs Powell is that, unlike Mrs Thorpe, she won't collapse under pressure.'

'That is why I decided questioning would be ineffective. She's of a much stronger character than the Thorpe woman.'

'I gathered that from her bone structure and other facial aspects. She does have a certain weakness but alongside this there is evidence of a basic strength which she can either keep hidden or utilize if the need should arise.'

He looked at her with admiration.

'This gift you have – it must be unique.'

She shook her head instantly.

'There are others with the gift of physiognomy,' she told him seriously. Then went on to say that her gift was in use more than that of others. 'Not many people are as interested in crime as I am. The criminal mind fascinates me, and I have always been very thankful for this gift since it has helped me so much in my estimates of character.'

'And in consequence been of valuable aid to the police,' he was quick to remind her, and she inclined her head in acknowledgement of his words of praise.

'So,' she murmured presently, 'our Mrs

Powell is going to get away with it.' Louise thought again of the woman's intention of putting the blame on Albert. She also wondered if Sally would be relieved to know that Mrs Powell would not be charged with murder.

'The loss of the fat legacy she was counting on will be a punishment in some measure. I gathered in the course of our conversation that she was given to understand by her husband, after he'd had the interview with the solicitor, that there was a lot of money to be divided by the six legatees.'

'He did expect a substantial amount,' she said reflectively. 'He knew that James Devlin had received a vast amount of compensation for the compulsory purchase of his house and land.'

'Well, one wouldn't have expected him to believe he'd been favoured in the will of a man he'd deliberately robbed. From what I've gathered, he was a pompous, arrogant sort of man.'

'He was certainly that.'

She became thoughtful and he said, 'It seems his wife is better off without him.'

Louisa smiled faintly and nodded her head. 'I wonder how she's feeling?'

'Elated, I expect. But she must have been anxious at the time you were asking her questions, the kind that would tell her at once that you suspected her of the crime.'

'She did show anxiety but soon recovered. She knew it would be almost impossible to prove anything against her. She had planned it all too well.'

The detective nodded thoughtfully.

'I couldn't have made any positive connection. She drives one of those insignificant little Fords and it's black. She'd park it in one of those little copses just off the main road. No one would notice it.'

'Yes, she was clever and calculating enough to be sure to hide the car from view. I rather think she arrived there early, that is, before he did. Then when she saw him walking along the cliff she would appear—'

'The path she would be on – and he also – was not very close to the edge,' he was forced to remind her, even though he knew there was nothing to be gained by it.

'I expect she manoeuvred him closer to the edge. She'd have taken him by surprise, remember, and I guess also that not much time was wasted in explanations. We'll never know what was said when they met but—'

'As you say, not much time would be wasted. Anyone who plans murder with such care to detail is not going to delay finally. My guess is that he was pushed only seconds after they met.'

Louisa nodded her head in agreement. The murder had been well planned, and carried out with the precision of an expert. She said again, 'She's going to get away with it.'

'She's laughing at us,' he said with a sigh. But then his eyes lit with humour as he added, 'But at least she's *not* laughing all the way to the bank!'

For a moment Louisa was thoughtful and then, aware of the question in the detective's eyes as he waited, she said musingly, 'Having learned of her character – the calculating way she has, the very strong quality of self-preservation, I suspect she had her husband well insured.' She glanced at him and added, 'You see, she'd had so many examples of his recklessness with money, that she knew that when he died he would leave her practically destitute.'

'So she safeguarded herself.' He pursed his lips. 'Seems feasible.'

'When I was telling you what she told me about her life with him, I might have forgotten to mention that he had mortgaged their house, the one in which they lived, in order to get money for his gambling.'

'Actually you did mention it. I felt sorry for her – at the time.'

She shot him a glance. 'And now?'

'Mrs Hooke, if I had the slightest hope that I had a chance of success, I'd put all my energies into a deep and thorough investigation that would put that woman into the dock. Does that answer your question?'

She nodded and smiled. 'Yes, it does.'

'If, as you surmise, she had her husband well insured, she doesn't need anyone to be sorry for her.'

'No. She'll survive – and prosper probably. But we shall never know.'

'It's been a strange business,' he mused. 'You people meeting here as complete strangers, and now leaving, never to meet again.'

'Never—? Oh, you don't know? Sally and I have sort of adopted James. He's coming to live close to us both, building a bungalow on a plot adjoining my garden. Sally lives only five minutes away. We're also taking Millie, who'll be living with me when I move into the cottage I'm buying. We'll be a family.' She paused before adding with a laugh, 'This case is the first since I came over from America, and as a result of it our family has increased to double. It's to be hoped it isn't a portent of things to come! However,' she added, 'I'll not be involved in another case for a long time – if ever.'

He leant right back in his chair and regarded her with an expression which she realized was curious.

'So you'll not let yourself get mixed up in this stolen-babies business that's going on somewhere in your part of the county?'

'Stolen babies?' sharply and with a certain eagerness of which she was unaware. 'Where is this happening, and how many babies have been stolen?'

350

'Two. Snatched from their prams within a week of each other. And it's in some place not far from Dorchester – which is your neck of the woods?'

'That's right. I live in Melcombe Porcorum, which is only a couple of miles or so from Dorchester.'

'It was in the *Mail*, and has the police baffled, so it sounds just up your street.'

Louisa made no comment, but she suddenly found herself eager to leave the manor and get back home.